The Struggles of Brown, Jones, and Robinson

ANTHONY TROLLOPE

The Struggles of Brown, Jones, and Robinson

BY ONE OF THE FIRM

G.K. Hall & Co. • Chivers Press
Thorndike, Maine USA   Bath, England

This Large Print edition is published by Thorndike Press, USA and by Chivers Press, England.

Originally published in 1870 and is now in Public Domain in the United States and the United Kingdom.

U.S. Hardcover 0-7838-9166-0 (Perennial Bestseller Series Edition)
U.K. Hardcover 0-7540-4376-2 (Chivers Large Print)

The text of this Large Print edition is unabridged.
Other aspects of the book may vary from the original edition.

Set in 16 pt. Plantin by PerfecType.

Printed in the United States on permanent paper.

British Library Cataloguing-in-Publication Data available

Library of Congress Cataloging-in-Publication Data

Trollope, Anthony, 1815–1882.
  The struggles of Brown, Jones, and Robinson / by one of the firm, Anthony Trollope.
      p.   cm.
  ISBN 0-7838-9166-0 (lg. print : hc : alk. paper)
  1. Men's furnishing goods — Fiction. 2. Clothing trade — Fiction.
3. Advertising — Fiction. 4. Businessmen — Fiction. 5. Large type
books. I. Title.
PR5684.S8 2000
823'.8—dc21   00-044940

CONTENTS

CHAPTER I

PREFACE

BY ONE OF THE FIRM

It will be observed by the literary and commercial world that, in this transaction, the name of the really responsible party does not show on the title-page. I — George Robinson — am that party. When our Mr Jones objected to the publication of these memoirs unless they appeared as coming from the firm itself, I at once gave way. I had no wish to offend the firm, and, perhaps, encounter a lawsuit for the empty honour of seeing my name advertised as that of an author. We had talked the matter over with our Mr Brown, who, however, was at that time in affliction, and not able to offer much that was available. One thing he did say; 'As we are partners,' said Mr Brown, 'let's be partners to the end.' 'Well,' said I, 'if you say so, Mr Brown, so it shall be.' I never supposed that Mr Brown would set the Thames on fire, and soon learnt that he was not the man to amass a fortune by British commerce. He was not made for the guild of Merchant Princes. But he was the senior member of our firm, and I always respected the old-fashioned doctrine of capital in the person of our Mr Brown.

When Mr Brown said, 'Let's be partners to the end; it won't be for long, Mr Robinson,' I never said another word. 'No,' said I, 'Mr Brown; you're not what you was — and you're down a peg; I'm not the man to take advantage and go against your last wishes. Whether for long or whether for short, we'll pull through in the same boat to the end. It shall be put on the title-page — "By One of the Firm."' 'God bless you, Mr Robinson,' said he; 'God bless you.'

And then Mr Jones started another objection. The reader will soon realize that anything I do is sure to be wrong with Mr Jones. It wouldn't be him else. He next declares that I can't write English, and that the book must be corrected, and put out by an editor? Now, when I inform the discerning British Public that every advertisement that has been posted by Brown, Jones, and Robinson, during the last three years has come from my own unaided pen, I think few will doubt my capacity to write the 'Memoirs of Brown, Jones, and Robinson,' without any editor whatsoever.

On this head I was determined to be firm. What! after preparing, and correcting, and publishing such thousands of advertisements in prose and verse and in every form of which the language is susceptible, to be told that I couldn't write English! It was Jones all over. If there is a party envious of the genius of another party in this sublunary world that party is our Mr Jones.

But I was again softened by a touching appeal from our senior partner. Mr Brown, though prosaic enough in his general ideas, was still sometimes given to the Muses; and now, with a melancholy and tender cadence, he quoted the following lines; —

Let dogs delight to bark and bite,
For 'tis their nature to.
But 'tis a shameful sight to see, when part-
      ners of one firm like we,
Fall out, and chide, and fight!

So I gave in again.

It was then arranged that one of Smith and Elder's young men should look through the manuscript, and make any few alterations which the taste of the public might require. It might be that the sonorous, and, if I may so express myself, magniloquent phraseology in which I was accustomed to invite the attention of the nobility and gentry to our last importations was not suited for the purposes of light literature, such as this. 'In fiction, Mr Robinson, your own unaided talents would doubtless make you great, said to me the editor of this Magazine; 'but if I may be allowed an opinion, I do think that in the delicate task of composing memoirs a little assistance may perhaps be not inexpedient.'

This was prettily worded; so what with this, and what with our Mr Brown's poetry, I gave way; but I reserved to myself the right of an epistolary preface in my own name. So here it is.

LADIES AND GENTLEMEN — I am not a bit ashamed of my part in the following transaction. I have done what little in me lay to further British commerce. British commerce is not now what it was. It is becoming open and free like everything else that is British; — open to the poor man as well as to the rich. That bugbear Capital is a crumbling old tower, and is pretty nigh brought to its last ruin. Credit is the polished shaft of the temple on which the new world of trade will be content to lean. That, I take it, is the one great doctrine of modern commerce. Credit, — credit, — credit. Get credit, and capital will follow. Doesn't the word speak for itself? Must not credit be respectable? And is not the word 're-spectable' the highest term of praise which can be applied to the British tradesman?

Credit is the polished shaft of the temple. But with what are you to polish it? The stone does not come from the quarry with its gloss on. Man's labour is necessary to give it that beauteous exterior. Then wherewith shall we polish credit? I answer the question at once. With the pumice-stone and sand-paper of advertisement.

Different great men have promulgated the different means by which they have sought to subjugate the world. 'Audacity — audacity — audacity,' was the lesson which one hero taught. 'Agitate — agitate — agitate,' was the counsel of a second. 'Register — register — register,' of a third. But I say — Advertise, advertise, advertise! And I say it again and again — Advertise, advertise, advertise! It is, or should be, the Shibboleth of British commerce. That it certainly will be so I, George Robinson, hereby venture to prophesy, feeling that on this subject something but little short of inspiration has touched my eager pen.

There are those, — men of the old school, who cannot rouse themselves to see and read the signs of the time, men who would have been in the last ranks, let them have lived when they would, — who object to it that it is untrue, — who say that advertisements do not keep the promises which they make. But what says the poet, — he whom we teach our children to read? What says the stern moralist to his wicked mother in the play? 'Assume a virtue if you have it not?' and so say I. 'Assume a virtue if you have it not.' It would be a great trade virtue in a haberdasher to have forty thousand pairs of best hose lying ready for sale in his warehouse. Let him assume that virtue if he have it not. Is not this the way in which we all live, and the only way in which it is possible to live comfortably. A gentleman gives a dinner party. His lady, who has to work all day like a dray-horse and scold the servants besides, to get things into order, loses her temper. We all pretty well know what that means. Well; up to the moment when she has to show, she is as bitter a piece of goods as may be. But, nevertheless, she comes down all smiles, al-

11

though she knows that at that moment the drunken cook is spoiling the fish. She assumes a virtue, though she has it not; and who will say she is not right?

Well; I say again and again to all young trades-men; — Advertise, advertise, advertise; — and don't stop to think too much about capital. It is a bugbear. Capital is a bugbear; and it is talked about by those who have it, — and by some that have not so much of it neither, — for the sake of putting down competition, and keeping the mar-ket to themselves.

There's the same game going on all the world over; and it's the natural game for mankind to play at. They who's up a bit is all for keeping down them who is down; and they who is down is so very soft through being down, that they've not spirit to force themselves up. Now I saw that very early in life. There is always going on a battle between aristocracy and democracy. Aristocracy likes to keep itself to itself; and democracy is just of the same opinion, only wishes to become aris-tocracy first.

We of the people are not very fond of dukes; but we'd all like to be dukes well enough our-selves. Now there are dukes in trade as well as in society. Capitalists are our dukes; and as they don't like to have their heels trod upon any more than the other ones, why they are always preach-ing up capital. It is their star and garter, their coronet, their ermine, their robe of state, their cap of maintenance, their wand of office, their noli me tangere. But stars and garters, caps and wands, and all other noli me tangeres, are gammon to those who can see through them. And capital is gammon. Capital is a very nice thing if you can get it. It is the desirable result of trade. A tradesman looks to end with a capital. But it's gammon to say that he can't begin without it. You might as well say a man can't marry unless he has first got a family. Why, he marries that he may have a family. It's putting the cart before the horse.

It's my opinion that any man can be a duke if so be it's born to him. It requires neither wit nor industry, nor any pushing or go-ahead whatsoever. A man may sit still in his arm-chair, half asleep half his time, and only half awake the other, and be as good a duke as need be. Well; it's just the same in trade. If a man is born to a dukedom there, if he begins with a large capital, why, I for one would not thank him to be successful. Any fool could do as much as that. He has only to keep on polishing his own star and garter, and there are lots of people to swear that there is no one like him.

But give me the man who can be a duke without being born to it. Give me the man who can go ahead in trade without capital; who can begin the world with a quick pair of hands, a quick brain to govern them, and can end with a capital.

Well, there you are; a young tradesman beginning the world without capital. Capital, though it's a bugbear, nevertheless it's a virtue. Therefore, as you haven't got it, you must assume it. That's credit. Credit I take to be the belief of other people in a thing that doesn't really exist. When you go into your friend Smith's house, and find Mrs S. all smiles, you give her credit for the sweetest of tempers. Your friend S. knows better; but then you see she's had wit enough to obtain credit. When I draw a bill at three months, and get it done, I do the same thing. That's credit. Give me credit enough, and I don't care a brass button for capital. If I could have but one wish, I would never ask a fairy for a second or a third. Let me have but unreserved credit, and I'll beat any duke of either aristocracy.

To obtain credit the only certain method is to advertise. Advertise, advertise, advertise. That is, assume, assume, assume. Go on assuming your virtue. The more you haven't got it, the more you must assume it. The bitterer your own heart is about that drunken cook and that idle husband who will do nothing to assist you, the sweeter you must smile. Smile sweet enough, and all the world will believe you. Advertise long enough, and credit will come.

But there must be some nous in your advertisements; there must be a system, and there must be some wit in your system. It won't suffice now-a-days to stick up on a blank wall a simple placard to say that you have forty thousand best hose just new arrived. Any wooden-headed fellow can do as much as that. That might have served in the olden times that we hear of, twenty years since; but the game to be successful in these days must be played in another sort of fashion. There must be some finish about your advertisements, something new in your style, something that will startle in your manner. If a man can make himself a real master of this art, we may say that he has learnt his trade, whatever that trade may be. Let him know how to advertise, and the rest will follow.

It may be that I shouldn't boast; but yet I do boast that I have made some little progress in this business. If I haven't yet practised the art in all its perfections, nevertheless I flatter myself I have learned how to practise it. Regarding myself as something of a master of this art, and being actuated by purely philanthropic motives in my wish to make known my experience, I now put these memoirs before the public.

It will, of course, be urged against me that I have not been successful in what I have already attempted, and that our house has failed. This is true. I have not been successful. Our house has failed. But with whom has the fault been? Certainly not in my department.

The fact is, and in this my preface I will not keep the truth back from a discerning public, that no firm on earth, — or indeed elsewhere, — could be successful in which our Mr Jones is one of the partners. There is an overweening vanity about that man which is quite upsetting. I confess I have been unable to stand it. Vanity is always allied to folly, and the relationship is very close in the person of our Mr Jones. Of Mr Brown I will never bring myself to say one disrespectful word. He is not now what he was once. From the bottom of my heart I pity his misfortunes. Think what it must be to be papa to a Goneril and a Regan, — without the Cordelia. I have always looked on Mrs Jones as a regular Goneril; and as for the Regan, why it seems to me that Miss Brown is likely to be Miss Regan to the end of the chapter.

No; of Mr Brown I will say nothing disrespectful; but he never was the man to be first partner in an advertising firm. That was our mistake. He had old-fashioned views about capital which were very burdensome. My mistake was this, — that in joining myself with Mr Brown, I compromised my principles, and held out, as it were, a left hand to capital. He had not much, as will be seen; but he thought a deal of what he had got, and talked a deal of it too. This impeded my wings. This prevented me from soaring. One cannot touch pitch and not be defiled. I have been untrue to myself in having had any dealings on the basis of capital; and hence has it arisen that hitherto I have failed.

I make these confessions hoping that they may be serviceable to trade in general. A man cannot learn a great secret, and the full use of a great secret, all at once. My eyes are now open. I shall not again make so fatal a mistake. I am still young. I have now learned my lesson more thoroughly, and I yet anticipate success with some confidence.

Had Mr Brown at once taken my advice, had his few thousand pounds been liberally expended in commencing a true system of advertising, we should have been, — I can hardly surmise where we should have been. He was for sticking altogether to the old system. Mr Jones was for mixing the old and the new, for laying in stock and advertising as well, with a capital of 4,000*l*! What my opinion is of Mr Jones I will not now say, but of Mr Brown I will never utter one word of disparagement.

I have now expressed what few words I wish to say on my own bottom. As to what has been done in the following pages by the young man who has been employed to look over these memoirs and put them into shape, it is not for me to speak. It may be that I think they might have read more natural-like had no other cook had a finger in the pie. The facts, however, are facts still. These have not been cooked.

Ladies and gentlemen, you who have so long distinguished our firm by a liberal patronage, to you I now respectfully appeal, and in showing to you a new article I beg to assure you with perfect confidence that there is nothing equal to it at the price at present in the market. The supply on hand is immense, but as a sale of unprecedented rapidity is anticipated, may I respectfully solicit your early orders? If not approved of the article shall be changed.

 Ladies and gentlemen,
   We have the honour to subscribe ourselves,
    With every respect,
   Your most obedient humble servants,
   BROWN, JONES, and ROBINSON,
      PER GEORGE ROBINSON.

CHAPTER II

THE EARLY HISTORY OF OUR MR BROWN, WITH SOME FEW WORDS OF MR JONES

O commerce, how wonderful are thy ways, how vast thy power, how invisible thy dominion! Who can restrain thee and forbid thy further progress? Kings are but as infants in thy hands, and emperors, despotic in all else, are bound to obey thee! Thou civilizest, hast civilized, and wilt civilize. Civilization is thy mission, and man's welfare thine appointed charge. The nation that most warmly fosters thee shall ever be the greatest in the earth; and without thee no nation shall endure for a day. Thou art our Alpha and our Omega, our beginning and our end; the marrow of our bones, the salt of our life, the sap of our branches, the corner-stone of our temple, the rock of our foundation. We are built on thee, and for thee, and with thee. To worship thee should be man's chiefest care, to know thy hidden ways his chosen study.

One maxim hast thou, O Commerce, great and true and profitable above all others; — one law which thy votaries should never transgress. 'Buy

in the cheapest market and sell in the dearest.'
May those divine words be ever found engraved
on the hearts of Brown, Jones, and Robinson!

Of Mr Brown, the senior member of our firm,
it is expedient that some short memoir should be
given. At the time at which we signed our articles
in 185— , Mr Brown had just retired from the
butter business. It does not appear that in his
early youth he ever had the advantage of an ap-
prenticeship, and he seems to have been employed in various branches of trade in the position, if one may say so, of an out-door messenger.
In this capacity he entered the service of Mr
McCockerell, a retail butter dealer in Smithfield.
When Mr McCockerell died our Mr Brown
married his widow, and thus found himself ele-
vated at once to the full-blown dignitary of a
tradesman. He and his wife lived together for
thirty years, and it is believed that in the temper
of his lady he found some alloy to the prosperity
which he had achieved. The widow McCockerell,
in bestowing her person upon Mr Brown, had
not intended to endow him also with entire dominion over her shop and chattels. She loved to
be supreme over her butter tubs, and she loved
also to be supreme over her till. Brown's views on
the rights of women were more in accordance
with the law of the land as laid down in the
statutes. He opined that a *femme couverte* could
own no property, not even a butter tub; — and
hence quarrels arose.

After thirty years of contests such as these Mr

Brown found himself victorious, made so not by the power of arguments, nor by that of his own right arm, but by the demise of Mrs Brown. That amiable lady died, leaving two daughters to lament their loss, and a series of family quarrels, by which she did whatever lay in her power to embarrass her husband, but by which she could not prevent him from becoming absolute owner of the butter business, and of the stock in trade.

The two young ladies had not been brought up to the ways of the counter; and as Mr Brown was not himself especially expert at that particular business in which his money was embarked, he prudently thought it expedient to dispose of the shop and goodwill. This he did to advantage; and thus at the age of fifty-five he found himself again on the world with 4,000*l.* in his pocket.

At this period one of his daughters was no longer under his own charge. Sarah Jane, the eldest of the two, was already Mrs Jones. She had been captivated by the black hair and silk waistcoat of Mr Jones, and had gone off with him in opposition to the wishes of both parents. This, she was aware, was not matter of much moment, for the opposition of one was sure to bring about a reconciliation with the other. And such was soon the case. Mrs Brown would not see her daughter, or allow Jones to put his foot inside the butter-shop. Mr Brown consequently took lodgings for them in the neighbourhood, and hence a close alliance sprung up between the future partners.

At this crisis Maryanne devoted herself to her mother. It was admitted by all who knew her that Maryanne Brown had charms. At that time she was about twenty-four years of age, and was certainly a fine young woman. She was, like her mother, a little too much inclined to corpulence, and there may be those who would not allow that her hair was auburn. Mr Robinson, however, who was then devotedly attached to her, was of that opinion, and was ready to maintain his views against any man who would dare to say that it was red.

There was a dash about Maryanne Brown at that period which endeared her greatly to Mr Robinson. She was quite above anything mean, and when her papa was left a widower in possession of four thousand pounds, she was one of those who were most anxious to induce him to go to work with spirit in a new business. She was all for advertising; that must be confessed of her, though her subsequent conduct was not all that it should have been. Maryanne Brown, when tried in the furnace, did not come out pure gold; but this, at any rate, shall be confessed in her behalf, that she had a dash about her, and understood more of the tricks of the trade than any other of her family.

Mrs McCockerell died about six months after her eldest daughter's marriage. She was generally called Mrs McCockerell in the neighbourhood of Smithfield, though so many years had passed since she had lost her right to that name. Indeed, she generally preferred being so styled, as Mr Brown was peculiarly averse to it. The name was wormwood to him, and this was quite sufficient to give it melody in her ears.

The good lady died about six months after her daughter's marriage. She was struck with apoplexy, and at that time had not been reconciled to her married daughter. Sarah Jane, nevertheless, when she heard what had occurred, came over to Smithfield. Her husband was then in employment as shopman at the large haberdashery house on Snow Hill, and lived with his wife in lodgings in Cowcross Street. They were supported nearly entirely by Mr Brown, and therefore owed to him at this crisis not only obedience, but dutiful affection.

When, however, Sarah Jane first heard of her mother's illness, she seemed to think that she couldn't quarrel with her father fast enough. Jones had an idea that the old lady's money must go to her daughters, that she had the power of putting it altogether out of the hands of her husband, and that having the power she would certainly exercise it. On this speculation he had married; and as he and his wife fully concurred in their financial views, it was considered expedient by them to lose no time in asserting their right. This they did as soon as the breath was out of the old lady's body.

Jones had married Sarah Jane solely with this view; and, indeed, it was highly improbable that he should have done so on any other consideration. Sarah Jane was certainly not a handsome girl. Her neck was scraggy, her arms lean, and her lips thin; and she resembled neither her father nor her mother. Her light brown, sandy hair, which always looked as though it were too thin and too short to adapt itself to any feminine usage, was also not of her family; but her disposition was a compound of the paternal and maternal qualities. She had all her father's painful hesitating timidity, and with it all her mother's grasping spirit. If there ever was an eye that looked sharp after the pence, that could weigh the ounces of a servant's meal at a glance, and foresee and prevent the expenditure of a farthing, it was the eye of Sarah Jane Brown. They say that it is as easy to save a fortune as to make one; and in this way, if in no other, Jones may be said to have got a fortune with his wife.

As soon as the breath was out of Mrs McCockerell's body, Sarah Jane was there, taking inventory of the stock. At that moment poor Mr Brown was very much to be pitied. He was a man of feeling, and even if his heart was not touched by his late loss, he knew what was due to decency. It behoved him now as a widower to forget the deceased lady's faults, and to put her under the ground with solemnity. This was done with the strictest propriety; and although he must, of course, have been thinking a good deal at that time as to whether he was to be a beggar or a rich man, nevertheless he conducted himself till after the funeral as though he hadn't a care on his mind, except the loss of Mrs B.

Maryanne was as much on the alert as her sister. She had been for the last six months her mother's pet, as Sarah Jane had been her father's darling. There was some excuse, therefore, for Maryanne when she endeavoured to get what she could in the scramble. Sarah Jane played the part of Goneril to the life, and would have denied her father the barest necessaries of existence, had it not ultimately turned out that the property was his own.

Maryanne was not well pleased to see her sister returning to the house at such a moment. She, at least, had been dutiful to her mother, or, if undutiful, not openly so. If Mrs McCockerell had the power of leaving her property to whom she pleased, it would only be natural that she should leave it to the daughter who had obeyed her, and not to the daughter who had added to personal disobedience the worse fault of having been on friendly terms with her father.

This, one would have thought, would have been clear at any rate to Jones, if not to Sarah Jane; but they both seemed at this time to have imagined that the eldest child had some right to the inheritance as being the eldest. It will be observed by this and by many other traits in his character that Mr Jones had never enjoyed the advantages of an education.

Mrs McCockerell never spoke after the fit first struck her. She never moved an eye, or stirred a limb, or uttered a word. It was a wretched household at that time. The good lady died on a Wednesday, and was gathered to her fathers at Kensal Green Cemetery on the Tuesday following. During the intervening days Mr Jones and Sarah Jane took on themselves as though they were owners of everything. Maryanne did try to prevent the inventory, not wishing it to appear that Mrs Jones had any right to meddle; but the task was too congenial to Sarah Jane's spirit to allow of her giving it over. She revelled in the work. It was a delight to her to search out hidden stores of useless wealth, — to bring forth to the light forgotten hoards of cups and saucers, and to catalogue every rag on the premises.

The house at this time was not a pleasant one. Mr Brown, finding that Jones, in whom he had trusted, had turned against him, put himself very much into the hands of a young friend of his, named George Robinson. Who and what George Robinson was will be told in the next chapter.

'There are three questions,' said Robinson, 'to be asked and answered. — Had Mrs B. the power to make a will? If so, did she make a will? And if so, what was the will she made?'

Mr Brown couldn't remember whether or no there had been any signing of papers at his marriage. A good deal of rum and water, he said, had been drunk; and there might have been signing too, — but he didn't remember it.

Then there was the search for the will. This was supposed to be in the hands of one Brisket, a butcher, for whom it was known Mrs

McCockerell had destined the hand of her younger daughter. Mr Brisket had been a great favourite with the old lady, and she had often been heard to declare that he should have the wife and money, or the money without the wife. This she said to coerce Maryanne into the match.

But Brisket, when questioned, declared that he had no will in his possession. At this time he kept aloof from the house and showed no disposition to meddle with the affairs of the family. Indeed, all through these trying days he behaved honestly, if not with high feeling. In recounting the doings of Brown, Jones, and Robinson, it will sometimes be necessary to refer to Mr Brisket. He shall always be spoken of as an honest man. He did all that in him lay to mar the bright hopes of one who was perhaps not the most insignificant of that firm. He destroyed the matrimonial hopes of Mr Robinson, and left him to wither like a blighted trunk on a lone waste. But he was, nevertheless, an honest man, and so much shall be said of him. Let us never forget that 'An honest man is the noblest work of God.'

Brisket, when asked, said that he had no will, and that he knew of none. In fact there was no will forthcoming, and there is no doubt that the old woman was cut off before she had made one. It may also be premised that had she made one it would have been invalid, seeing that Mr Brown, as husband, was, in fact, the owner of the whole affair.

Sarah Jane and Maryanne, when they found that no document was forthcoming, immediately gave out that they intended to take on themselves the duties of joint heiresses, and an alliance, offensive and defensive, was sworn between them. At this time Mr Brown employed a lawyer, and the heiresses, together with Jones, employed another. There could be no possible doubt as to Mr Brown being the owner of the property, however infatuated on such a subject Jones and his wife may have been. No lawyer in London could have thought that the young women had a leg to stand upon. Nevertheless, the case was undertaken, and Brown found himself in the middle of a lawsuit. Sarah Jane and Maryanne both remained in the house in Smithfield to guard the property on their own behalf. Mr Brown also remained to guard it on his behalf. The business for a time was closed. This was done in opposition both to Mr Brown and Maryanne; but Mrs Jones could not bring herself to permit the purchase of a firkin of butter, unless the transaction could be made absolutely under her own eyes; and, even then, she would insist on superintending the retail herself and selling every pound, short weight. It was the custom of the trade, she said; and to depart from it would ruin them.

Things were in this condition, going from bad to worse, when Jones came over one evening, and begged an interview with Mr Brown. That interview was the commencement of the partnership. From such small matters do great events arise.

At that interview Mr Robinson was present. Mr Brown indeed declared that he would have no conversation with Jones on business affairs, unless in the presence of a third party. Jones represented that if they went on as they were now doing, the property would soon be swallowed up by the lawyers. To this Mr Brown, whose forte was not eloquence, tacitly assented with a deep groan.

'Then,' said Jones, 'let us divide it into three portions. You shall have one; Sarah Jane a second; and I will manage the third on behalf of my sister-in-law, Maryanne. If we arrange it well, the lawyers will never get a shilling.'

The idea of a compromise appeared to Mr Brown to be not uncommendable; but a compromise on such terms as those could not of course be listened to. Robinson strongly counselled him to nail his colours to the mast, and kick Mr Jones downstairs. But Mr Brown had not spirit for this.

'One's children is one's children,' said he to Robinson, when they went apart into the shop to talk the matter over. 'The fruit of one's loins, and the prop of one's age.'

Robinson could not help thinking that Sarah Jane was about as bad a prop as any that ever a man leant on; but he was too generous to say so. The matter was ended at last by a compromise. 'Go on with the business together,' said Robinson; 'Mr Brown keeping, of course, a preponderating share in his own hands.'

'I don't like butter,' said Jones. 'Nothing great can be done in butter.'

'It is a very safe line,' said Mr Brown, 'if the connection is good.'

The connection must have been a good deal damaged,' said Robinson, 'seeing that the shop has been closed for a fortnight. Besides, it's a woman's business; — and you have no woman to manage it,' added he, fearing that Mrs Jones might be brought in, to the detriment of all concerned.

Jones suggested haberdashery; Robinson, guided by a strong idea that there is a more absolute opening for the advertising line in haberdashery than in any other business, assented.

'Then let it be haberdashery,' said Mr Brown, with a sigh. And so that was settled.

CHAPTER III
THE EARLY HISTORY OF MR ROBINSON

And haberdashery it was. But here it may be as well to say a few words as to Mr Robinson, and to explain how he became a member of the firm. He had been in his boyhood, — a bill-sticker; and he defies the commercial world to show that he ever denied it. In his earlier days he carried the paste and pole, and earned a livelihood by putting up notices of theatrical announcements on the hoardings of the metropolis. There was, however, that within him which Nature did not intend to throw away on the sticking of bills, as was found out quickly enough by those who employed him. The lad, while he was running the streets with his pole in his hand, and his pot round his neck, learned first to read, and then to write what others might read. From studying the bills which he carried, he soon took to original composition; and it may be said of him, that in fluency of language and richness of imagery few surpassed him. In person Mr Robinson was a genteel young man, though it cannot be said of

31

him that he possessed manly beauty. He was slight and active, intelligent in his physiognomy, and polite in his demeanour. Perhaps it may be unnecessary to say anything further on this head.

Mr Robinson had already established himself as an author in his own line, and was supporting himself decently by his own unaided abilities, when he first met Maryanne Brown in the Regent's Park. She was then walking with her sister, and resolutely persisted in disregarding all those tokens of admiration which he found himself unable to restrain.

There certainly was a dash about Maryanne Brown that at certain moments was invincible. Hooped petticoats on the back of her sister looked like hoops, and awkward hoops. They were angular, lopsided, and lumpy. But Maryanne wore her hoops as a duchess wears her crinoline. Her well-starched muslin dress would swell off from her waist in a manner that was irresistible to George Robinson. 'Such grouping!' as he said to his friend Walker. 'Such a flow of drapery! such tournure! Ah, my dear fellow, the artist's eye sees these things at a glance.' And then, walking at a safe distance, he kept his eyes on them.

'I'm sure that fellow's following us,' said Sarah Jane, looking back at him with all her scorn.

There's no law against that, I suppose,' said Maryanne, tartly. So much as that Mr Robinson did succeed in hearing.

The girls entered their mother's house; but as

they did so, Maryanne lingered for a moment in the doorway. Was it accident, or was it not? Did the fair girl choose to give her admirer one chance, or was it that she was careful not to crush her starch by too rapid an entry?

'I shall be in Regent's Park on Sunday afternoon,' whispered Robinson, as he passed by the house, with his hand to his mouth. It need hardly be said that the lady vouchsafed him no reply.

On the following Sunday George Robinson was again in the park, and after wandering among its rural shades for half a day, he was rewarded by seeing the goddess of his idolatry. Miss Brown was there with a companion, but not with Sarah Jane. He had already, as though by instinct, conceived in his heart as powerful an aversion for one sister as affection for the other, and his delight was therefore unbounded when he saw that she he loved was there, while she he hated was away.

'Twere long to tell, at the commencement of this narrative, how a courtship was commenced and carried on; how Robinson sighed, at first in vain and then not in vain; how good-natured was Miss Twizzle, the bosom friend of Maryanne; and how Robinson for a time walked and slept and fed on roses.

There was at that time a music class held at a certain elegant room near Osnaburgh Church in the New Road, at which Maryanne and her friend Miss Twizzle were accustomed to attend. Those lessons were sometimes prosecuted in the evening, and those evening studies sometimes resulted in a little dance. We may say that after a while that was their habitual tendency, and that the lady pupils were permitted to introduce their male friends on condition that the gentlemen paid a shilling each for the privilege. It was in that room that George Robinson passed the happiest hours of his chequered existence. He was soon expert in all the figures of the mazy dance, and was excelled by no one in the agility of his step or the endurance of his performances. It was by degrees rumoured about that he was something higher than he seemed to be, and those best accustomed to the place used to call him the Poet. It must be remembered that at this time Mrs McCockerell was still alive, and that as Sarah Jane had then become Mrs Jones, Maryanne was her mother's favourite, and destined to receive all her mother's gifts. Of the name and person of William Brisket, George Robinson was then in happy ignorance, and the first introduction between them took place in the Hall of Harmony.

'Twas about eleven o'clock in the evening, when the light feet of the happy dancers had already been active for some hour or so in the worship of their favourite muse, that Robinson was standing up with his arm round his fair one's waist, immediately opposite to the door of entrance. His right arm still embraced her slight girdle, whilst with his left hand he wiped the perspiration from his brow. She leaned against him palpitating, for the motion of the music had been quick, and there had been some amicable contest among the couples. It is needless to say that George Robinson and Maryanne Brown had suffered no defeat. At that moment a refreshing breeze of the night air was wafted into the room from the opened door, and Robinson, looking up, saw before him a sturdy, thickset man, with mottled beefy face, and by his side there stood a spectre. 'It's your sister,' whispered he to Maryanne, in a tone of horror.

'Oh, laws! there's Bill,' said she, and then she fainted. The gentleman with the mottled face was indeed no other than Mr Brisket, the purveyor of meat, for whose arms Mrs McCockerell had destined the charms of her younger daughter. Conduct baser than that of Mrs Jones on this occasion is not perhaps recorded in history. She was no friend of Brisket's. She had it not at heart to forward her mother's views. At this period of their lives she and her mother never met. But she had learned her sister's secret, and having it in her power to crush her sister's happiness, had availed herself of the opportunity.

'There he is,' said she, quite aloud, so that the whole room should hear. 'He's a bill-sticker!' and she pointed the finger of scorn at her sister's lover.

'I'm one who have always earned my own living,' said Robinson, 'and never had occasion to hang on to any one.' This he said knowing that Jones's lodgings were paid for by Mr Brown.

Hereupon Mr Brisket walked across the room, and as he walked there was a cloud of anger on his brow. 'Perhaps, young man,' he said, — and as he spoke he touched Robinson on the shoulder, — 'perhaps, young man, you wouldn't mind having a few words with me outside the door.'

'Sir,' said the other with some solemnity, 'I am not aware that I have the honour of your acquaintance.'

'I'm William Brisket, butcher,' said he; 'and if you don't come out when I asks you, by jingo, I'll carry you.'

The lady had fainted. The crowd of dancers was standing round with inquiring faces. That female spectre repeated the odious words, still pointing at him with her finger, 'He's a billsticker!' Brisket was full fourteen stone, whereas Robinson might perhaps be ten. What was Robinson to do? 'Are you going to walk out, or am I going to carry you?' said the Hercules of the slaughterhouse.

'I will do anything,' said Robinson, 'to relieve a lady's embarrassment.'

They walked out on to the landing-place, whither not a few of the gentlemen and some of the ladies followed them.

'I say, young man,' said Brisket, 'do you know who that young woman is?'

'I certainly have the honour of her acquaintance,' said Robinson.

'But perhaps you haven't the honour of knowing that she's my wife, — as is to be. Now you know it.' And then the coarse monster eyed him from head to foot. 'Now you may go home to your mother,' said he. 'But don't tell her anything of it, because it's a secret.'

He was fifteen stone at least, and Robinson was hardly ten. Oh, how vile is the mastery which matter still has over mind in many of the concerns of life! How can a man withstand the assault of a bull? What was Robinson to do? He walked downstairs into the street, leaving Maryanne behind with the butcher.

Some days after this he contrived a meeting with his love, and he then learned the history of that engagement. 'She hated Brisket,' she said. 'He was odious to her. He was always greasy and smelt of meat; — but he had a respectable business.'

'And is my Maryanne mercenary?' asked Robinson.

'Now, George,' said she, 'it's no use you scolding me, and I won't be scolded. Ma says that I must be civil to him, and I'm not going to quarrel with Ma. At any rate not yet.'

'But surely, Maryanne —'

'It's no good you surelying me, George, for I won't be surelyed. If you don't like me you can leave me.'

'Maryanne, I adore you.'

That's all very well, and I hope you do; but why did you make a row with that man the other night?'

'But, dearest love, he made the row with me.'

'And when you did make it,' continued Maryanne, 'why didn't you see it out?' Robinson did not find it easy to answer this accusation. That matter has still dominion over mind, though the days are coming when mind shall have dominion over matter, was a lesson which, in after days, it would be sweet to teach her. But at the present moment the time did not serve for such teaching. 'A man must look after his own, George, or else he'll go to the wall,' she said, with a sneer. And then he parted from her in anger.

But his love did not on that account wax cool, and so in his misery he had recourse to their mutual friend, Miss Twizzle. 'The truth is this,' said Miss Twizzle, 'I believe she'd take him, because he's respectable and got a business.'

'He's horribly vulgar,' said Robinson.

'Oh, bother!' said Miss Twizzle. 'I know nothing about that. He's got a business, and whoever marries Brisket won't have to look for a bed to sleep on. But there's a hitch about the money.'

Then Mr Robinson learned the facts. Mrs McCockerell, as she was still called, had promised to give her daughter five hundred pounds as her marriage portion, but Mr Brisket would not go to the altar till he got the money. 'He wanted to extend himself,' he said, 'and would not marry till he saw his way.' Hence had arisen that delay which Maryanne had solaced by her attendance at the music-hall.

'But if you're in earnest,' said Miss Twizzle, 'don't you be down on your luck. Go to old

Brown, and make friends with him. He'll stand up for you, because he knows his wife favours Brisket.'

George Robinson did go to Mr Brown, and on the father the young man's eloquence was not thrown away. 'She shall be yours, Mr Robinson,' he said, after the first fortnight. 'But we must be very careful with Mrs B.'

After the second fortnight Mrs B was no more! And in this way it came to pass that George Robinson was present as Mr Brown's adviser when that scheme respecting the haberdashery was first set on foot.

CHAPTER IV

NINE TIMES NINE IS EIGHTY-ONE. SHOWING HOW BROWN, JONES, AND ROBINSON SELECTED THEIR HOUSE OF BUSINESS

And haberdashery it was. But there was much yet to be done before any terms for a partnership could be settled. Mr Jones at first insisted that he and his father-in-law should begin business on equal terms. He considered that any questions as to the actual right in the property would be mean after their mutual agreement to start in the world as friends. But to this Mr Brown, not unnaturally, objected.

'Then I shall go back to my lawyer,' said Jones. Whereupon he did leave the room, taking his hat with him; but he remained below in the old shop.

'If I am to go into partnership with that man alone,' said Mr Brown, turning to his young friend almost in despair, 'I may prepare for the Gazette at once. — And for my grave!' he added, solemnly.

'I'll join you,' said Robinson. 'I haven't got any money. You know that. But then neither has he.'

'I wish you had a little,' said Mr Brown. 'Capital is capital, you know.'

'But I've got that which is better than capital,' said Robinson, touching his forehead with his forefinger. 'And if you'll trust me, Mr Brown, I won't see you put upon.' The promise which Mr Robinson then gave he kept ever afterwards with a marked fidelity.

'I will trust you,' said Mr Brown. 'It shall be Brown, Jones, and Robinson.'

'And Brown, Jones, and Robinson shall carry their heads high among the greatest commercial firms of this wealthy metropolis,' said Robinson, with an enthusiasm which was surely pardonable at such a moment.

Mr Jones soon returned with another compromise; but it was of a low, peddling nature. It had reference to sevenths and eighths, and went into the payments of the household bills. 'I, as one of the partners, must object to any such arrangements,' said Robinson.

'You! — you one of the partners!' said Jones.

'If you have no objection — certainly!' said Robinson. 'And if you should have any objection, — equally so.'

'You! — a bill-sticker!' said Jones.

In the presence of William Brisket, George Robinson had been forced to acknowledge that matter must still occasionally prevail over mind; but he felt no such necessity in the presence of Jones. 'I'll tell you what it is,' said Robinson; 'I've never denied my former calling. Among friends I often talk about it. But mind you, Mr Jones, I won't bear it from you! I'm not very big myself, but I think I could stand up before you!'

But in this quarrel they were stopped by Mr Brown. 'Let dogs delight,' he said or sung, 'to bark and bite; —' and then he raised his two fat hands feebly, as though deprecating any further wrath. As usual on such occasions Mr Robinson yielded, and then explained in very concise language the terms on which it was proposed that the partnership should be opened. Mr Brown should put his 'capital' into the business, and be entitled to half the profits. Mr Jones and Mr Robinson should give the firm the advantage of their youth, energies, and genius, and should each be held as the possessor of a quarter. That Mr Jones made long and fierce objections to this, need hardly be stated. It is believed that he did, more than once, go back to his lawyer. But Mr Brown, who, for the time, put himself in the hands of his youngest partner, remained firm, and at last the preliminaries were settled.

The name of the house, the nature of the business, and the shares of the partners were now settled, and the site of the future labours of the firm became the next question. Mr Brown was in favour of a small tenement in Little Britain, near to the entrance into Smithfield.

'There would not be scope there,' said Robinson.

'And no fashion,' said Jones.

'It's safe and respectable,' pleaded Mr Brown. There have been shops in Little Britain these sixty years in the same families.'

But Robinson was of opinion that the fortunes of the firm might not improbably be made in six, if only they would commence with sufficient distinction. He had ascertained that large and commanding premises might be had in St Paul's Churchyard, in the frontage of which the square feet of plate glass could be counted by the hundred. It was true that the shop was nearly all window; but then, as Mr Robinson said, an extended front of glass was the one thing necessary. And it was true also that the future tenants must pay down a thousand pounds before they entered; — but then, as he explained, how could they better expend the trifle of money which they possessed?

'Trifle of money!' said Mr Brown, thinking of the mountains of butter and years of economy which had been required to put together those four thousand pounds; — thinking also, perhaps, of the absolute impecuniosity of his young partner who thus spoke.

Jones was for the West End and Regent Street. There was a shop only two doors off Regent Street, which could be made to look as if it was almost in Regent Street. The extension of a side piece of plate glass would show quite into Regent Street. He even prepared a card, describing the house as '2 doors from Regent Street,' printing the figure and the words 'Regent Street' very large, and the Intermediate description very small. It was ever by such stale, inefficient artifices as these that he sought success.

'Who'll care for your card?' said Robinson.

'When a man's card comes to be of use to him, the thing's done. He's living in his villa by that time, and has his five thousand a-year out of the profits.'

'I hope you'll both have your willas before long,' said Brown, trying to keep his partners in good humour. 'But a cottage *horney* will be enough for me. I'd like to be able to give my children their bit of dinner on Sunday hot and comfortable. I want no more than that.'

That was a hard battle, and it resulted in no victory. The dingy shop in Little Britain was, of course, out of the question; and Mr Brown assisted Robinson in preventing that insane attempt at aping the unprofitable glories of Regent Street. The matter ended in another compromise, and a house was taken in Bishopsgate Street, of which the frontage was extensive and commanding, but as to which it must certainly be confessed that the back part of the premises was inconveniently confined.

'It isn't exactly all I could wish,' said Robinson, standing on the pavement as he surveyed it. 'But it will do. With a little originality and some dash, we'll make it do. We must give it a name.'

'A name?' said Mr Brown; 'it's 81, Bishopsgate Street; ain't it? They don't call houses names in London.'

'That's just why we'll have a name for ours, Mr Brown.'

'The "Albert Emporium,"' suggested Jones; 'or "Victoria Mart."'

Mr Jones, as will be seen, was given to tuft-hunting to the backbone. His great ambition was to have a lion and a unicorn, and to call himself haberdasher to a royal prince. He had never realized the fact that profit, like power, comes from the people, and not from the court. 'I wouldn't put up the Queen's arms if the Queen came and asked me,' Robinson once said in answer to him. 'That game has been played out, and it isn't worth the cost of the two wooden figures.'

'"The Temple of Fashion" would do very well,' said Jones.

'The Temple of Fiddlestick!' said Robinson.

'Of course you say so,' said Jones.

'Let dogs delight —' began Mr Brown, standing as we were in the middle of the street.

'I'll tell you what,' said Robinson; 'there's nothing like colour. We'll call it Magenta House, and we'll paint it magenta from the roof to the window tops.

This beautiful tint had only then been invented, and it was necessary to explain the word to Mr Brown. He merely remarked that the oil and paint would come to a deal of money, and then gave way. Jones was struck dumb by the brilliancy of the idea, and for once forgot to object.

'And, I'll tell you what,' said Robinson — 'nine times nine is eighty-one.

'Certainly, certainly,' said Mr Brown, who delighted to agree with his younger partner when circumstances admitted it. 'You are right there, certainly.' Jones was observed to go through the multiplication table mentally, but he could detect no error.

'Nine times nine is eighty-one,' repeated Robinson with confidence, 'and we'll put that fact up over the first-floor windows.

And so they did. The house was painted magenta colour from top to bottom. And on the front in very large figures and letters was stated the undoubted fact that nine times nine is 81. 'If they will only call us "The nine times nine", the thing is done,' said Robinson. Nevertheless, the house was christened Magenta House. 'And now about glass,' said Robinson, when the three had retired to the little back room within.

Mr Robinson, however, admitted afterwards that he was wrong about the colour and the number. Such methods of obtaining attention were, he said, too easy of imitation, and devoid of any inherent attraction of their own. People would not care for nine times nine in Bishopsgate Street, if there were nine times nines in other streets as well. 'No,' said he; 'I was but beginning, and made errors as beginners do. Outside there should be glass, gas, gold, and glare. Inside there should be the same, with plenty of brass, and if possible a little wit. If those won't do it, nothing will.' All the same the magenta colour and the nine times nine did have their effect. 'Nine times nine is eighty-one,' was printed on the top of all the flying advertisements issued by the firm, and the printing was all done in magenta.

Mr Brown groaned sorely over the expenditure that was necessary in preparation of the premises. His wish was that this should be paid for in ready money; and indeed it was necessary that this should be done to a certain extent. But the great object should have been to retain every available shilling for advertisements. In the way of absolute capital, — money to be paid for stock, — 4,000*l*. was nothing. But 4,000*l*. scattered broadcast through the metropolis on walls, omnibuses, railway stations, little books, pavement chalkings, illuminated notices, porters' backs, gilded cars, and men in armour, would have driven nine times nine into the memory of half the inhabitants of London. The men in armour were tried. Four suits were obtained in Poland Street, and four strong men were hired who rode about town all day on four brewers' horses. They carried poles with large banners, and on the banners were inscribed the words which formed the shibboleth of the firm; —

MAGENTA HOUSE,
9 TIMES 9 IS 81,
BISHOPSGATE STREET.

And four times a day these four men in armour met each other in front of the windows of the house, and stood there on horseback for fifteen minutes, with their backs to the curbstone. The forage, however, of the horses became so terribly large an item of expenditure that Mr Brown's heart failed him. His heart failed him, and he himself went off late one evening to the livery stable-keeper who supplied the horses, and in Mr Robinson's absence, the armour was sent back to Poland Street.

'We should have had the police down upon us, George,' said Mr Brown, deprecating the anger of his younger partner.

'And what better advertisement could you have wished?' said Robinson. 'It would have been in all the papers, and have cost nothing.'

'But you don't know, George, what them beastesses was eating! It was frightful to hear of! Four-and-twenty pounds of corn a day each of 'em, because the armour was so uncommon heavy.' The men in armour were then given up, but they certainly were beginning to be effective. At 6 P.M., when the men were there, it had become impossible to pass the shop without going into the middle of the street, and on one or two occasions the policemen had spoken to Mr Brown. Then there was a slight accident with a child, and the newspapers had interfered.

But we are anticipating the story, for the men in armour did not begin their operations till the shop had been opened.

'And now about glass,' said Robinson, as soon as the three partners had retired from the outside flags into the interior of the house.

'It must be plate, of course,' said Jones. Plate!

He might as well have said when wanting a house, that it must have walls.

'I rather think so,' said Robinson; 'and a good deal of it.'

'I don't mind a good-sized common window,' said Brown.

'A deal better have them uncommon,' said Robinson, interrupting him. 'And remember, sir, there's nothing like glass in these days. It has superseded leather altogether in that respect.'

'Leather!' said Mr Brown, who was hardly quick enough for his junior partner.

'Of all our materials now in general use,' said Robinson, 'glass is the most brilliant, and yet the cheapest; the most graceful and yet the strongest. Though transparent it is impervious to wet. The eye travels through it, but not the hailstorm. To the power of gas it affords no obstacle, but is as efficient a barrier against the casualties of the street as an iron shutter. To that which is ordinary it lends a grace; and to that which is graceful it gives a double lustre. Like a good advertisement, it multiplies your stock tenfold, and like a good servant, it is always eloquent in praise of its owner. I look upon plate glass, sir, as the most glorious product of the age; and I regard the tradesman who can surround himself with the greatest quantity of it, as the most in advance of the tradesmen of his day. Oh, sir, whatever we do, let us have glass.'

'It's beautiful to hear him talk,' said Mr Brown; 'but it's the bill I'm a thinking of.'

'If you will only go enough ahead, Mr Brown, you'll find that nobody will trouble you with such bills.'

'But they must be paid some day, George.'

'Of course they must; but it will never do to think of that now. In twelve months or so, when we have set the house well going, the payment of such bills as that will be a mere nothing, — a thing that will be passed as an item not worth notice. Faint heart never won fair lady, you know, Mr Brown.' And then a cloud came across George Robinson's brow as he thought of the words he had spoken; for his heart had once been faint, and his fair lady was by no means won.

'That's quite true,' said Jones; 'it never does. Ha! ha! ha!'

Then the cloud went away from George Robinson's brow, and a stern frown of settled resolution took its place. At that moment he made up his mind, that when he might again meet that giant butcher he would forget the difference in their size, and accost him as though they two were equal. What though some fell blow, levelled as at an ox, should lay him low for ever. Better that, than endure from day to day the unanswered taunts of such a one as Jones!

Mr Brown, though he was not quick-witted, was not deficient when the feelings of man and man were concerned. He understood it all, and taking advantage of a moment when Jones had stepped up the shop, he pressed Robinson's hand and said, 'You shall have her, George. If a father's word is worth anything, you shall have her.' But in this case, — as in so many others, — a father's word was not worth anything.

'But to business!' said Robinson, shaking off from him all thoughts of love.

After that Mr Brown had not the heart to oppose him respecting the glass, and in that matter he had everything nearly his own way. The premises stood advantageously at the corner of a little alley, so that the window was made to jut out sideways in that direction, and a full foot and a half was gained. On the other side the house did not stand flush with its neighbour, — as is not unfrequently the case in Bishopsgate Street, — and here also a few inches were made available. The next neighbour, a quiet old man who sold sticks, threatened a lawsuit; but that, had it been instituted, would have got into the newspapers and been an advertisement. There was considerable trouble about the entrance. A wide, commanding centre doorway was essential; but this, if made in the desirable proportions, would have terribly crippled the side windows. To obviate this difficulty, the exterior space allotted for the entrance between the frontage of the two windows was broad and noble, but the glass splayed inwards towards the shop, so that the absolute door was decidedly narrow.

'When we come to have a crowd, they won't get in and out,' said Jones.

'If we could only crush a few to death in the

doorway our fortune would be made,' said Robinson.

'God forbid!' said Mr Brown; 'God forbid! Let us have no bloodshed, whatever we do.'

In about a month the house was completed, and much to the regret of both the junior partners, a considerable sum of ready money was paid to the tradesmen who performed the work. Mr Jones was of opinion that by sufficient cunning such payments might be altogether evaded. No such thought rested for a moment in the bosom of Mr Robinson. All tradesmen should be paid, and paid well. But the great firm of Brown, Jones, and Robinson would be much less likely to scrutinize the price at which plate glass was charged to them per square foot, when they were taking their hundreds a day over the counter, than they would be now when every shilling was of importance to them.

'For their own sake you shouldn't do it,' said he to Mr Brown. 'You may be quite sure they don't like it.'

'I always liked it myself,' said Mr Brown. And thus he would make his dribbling payments, by which an unfortunate idea was generated in the neighbourhood that money was not plentiful with the firm.

CHAPTER V
THE DIVISION OF LABOUR

There were two other chief matters to which it was now necessary that the Firm should attend; the first and primary being the stock of advertisements which should be issued; and the other, or secondary, being the stock of goods which should be obtained to answer the expectations raised by those advertisements.

'But, George, we must have something to sell,' said Mr Brown, almost in despair. He did not then understand, and never since has learned the secrets of that commercial science which his younger partner was at so much pains to teach. There are things which no elderly man can learn; and there are lessons which are full of light for the new recruit, but dark as death to the old veteran.

'It will be so doubtless with me also,' said Robinson, soliloquizing on the subject in his melancholy mood. 'The day will come when I too must be pushed from my stool by the workings of younger genius, and shall sink, as poor

Mr Brown is now sinking, into the foggy depths of fogeydom. But a man who is a man —' and then that melancholy mood left him, 'can surely make his fortune before that day comes. When a merchant is known to be worth half a million, his fogeydom is respected.'

That necessity of having something to sell almost overcame Mr Brown in those days. 'What's the good of putting down 5,000 Kolinski and Minx Boas in the bill, if we don't possess one in the shop?' he asked; 'we must have some if they're asked for.' He could not understand that for a first start effect is everything. If customers should want Kolinski Boas, Kolinski Boas would of course be forthcoming, — to any number required; either Kolinski Boas, or quasi Kolinski, which in trade is admitted to be the same thing. When a man advertises that he has 40,000 new paletots, he does not mean that he has got that number packed up in a box. If required to do so, he will supply them to that extent, — or to any further extent. A long row of figures in trade is but an elegant use of the superlative. If a tradesman can induce a lady to buy a diagonal Osnabruck cashmere shawl by telling her that he has 1,200 of them, who is injured? And if the shawl is not exactly a real diagonal Osnabruck cashmere, what harm is done as long as the lady gets the value for her money? And if she don't get the value for her money, whose fault is that? Isn't it a fair stand-up fight? And when she tries to buy for 4*l.*, a shawl which she thinks is worth about

8*l.*, Isn't she dealing on the same principles herself? If she be lucky enough to possess credit, the shawl is sent home without payment, and three years afterwards fifty per cent, is perhaps offered for settlement of the bill. It is a fair fight, and the ladies are very well able to take care of themselves.

And Jones also thought they must have something to sell. 'Money is money,' said he, 'and goods is goods. What's the use of windows if we haven't anything to dress them? And what's the use of capital unless we buy a stock?'

With Mr Jones, George Robinson never cared to argue. The absolute impossibility of pouring the slightest ray of commercial light into the dim chaos of that murky mind had long since come home to him. He merely shook his head, and went on with the composition on which he was engaged. It need hardly be explained here that he had no idea of encountering the public throng on their opening day, without an adequate assortment of goods. Of course there must be shawls and cloaks; of course there must be muffs and boas; of course there must be hose and handkerchiefs. That dressing of the windows was to be the special care of Mr Jones, and Robinson would take care that there should be the wherewithal. The dressing of the windows, and the parading of the shop, was to be the work of Jones. His ambition had never soared above that, and while serving in the house on Snow Hill, his utmost envy had been excited by the youthful aspirant who there walked the boards, and with an oily courtesy handed chairs to the ladies. For one short week he had been allowed to enter this Paradise. 'And though I looked so sweet on them,' said he, 'I always had my eye on them. It's a grand thing to be down on a well-dressed woman as she's hiding a roll of ribbon under her cloak.' That was his idea of grandeur!

A stock of goods was of course necessary, but if the firm could only get their name sufficiently established, that matter would be arranged simply by written orders to two or three wholesale houses. Competition, that beautiful science of the present day, by which every plodding cart-horse is converted into a racer, makes this easy enough. When it should once become known that a firm was opening itself on a great scale in a good thoroughfare, and advertising on real, intelligible principles, there would be no lack of goods.

'You can have any amount of hose you want, out of Cannon Street,' said Mr Robinson, 'in forty-five minutes. They can be brought in at the back while you are selling them over the counter.

'Can they?' said Mr Brown: 'perhaps they can. But nevertheless, George, I think I'll buy a few. It'll be an ease to my mind.'

He did so; but it was a suicidal act on his part. One thing was quite clear, even to Mr Jones. If the firm commenced business to the extent which they contemplated, it was out of the question that they should do everything on the ready-money principle. That such a principle is antiquated, absurd, and uncommercial; that it is opposed to the whole system of trade as now adopted in this metropolis, has been clearly shown in the preface to these memoirs. But in this instance, in the case of Brown, Jones, and Robinson, the doing so was as impracticable as it would have been foolish, if practicable. Credit and credit only was required. But of all modes of extinguishing credit, or crushing, as it were, the young baby in its cradle, there is none equal to that of spending a little ready money, and then halting. In trade as in love, to doubt, — or rather, to seem to doubt, — is to be lost. When you order goods, do so as though the bank were at your back. Look your victim full in the face, and write down your long numbers without a falter in your pen. And should there seem a hesitation on his part, do not affect to understand it. When the articles are secured, you give your bills at six months' date; then your credit at your bankers, — your discount system, — commences. That is another affair. When once your bank begins that with you, — and the banks must do so, or they may put up their shutters, — when once your bank has commenced, it must carry on the game. You are floated then, placed well in the centre of the full stream of commerce, and it must be your own fault if you do not either retire with half a million, or become bankrupt with an éclat, which is worth more than any capital in refitting you for a further attempt. In the meantime it need hardly be said that you yourself are living on the very fat of the land.

But birds of a feather should flock together, and Mr Brown and Mr Robinson were not exactly of the same plumage.

It was finally arranged that Mr Robinson should have carte blanche at his own particular line of business, to the extent of fifteen hundred pounds, and that Mr Brown should go into the warehouse and lay out a similar sum in goods. Both Jones and Mrs Jones accompanied the old man, and a sore time he had of it. It may here be remarked, that Mrs Jones struggled very hard to get a footing in the shop, but on this point it should be acknowledged that her husband did his duty for a while.

'It must be you or I, Sarah Jane,' said he; 'but not both.'

'I have no objection in life,' said she; 'you can stay at home, if you please.

'By no means, he replied. 'If you come here, and your father permits it, I shall go to America. Of course the firm will allow me for my share.' She tried it on very often after that, and gave the firm much trouble, but I don't think she got her hand into the cash drawer above once or twice during the first twelve months.

The division of labour was finally arranged as follows. Mr Brown was to order the goods; to hire the young men and women, look after their morality, and pay them their wages; to listen to any special applications when a desire might be expressed to see the firm; and to do the heavy respectable parental business. There was a little back room with a skylight, in which he was to sit; and when he was properly got up, his manner of shaking his head at the young people who misbehaved themselves, was not ineffective. There is always danger when young men and women are employed together in the same shop, and if possible this should be avoided. It is not in human nature that they should not fall in love, or at any rate amuse themselves with ordinary flirtations. Now the rule is that not a word shall be spoken that does not refer to business. 'Miss O'Brien, where is the salmon-coloured sarsenet? or, Mr Green, I'll trouble you for the ladies' sevens.' Nothing is ever spoken beyond that. 'Morals, morals, above everything!' Mr Brown was once heard to shout from his little room, when a whisper had been going round the shop as to a concerted visit to the Crystal Palace. Why a visit to the Crystal Palace should be immoral, when talked of over the counter, Mr Brown did not explain on that occasion.

'A very nice set of young women,' the compiler of these memoirs once remarked to a commercial gentleman in a large way, who was showing him over his business, 'and for the most part very good-looking.'

'Yes, sir, yes; we attend to their morals especially. They generally marry from us, and become the happy mothers of families.'

'Ah,' said I, really delighted in my innocence.

'They've excellent opportunities for that, because there are so many decent young men about.'

He turned on me as though I had calumniated his establishment with a libel of the vilest description. 'If a whisper of such a thing ever reaches us, sir,' said he, quite alive with virtuous indignation; 'if such a suspicion is ever engendered, we send them packing at once! The morals of our young women, sir —' And then he finished his sentence simply by a shake of his head. I tried to bring him into an argument, and endeavoured to make him understand that no young woman can become a happy wife unless she first be allowed to have a lover. 'Morals, sir!' he repeated. 'Morals above everything. In such an establishment as this, if we are not moral, we are nothing.' I supposed he was right, but it seemed to me to be very hard on the young men and women. I could only hope that they walked home together in the evening.

In the new firm in Bishopsgate Street, Mr Brown, of course, took upon himself that branch of business, and some little trouble he had, because his own son-in-law and partner would make eyes to the customers.

'Mr Jones,' he once said before them all; 'you'll bring down my gray hairs with sorrow to the grave; you will, indeed.' And then he put up his fat hand, and gently stroked the white expense of his bald pate. But that was a very memorable occasion.

Such was Mr Brown's business. To Mr Jones was allocated the duty of seeing that the shop was duly dressed, of looking after the customers, including that special duty of guarding against shoplifting, and of attending generally to the retail business. It cannot be denied that for this sort of work he had some specialties. His eye was sharp, and his ear was keen, and his feelings were blunt. In a certain way, he was good-looking, and he knew how to hand a chair with a bow and smile, which went far with the wives and daughters of the East End little tradesmen, — and he was active enough at his work. He was usually to be seen standing in the front of the shop, about six yards within the door, rubbing his hands together, or arranging his locks, or twiddling with his brass watch-chain. Nothing disconcerted him, unless his wife walked into the place; and then, to the great delight of the young men and women, he was unable to conceal his misery. By them he was hated, — as was perhaps necessary in his position. He was a tyrant, who liked to feel at every moment the relish of his power. To the poor girls he was cruel, treating them as though they were dirt beneath his feet. For Mr Jones, though he affected the reputation of an admirer of the fair sex, never forgot himself by being even civil to a female who was his paid servant. Woman's smile had a charm for him, but no charm equal to the servility of dependence.

But on the shoulders of Mr Robinson fell the great burden of the business. There was a question as to the accounts; these, however, he undertook to keep in his leisure moments, thinking but little of the task. But the work of his life was to be the advertising department. He was to draw up the posters; he was to write those little books which, printed on magenta-coloured paper, were to be thrown with reckless prodigality into every vehicle in the town; he was to arrange new methods of alluring the public into that emporium of fashion. It was for him to make a credulous multitude believe that at that shop, number Nine Times Nine in Bishopsgate Street, goods of all sorts were to be purchased at prices considerably less than the original cost of their manufacture. This he undertook to do; this for a time he did do; this for years to come he would have done, had he not experienced an interference in his own department, by which the whole firm was ultimately ruined and sent adrift.

'The great thing is to get our bills into the hands of the public,' said Robinson.

'You can get men for one and nine a day to stand still and hand 'em out to the passers-by,' said Mr Brown.

'That's stale, sir, quite stale; novelty in advertising is what we require; — something new and startling.'

'Put a chimney-pot on the man's head,' said Mr Brown, 'and make it two and three.'

'That's been tried,' said Robinson.

'Then put two chimney-pots,' said Mr Brown.

Beyond that his imagination did not carry him.

Chimney-pots and lanterns on men's heads avail nothing. To startle men and women to any purpose, and drive them into Bishopsgate Street, you must startle them a great deal. It does not suffice to create a momentary wonder. Mr Robinson, therefore, began with eight footmen in full livery, with powdered hair and gold tags to their shoulders. They had magenta-coloured plush knee-breeches, and magenta-coloured silk stockings. It was in May, and the weather was fine, and these eight excellently got-up London footmen were stationed at different points in the city, each with a silken bag suspended round his shoulder by a silken cord. From these bags they drew forth the advertising cards of the house, and presented them to such of the passers-by as appeared from their dress and physiognomy to be available for the purpose. The fact has now been ascertained that men and women who have money to spend will not put out their hands to accept common bills from street advertisers. In an ordinary way the money so spent is thrown away. But from these men, arrayed in gorgeous livery, a duchess would have stayed her steps to accept a card. And duchesses did stay their steps, and cards from the young firm of Brown, Jones, and Robinson were, as the firm was credibly informed, placed beneath the eyes of a very illustrious personage indeed.

The nature of the card was this. It was folded into three, and when so folded, was of the size of an ordinary playing card. On the outside, which bore a satin glaze with a magenta tint, there was a blank space as though for an address, and the compliments of the firm in the corner; when opened there was a separate note inside, in which the public were informed in very few words, that 'Messrs. Brown, Jones, and Robinson were prepared to open their house on the 15th of May, intending to carry on their trade on principles of commerce perfectly new, and hitherto untried. The present rate of money in the city was five per cent., and it would be the practice of the firm to charge five and a half per cent. on every article sold by them. The very quick return which this would give them, would enable B. J. and R. to realize princely fortunes, and at the same time to place within the reach of the public goods of the very best description at prices much below any that had ever yet been quoted.' This also was printed on magenta-coloured paper, and 'nine times nine is eighty-one' was inserted both at the top and the bottom.

On the inside of the card, on the three folds, were printed lists of the goods offered to the public. The three headings were 'cloaks and shawls,' 'furs and velvets,' 'silks and satins;' and in a small note at the bottom it was stated that the stock of hosiery, handkerchiefs, ribbons, and gloves, was sufficient to meet any demand which the metropolis could make upon the firm.

When that list was first read out in conclave to the partners, Mr Brown begged almost with tears in his eyes, that it might be modified. 'George,' said he, 'we shall be exposed.'

'I hope we shall,' said Robinson. 'Exposition is all that we desire.'

'Eight thousand African monkey muffs! Oh, George, you must leave out the monkey muffs.'

'By no means, Mr Brown.'

'Or bring them down to a few hundreds. Two hundred African monkey muffs would really be a great many.'

'Mr Brown,' said Robinson on that occasion; — and it may be doubted whether he ever again spoke to the senior partner of his firm in terms so imperious and decisive; 'Mr Brown, to you has been allotted your share in our work, and when you insisted on throwing away our ready money on those cheap Manchester prints, I never said a word. It lay in your department to do so. The composition of this card lies in mine, and I mean to exercise my own judgment.' And then he went on, 'Eight thousand real African monkey muffs; six thousand ditto, ditto, ditto, very superior, with long fine hair.' Mr Brown merely groaned, but he said nothing further.

'Couldn't you say that they are such as are worn by the Princess Alice?' suggested Jones.

'No, I could not,' answered Robinson. 'You may tell them that in the shop if you please. That will lie in your department.

In this way was the first card of the firm drawn out, and in the space of a fortnight, nineteen thousand of them were disseminated through the metropolis. When it is declared that each of those cards cost B. J. and R. threepence three farthings, some idea may be formed of the style in which they commenced their operations.

CHAPTER VI
IT IS OUR OPENING DAY

And now the day had arrived on which the firm was to try the result of their efforts. It is believed that the 15th of May in that year will not easily be forgotten in the neighbourhood of Bishopsgate Street. It was on this day that the experiment of the men in armour was first tried, and the four cavaliers, all mounted and polished as bright as brass, were stationed in the front of the house by nine o'clock. There they remained till the doors and shop windows were opened, which ceremony actually took place at twelve. It had been stated to the town on the preceding day by a man dressed as Fame, with a long horn, who had been driven about in a gilt car, that this would be done at ten. But peeping through the iron shutters at that hour, the gentlemen of the firm saw that the crowd was as yet by no means great. So a huge poster was put up outside each window: —

'POSTPONED TILL ELEVEN

At eleven this was done again; but at twelve the house was really opened. At that time the car with Fame and the long horn was stationed in front of the men in armour, and there really was a considerable concourse of people.

'This won't do, Mr Brown,' a policeman had said. 'The people are half across the street.

'Success! success!' shouted Mr Robinson, from the first landing on the stairs. He was busy correcting the proofs of their second set of notices to the public.

'Shall we open, George?' whispered Mr Brown, who was rather flurried.

'Yes; you may as well begin,' said he. 'It must be done sooner or later.' And then he retired quietly to his work. He had allowed himself to be elated for one moment at the interference of the police, but after that he remained above, absorbed in his work; or if not so absorbed, disdaining to mix with the crowd below. For there, in the centre of the shop, leaning on the arm of Mr William Brisket, stood Maryanne Brown.

As regards grouping, there was certainly some propriety in the arrangements made for receiving the public. When the iron shutters were wound up, the young men of the establishment stood in a row behind one of the counters, and the young women behind the other. They were very nicely got up for the occasion. The girls were all decorated with magenta-coloured ribbons, and the young men with magenta neckties. Mr Jones had been very anxious to charge them for these articles in their wages, but Mr Brown's good feeling had prevented this. 'No, Jones, no; the master always finds the livery.' There had been something in the words, master and livery, which had tickled the ears of his son-in-law, and so the matter had been allowed to pass by.

In the centre of the shop stood Mr Brown, very nicely dressed in a new suit of black. That bald head of his, and the way he had of rubbing his hands together, were not ill-calculated to create respect. But on such occasions it was always necessary to induce him to hold his tongue. Mr Brown never spoke effectively unless he had been first moved almost to tears. It was now his special business to smile, and he did smile. On his right hand stood his partner and son-in-law Jones, mounted quite irrespectively of expense. His waistcoat and cravat may be said to have been gorgeous, and from his silky locks there came distilled a mixed odour of musk and patchouli. About his neck also the colours of the house were displayed, and in his hand he waved a magenta handkerchief. His wife was leaning on his arm, and on such an occasion as this even Robinson had consented to her presence. She was dressed from head to foot in magenta. She wore a magenta bonnet, and magenta stockings, and it was said of her that she was very careful to allow the latter article to be seen. The only beauty of which

Sarah Jane could boast, rested in her feet and ankles.

But on the other side of Mr Brown stood a pair, for whose presence there George Robinson had not expressed his approbation, and as to one of whom it may be said that better taste would have been shown on all sides had he not thus intruded himself. Mr Brisket had none of the rights of proprietorship in that house, nor would it be possible that he should have as long as the name of the firm contained within itself that of Mr Robinson. Had Brown, Jones, and Brisket agreed to open shop together, it would have been well for Brisket to stand there with that magenta shawl round his neck, and waving that magenta towel in his hand. But as it was, what business had he there?

'What business has he there? Ah, tell me that; what business has he there?' said Robinson to himself, as he sat moodily in the small back room upstairs. Ah, tell me that, what business has he here? Did not the old man promise that she should be mine? Is it for him that I have done all; for him that I have collected the eager crowd of purchasers that throng the hall of commerce below, which my taste has decorated? Or for her — ? Have I done this for her, — the false one? But what recks it? She shall live to know that had she been constant to me she might have sat — almost upon a throne!' And then he rushed again to his work, and with eager pen struck off those well-known lines about the house which some short time after ravished the ears of the metropolis.

In a following chapter of these memoirs it will be necessary to go back for a while to the domestic life of some of the persons concerned, and the fact of Mr Brisket's presence at the opening of the house will then be explained. In the meantime the gentle reader is entreated to take it for granted that Mr William Brisket was actually there, standing on the left hand of Mr Brown, waving high above his head a huge magenta cotton handkerchief, and that on his other arm was hanging Maryanne Brown, leaning quite as closely upon him as her sister did upon the support which was her own. For one moment George Robinson allowed himself to look down upon the scene, and he plainly saw that clutch of the hand upon the sleeve. 'Big as he is,' said Robinson to himself, 'pistols would make us equal. But the huge ox has no sense of chivalry.'

It was unfortunate for the future intrinsic comfort of the firm that that member of it who was certainly not the least enterprising should have found himself unable to join in the ceremony of opening the house; but, nevertheless, it must be admitted that that ceremony was imposing. Maryanne Brown was looking her best, and dressed as she was in the correctest taste of the day, wearing of course the colours of the house, it was not unnatural that all eyes should be turned on her. 'What a big man that Robinson is!' some one in the crowd was heard to observe.

Yes; that huge lump of human clay that called itself William Brisket, the butcher of Aldersgate
Street, was actually taken on that occasion for
the soul, and life, and salt of an advertising
house. Of Mr William Brisket, it may here be
said, that he had no other idea of trade than that
of selling at so much per pound the beef which
he had slaughtered with his own hands.

But that ceremony was imposing. 'Ladies and
gentlemen,' said those five there assembled —
speaking as it were with one voice, — 'we bid you
welcome to Magenta House. Nine times nine is
eighty-one. Never forget that.' Robinson had
planned the words, but he was not there to assist
at their utterance! 'Ladies and gentlemen, again,
we bid you welcome to Magenta House.' And
then they retired backwards down the shop, allowing the crowd to press forward, and all
packed themselves for awhile into Mr Brown's
little room at the back.

'It was smart,' said Mr Brisket.

'And went off uncommon well,' said Jones,
shaking the scent from his head. 'All the better,
too, because that chap wasn't here.'

'He's a clever fellow,' said Brisket.

'And you shouldn't speak against him behind
his back, Jones. Who did it all? And who couldn't
have done it if he hadn't been here?' When these
words were afterwards told to George Robinson,
he forgave Mr Brown a great deal.

The architect, acting under the direction of Mr
Robinson, had contrived to arch the roof, sup-

porting it on five semicircular iron girders, which were left there visible to the eye, and which were of course painted magenta. On the foremost of these was displayed the name of the firm, — Brown, Jones, and Robinson. On the second, the name of the house, — Magenta House. On the third the number, — Nine times nine is eighty one. On the fourth, an edict of trade against which retail houses in the haberdashery line should never sin, — 'Terms: Ready cash.' And on the last, the special principle of our trade, — 'Five-and-a-half per cent. profit.' The back of the shop was closed in with magenta curtains, through which the bald head of Mr Brown would not unfrequently be seen to emerge; and on each side of the curtains there stood a tall mirror, reaching up to the very ceiling. Upon the whole, the thing certainly was well done.

'But the contractor,' — the man who did the work was called the contractor, — 'the contractor says that he will want the rest of his money in two months,' said Mr Brown, whining.

'He would not have wanted any for the next twelve months,' answered Robinson, 'if you had not insisted on paying him those few hundreds.'

'You can find fault with the bill, you know,' said Jones, 'and delay it almost any time by threatening him with a lawyer.'

'And then he will put a distress on us,' said Mr Brown.

'And after that will be very happy to take our bill at six months,' said Robinson. And so that matter was ended for the time.

Those men in armour stood there the whole of that day, and Fame in his gilded car used his trumpet up and down Bishopsgate Street with such effect, that the people living on each side of the street became very sick of him. Fame himself was well acted, — at 16*s.* the day, — and when the triumphal car remained still, stood balanced on one leg, with the other stretched out behind, in a manner that riveted attention. But no doubt his horn was badly chosen. Mr Robinson insisted on a long single-tubed instrument, saying that it was classical; but a cornet à piston would have given more pleasure.

A good deal of money was taken on that day; but certainly not so much as had been anticipated. Very many articles were asked for, looked at, and then not purchased. But this, though it occasioned grief to Mr Brown, was really not of much moment. That the thing should be talked of, — if possible mentioned in the newspapers — was the object of the firm.

'I would give my bond for 2,000*l.*,' said Robinson, 'to get a leader in the Jupiter.'

The first article demanded over the counter was a real African monkey muff, very superior, with long fine hair.

'The ships which are bringing them have not yet arrived from the coast,' answered Jones, who luckily stepped up at the moment. 'They are expected in the docks to-morrow.

CHAPTER VII

MISS BROWN PLEADS HER OWN CASE, AND MR ROBINSON WALKS ON BLACKFRIARS BRIDGE

At the time of Mrs McCockerell's death Robinson and Maryanne Brown were not on comfortable terms with each other. She had twitted him with being remiss in asserting his own rights in the presence of his rival, and he had accused her of being fickle, if not actually false.

'I shall be just as fickle as I please,' she said. 'If it suits me I'll have nine to follow me; but there shan't be one of the nine who won't hold up his head and look after his own.'

'Your conduct, Maryanne —.'

'George, I won't be scolded, and that you ought to know. If you don't like me, you are quite welcome to do the other thing.' And then they parted. This took place after Mr Brown's adherence to the Robinson interest, and while Brisket was waiting passively to see if that five hundred pounds would be forthcoming.

Their next meeting was in the presence of Mr Brown; and on that occasion all the three spoke out their intentions on the subject of their future family arrangements, certainly with much plain language, if not on every side with positive truth. Mr Robinson was at the house in Smithfield, giving counsel to old Mr Brown as to the contest which was then being urged between him and his son-in-law. At that period the two sisters conceived that their joint pecuniary interests required that they should act together; and it must be acknowledged that they led poor Mr Brown a sad life of it. He and Robinson were sitting upstairs in the little back room looking out into Spavinhorse Yard, when Maryanne abruptly broke in upon them.

'Father,' she said, standing upright in the middle of the room before them, 'I have come to know what it is that you mean to do?'

'To do, my dear?' said old Mr Brown.

'Yes; to do. I suppose something is to be done some day. We ain't always to go on shilly-shallying, spending the money, and ruining the business, and living from hand to mouth, as though there was no end to anything. I've got myself to look to, and I don't mean to go into the workhouse if I can help it!'

'The workhouse, Maryanne!'

'I said the workhouse, father, and I meant it. If everybody had what was justly their own, I shouldn't have to talk in that way. But as far as I can see, them sharks, the lawyers, will have it all. Now, I'll tell you what it is —'

Hitherto Robinson had not said a word; but at this moment he thought it right to interfere.

'Maryanne!' he said, — and, in pronouncing the well-loved name, he threw into it all the affection of which his voice was capable, —' Maryanne!'

'"Miss Brown" would be a deal properer, and also much more pleasing, if it's all the same to you, sir!'

How often had he whispered 'Maryanne' into her ears, and the dear girl had smiled upon him to hear herself so called! But he could not remind her of this at the present moment. 'I have your father's sanction,' said he —

'My father is nothing to me, — not with reference to what young man I let myself be called "Maryanne" by. And going on as he is going on, I don't suppose that he'll long be much to me in any way.'

'Oh, Maryanne!' sobbed the unhappy parent.

'That's all very well, sir, but it won't keep the kettle a-boiling!'

'As long as I have a bit to eat of, Maryanne, and a cup to drink of, you shall have the half.'

'And what am I to do when you won't have neither a bit nor a cup? That's what you're coming to, father. We can all see that. What's the use of all them lawyers?'

'That's Jones's doing,' said Robinson.

'No; it isn't Jones's doing. And of course Jones must look after himself. I'm not partial to Jones. Everybody knows that. When Sarah Jane disgraced herself, and went off with him, I never said a word in her favour. It wasn't I who brought a viper into the house and warmed it in my bosom.' It was at this moment that Jones was be-having with the most barefaced effrontery, as well as the utmost cruelty, towards the old man, and Maryanne's words cut her father to the very soul. 'Jones might have been anywhere for me,' she continued; 'but there he is downstairs, and Sarah Jane is with him. Of course they are look-ing for their own.'

'And what is it you want, Maryanne?'

'Well; I'll tell you what I want. My dear sainted mother's last wish was that — I should become Mrs Brisket!'

'And do you mean to say,' said Robinson — 'do you mean to say that that is now your wish?' And he looked at her till the audacity even of her eyes sank beneath the earnestness of his own. But though for the moment he quelled her eye, nothing could quell her voice.

'I mean to say,' said she, speaking loudly, and with her arms akimbo, 'that William Brisket is a very respectable young man, with a trade, — that he's got a decent house for a young woman to live in, and a decent table for her to sit at. And he's always been brought up decent, having been a regular 'prentice to his uncle, and all that sort of thing. He's never been wandering about like a vagrant, getting his money nobody knows how. William Brisket's as well known in Aldersgate Street as the Post Office. And moreover,' she added, after a pause, speaking these last words in a somewhat milder breath — 'And moreover, it was my sainted mother's wish!'

'Then go to him!' said Robinson, rising suddenly, and stretching out his arm against her. 'Go to him, and perform your — sainted mother's wish! Go to the — butcher! revel in his shambles, and grow fat and sleek in his slaughter-house! From this moment George Robinson will fight the world alone. Brisket, indeed! If it be accounted manliness to have killed hecatombs of oxen, let him be called manly!'

'He would have pretty nigh killed you, young man, on one occasion, if you hadn't made yourself scarce.'

'But heavens!' exclaimed Robinson, 'if he'll come forth, I'll fight him to-morrow; — with cleavers, if he will!'

'George, George, don't say that,' exclaimed Mr Brown. '"Let dogs delight to bark and bite."'

'You needn't be afraid,' said Maryanne. 'He doesn't mean fighting,' and she pointed to Robinson. 'William would about eat him, you know, if they were to come together.'

'Heaven forbid!' said Mr Brown.

'But what I want to know is this,' continued the maiden; 'how is it to be about that five hundred pounds which my mother left me?'

'But, my dear, your mother had not five hundred pounds to leave.'

'Nor did she make any will if she had,' said Robinson.

'Now don't put in your oar, for I won't have it,' said the lady. 'And you'd show a deal more correct feeling if you wasn't so much about the

79

house just at present. My darling mamma,' — and then she put her handkerchief up to her eyes — 'always told William that when he and I become one, there should be five hundred pounds down; — and of course he expects it. Now, sir, you often talk about your love for your children.'

'I do love them; so I do. What else have I?'

'Now's the time to prove it. Let me have that sum of five hundred pounds, and I will always take your part against the Joneses. Five hundred pounds isn't so much, — and surely I have a right to some share. And you may be sure of this; when we're settled, Brisket is not the man to come back to you for more, as some would do.' And then she gave another look at Robinson.

'I haven't got the money; have I, George?' said the father.

'That question I cannot answer,' replied Robinson. 'Nor can I say how far it might be prudent in you to debar yourself from all further progress in commerce if you have got it. But this I can say; do not let any consideration for me prevent you from giving a dowry with your daughter to Mr Brisket; if she loves him —'

'Oh, it's all bother about love,' said she; 'men and women must eat, and they must have something to give their children, when they come.'

'But if I haven't got it, my dear?'

'That's nonsense, father. Where has the money gone to? Whatever you do, speak the truth. If you choose to say you won't —'

'Well, then, I won't,' said he, roused suddenly

to anger. 'I never made Brisket any promise!'

'But mother did; she as is now gone, and far away; and it was her money, — so it was.'

'It wasn't her money; — it was mine!' said Mr Brown.

'And that's all the answer I'm to get? Very well. Then I shall know where to look for my rights. And as for that fellow there, I didn't think it of him, that he'd be so mean. I knew he was a coward always.'

'I am neither mean nor a coward,' said Robinson, jumping up, and speaking with a voice that was audible right across Spavinhorse Yard, and into the tap of the 'Man of Mischief' public-house opposite. 'As for meanness, if I had the money, I would pour it out into your lap, though I knew that it was to be converted into beef and mutton for the benefit of a hated rival. And as for cowardice, I repel the charge, and drive it back into the teeth of him who, doubtless, made it. I am no coward.'

'You ran away when he bid you!'

'Yes; because he is big and strong, and had I remained, he would have knocked me about, and made me ridiculous in the eyes of the spectators. But I am no coward. If you wish it, I am ready to fight him.'

'Oh, dear, no. It can be nothing to me.'

'He will make me one mash of gore,' said Robinson, still holding out his hand. 'But if you wish it, I care nothing for that. His brute strength will, of course, prevail; but I am indifferent as to

81

that, if it would do you a pleasure.'

'Pleasure to me! Nothing of the kind, I can assure you.'

'Maryanne, if I might have my wish, it should be this. Let us both sit down, with our cigars lighted, — ay, and with tapers in our hands, — on an open barrel of gunpowder. Then let him who will sit there longest receive this fair hand as his prize.' And as he finished, he leaned over her, and took up her hand in his.

'Laws, Robinson!' she said; but she did not on the moment withdraw her hand. 'And if you were both blew up, what'd I do then?'

'I won't hear of such an arrangement,' said Mr Brown. 'It would be very wicked. If there's another word spoke about it, I'll go to the police at once!'

On that occasion Mr Brown was quite determined about the money; and, as we heard afterwards, Mr Brisket expressed himself as equally resolute. 'Of course, I expect to see my way, said he; 'I can't do anything of that sort without seeing my way.' When that overture about the gunpowder was repeated to him, he is reported to have become very red. 'Either with gloves or without, or with the sticks, I'm ready for him,' said he; 'but as for sitting on a barrel of gunpowder, it's a thing as nobody wouldn't do unless they was in Bedlam.'

When that interview was over, Robinson walked forth by himself into the evening air, along Giltspur Street, down the Old Bailey, and so on by Bridge Street, to the middle of Blackfriars Bridge; and as he walked, he strove manfully to get the better of the passion which was devouring the strength of his blood, and the marrow of his bones.

'If she be not fair for me,' he sang to himself, 'what care I how fair she be?' But he did care; he could not master that passion. She had been vile to him, unfeminine, untrue, coarsely abusive; she had shown herself to be mercenary, incapable of true love, a scold, fickle, and cruel. But yet he loved her. There was a gallant feeling at his heart that no misfortune could conquer him, — but one; that misfortune had fallen upon him, — and he was conquered.

'Why is it,' he said as he looked down into the turbid stream — 'why is it that bloodshed, physical strife, and brute power are dear to them all? Any fool can have personal bravery; 'tis but a sign of folly to know no fear. Grant that a man has no imagination, and he cannot fear; but when a man does fear, and yet is brave —' Then for awhile he stopped himself. 'Would that I had gone at his throat like a dog!' he continued, still in his soliloquy. 'Would that I had! Could I have torn out his tongue, and laid it as a trophy at her feet, then she would have loved me.' After that he wandered slowly home, and went to bed.

CHAPTER VIII

MR BRISKET THINKS HE SEES HIS WAY, AND MR ROBINSON AGAIN WALKS ON BLACKFRIARS BRIDGE

For some half-hour on that night, as Robinson had slowly walked backwards and forwards across the bridge, ideas of suicide had flitted across his mind. Should he not put an end to all this, — to all this and so much else that harassed him and made life weary. ' " 'Tis a consummation devoutly to be wished," ' he said, as he looked down into the dark river. And then he repeated a good deal more, expressing his desire to sleep, but acknowledging that his dreams in that strange bed might be the rub. 'And thus "calamity must still live on," ' he said, as he went home to his lodgings.

Then came those arrangements as to the partnership and the house in Bishopsgate Street, which have already been narrated. During the weeks which produced these results, he frequently saw Maryanne in Smithfield, but never spoke to her, except on the ordinary topics of the day. In his demeanour he was courteous to her, but he never once addressed her except as Miss

Brown, and always with a politeness which was as cold as it was studied. On one or two occasions he thought that he observed in her manner something that showed a wish for reconciliation; but still he said nothing to her. 'She has treated me like a dog,' he said to himself, 'and yet I love her. If I tell her so, she will treat me worse than a dog.' Then he heard, also, that Brisket had declared more than once that he could not see his way. 'I could see mine,' he said, 'as though a star guided me, if she should but stretch forth her hand to me and ask me to forgive her.'

It was some week or two after the deed of partnership had been signed, and when the house at No. 81 had been just taken, that Miss Twizzle came to Robinson. He was, at the moment, engaged in composition for an illustrious house in the Minories that shall be nameless; but he immediately gave his attention to Miss Twizzle, though at the moment he was combating the difficulties of a rhyme which it had been his duty to repeat nineteen times in the same poem. 'I think that will do,' said he, as he wrote it down. 'And yet it's lame, — very lame:

But no lady ever loses
By going to the shop of —'

And then Miss Twizzle entered.

'I see you are engaged,' said she, 'and, perhaps, I had better call another time.'

'By no means, Miss Twizzle; pray be seated.

How is everything going on at the Hall of Harmony?'

'I haven't been there, Mr Robinson, since that night as Mr Brisket did behave so bad. I got such a turn that night, as I can't endure the sight of the room ever since. If you'll believe me, I can't.'

'It was not a pleasant occurrence,' said Robinson. 'I felt it very keenly. A man's motives are so vilely misconstrued, Miss Twizzle. I have been accused of — of — cowardice.'

'Not by me, Mr Robinson. I did say you should have stuck up a bit; but I didn't mean anything like that.'

'Well; it's over now. When are they to be married, Miss Twizzle?'

'Now, Mr Robinson, don't you talk like that. You wouldn't take it all calm that way if you thought she was going to have him.'

'I mean to take it very calm for the future.'

'But I suppose you're not going to give her up. It wouldn't be like you, that wouldn't.'

'She has spurned me, Miss Twizzle; and after that —.'

'Oh, spurn! that's all my eye. Of course she has. There's a little of that always, you know, — just for the fun of the thing. The course of love shouldn't run too smooth. I wouldn't give a straw for a young man if he wouldn't let me spurn him sometimes.'

'But you wouldn't call him a — a —'

'A what? A coward, is it? Indeed but I would, or anything else that came uppermost. Laws!

what's the good of keeping company if you ain't to say just what comes uppermost at the moment. 'Twas but the other day I called my young man a raskil.'

'It was in sport, no doubt.'

'I was that angry at the time I could have tore him limb from limb; I was, indeed. But he says, "Polly," says he, "if I'm a he-raskil, you're a she-raskil; so that needn't make any difference between us." And no more it didn't. He gets his salary rose in January, and then we shall be married.'

'I wish you all the happiness that married life can bestow,' said Robinson.

'That's very prettily said, and I wish the same to you. Only you mustn't be so down like. There's Maryanne; she says you haven't a word for her now.'

'She'll find as many words as she likes in Aldersgate Street, no doubt.'

'Now, Robinson, if you're going to go on like that, you are not the man I always took you for. You didn't suppose that a girl like Maryanne isn't to have her bit of fun as long as it lasts. Them as is as steady as old horses before marriage usually has their colt's fling after marriage. Maryanne's principles is good, and that's everything; — ain't it?'

'I impute nothing to Miss Brown, except that she is false, and mercenary, and cruel.'

'Exactly; just a she-raskil, as Tom called me. I was mercenary and all the rest of it. But, laws!

what's that between friends? The long and short of it is this; is Barkis willing? If Barkis is willing then a certain gentleman as we know in the meat trade may suit himself elsewhere. Come; answer that. Is Barkis willing?'

For a minute or two Robinson sat silent, thinking of the indignities he had endured. That he loved the girl, — loved her warmly, with all his heart, — was only too true. Yes; he loved her too well. Had his affection been of a colder nature, he would have been able to stand off for awhile, and thus have taught the lady a lesson which might have been of service. But, in his present mood, the temptation was too great for him, and he could not resist it. 'Barkis is willing,' said he. And thus, at the first overture, he forgave her all the injury she had done him. A man never should forgive a woman unless he has her absolutely in his power. When he does so, and thus wipes out all old scores, he merely enables her to begin again.

But Robinson had said the word, and Miss Twizzle was not the woman to allow him to go back from it. 'That's well,' said she. 'And now I'll tell you what. Tom and I are going to drink tea in Smithfield, with old Brown, you know. You'll come too; and then, when old Brown goes to sleep, you and Maryanne will make it up.' Of course she had her way; and Robinson, though he repented himself of what he was doing before she was out of the room, promised to be there.

And he was there. When he entered Mr

Brown's sitting-room he found Maryanne and Miss Twizzle, but Miss Twizzle's future lord had not yet come. He did not wait for Mr Brown to go to sleep, but at once declared the purpose of his visit.

'Shall I say "Maryanne?"' said he, putting out his hand; 'or is it to be "Miss Brown?"'

'Well, I'm sure,' said she; 'there's a question! If "Miss Brown" will do for you, sir, it will do uncommon well for me.'

'Call her "Maryanne," and have done with it,' said Miss Twizzle. 'I hate all such nonsense, like poison.'

'George,' said the old man, 'take her, and may a father's blessing go along with her. We are partners in the haberdashery business, and now we shall be partners in everything.' Then he rose up, as though he were going to join their hands.

'Oh, father, I know a trick worth two of that!' said Maryanne. 'That's not the way we manage these things now-a-days, is it, Polly?'

'I don't know any better way,' said Polly, 'when Barkis is willing.'

'Maryanne,' said Robinson, 'let bygones be bygones.'

'With all my heart,' said she. 'All of them, if you like.'

'No, not quite all, Maryanne. Those moments in which I first declared what I felt for you can never be bygones for me. I have never faltered in my love; and now, if you choose to accept my hand in the presence of your father, there it is.'

'God bless you, my boy! God bless you!' said Mr Brown.

'Come, Maryanne,' said Miss Twizzle, 'he has spoke out now, quite manly; and you should give him an answer.'

'But he is so imperious, Polly! If he only sees me speaking to another, in the way of civility — as, of course, I must, — he's up with his grand ways, and I'm put in such a trembling that I don't know how to open my mouth.'

Of course, every one will know how the affair ended on that evening. The quarrels of lovers have ever been the renewal of love. Miss Brown did accept Mr Robinson's vows; Mr Brown did go to sleep; Tom, whose salary was about to be raised to the matrimonial point, did arrive; and the evening was passed in bliss and harmony.

Then, again, for a week or two did George Robinson walk upon roses. It could not now be thrown in his teeth that some other suitor was an established tradesman; for such also was his proud position. He was one of that firm whose name was already being discussed in the commercial world, and could feel that the path to glory was open beneath his feet. It was during these days that those original ideas as to the name and colour of the house, and as to its architectural ornamentation, came from his brain, and that he penned many of those advertisements which afterwards made his reputation so great. It was then that he so plainly declared his resolve to have his own way in his own department, and startled his partners by the firmness of his purpose. It need hardly be said that gratified love was the source from whence he drew his inspiration.

'And now let us name the day,' said Robinson, as soon as that other day, — the opening day for Magenta House, — had been settled. All nature would then be smiling. It would be the merry month of May; and Robinson suggested that, after the toil of the first fortnight of the opening, a day's holiday for matrimonial purposes might well be accorded to him. 'We'll go to the bowers of Richmond, Maryanne,' said he.

'God bless you, my children,' said Mr Brown. 'And as for the holiday, Jones shall see the shutters down, and I will see them up again.'

'What!' said Maryanne. 'This next first of June as ever is? I'll do no such thing.'

'Why not, my own one?'

'I never heard the like! Where am I to get my things? And you will have no house taken or anything. If you think I'm going into lodgings like Sarah Jane, you're mistook. I don't marry unless I have things comfortable about me, — furniture, and all that. While you were in your tantrums, George, I once went to see William Brisket's house.'

'— William Brisket!' said Robinson. Perhaps, he was wrong in using such a phrase, but it must be confessed that he was sorely tried. Who but a harpy would have alluded to the comforts of a rival's domestic establishment at such a moment as that? Maryanne Brown was a harpy, and is a harpy to this day.

'There, father,' said she, 'look at that! just listen to him! You wouldn't believe me before. What's a young woman to look for with a man as can go on like that? — cursing and swearing before one's face, — quite awful!'

'He was aggravated, Maryanne,' said the old man.

'Yes, and he'll always be being aggravated. If he thinks as I ain't going to speak civil to them as has always spoke civil to me, he's in the wrong of it. William Brisket never went about cursing at me in that way.'

'I didn't curse at you, Maryanne.'

'If William Brisket had anything to say of a rival, he said it out honest. "Maryanne," said he to me once, "if that young man comes after you any more, I'll polish his head off his shoulders." Now, that was speaking manly; and, if you could behave like that, you'd get yourself respected. But as for them rampagious Billingsgate ways before a lady, I for one haven't been used to it, and I won't put up with it!' And so she bounced out of the room.

'You shouldn't have swore at her, George,' said Mr Brown.

'Swear at her!' said Robinson, putting his hand up to his head, as though he found it almost impossible to collect his scattered thoughts. 'But it doesn't matter. The world may swear at her for me now; and the world will swear at her!' So saying, he left the house, went hastily down Snow Hill, and again walked moodily on the bridge of Blackfriars. ''Tis a consummation devoutly to be wished,' said he: '— devoutly! — devoutly! And when they take me up, — up to her, would it be loving, or would it be loathing? — A nasty, cold, moist, unpleasant body!' he went on. 'Ah me! It would be loathing! He hadn't a father; he hadn't a mother; he hadn't a sister; he hadn't a brother; — but he had a dearer one still, and a nearer one yet, than all other. — "To be or not to be; that is the question." — He must in ground unsanctified be lodged, till the last trumpet! Ah, there's the rub! But for that, who would these fardels bear?' Then he made up his mind that the fardels must still be borne, and again went home to his lodgings.

This had occurred some little time before the opening of the house, and on the next morning George Robinson was at his work as hard, — ay, harder — than ever. He had pledged himself to the firm, and was aware that it would ill become him to allow private sorrows to interfere with public duties. On that morrow he was more enterprising than ever, and it was then that he originated the idea of the four men in armour, and of Fame with her classical horn and gilded car.

'She'll come round again, George,' said Mr Brown, 'and then take her at the hop.'

'She'll hop no more for me,' said George Robinson, sternly. But on this matter he was weak as water, and this woman was able to turn him round her little finger.

On the fourteenth of May, the day previous to the opening of the house, Robinson was seated upstairs alone, still at work on some of his large posters. There was no sound to be heard but the hammers of the workmen below; and the smell of the magenta paint, as it dried, was strong in his nostrils. It was then that one of the workmen came up to him, saying that there was a gentleman below who wished to see him. At this period Robinson was anxious to be called on by commercial gentlemen, and at once sent down civil word, begging that the gentleman would walk up. With heavy step the gentleman did walk up, and William Brisket was shown into the room.

'Sir,' said George Robinson as soon as he saw him, 'I did not expect this honour from you.' And then he bethought himself of his desire to tear out the monster's tongue, and began to consider whether he might do it now.

'I don't know much about honour,' said Brisket; 'but it seems to me an understandin's wanted 'twixt you and I.'

'There can be none such,' said Robinson.

'Oh, but there must.'

'It is not within the compass of things. You, sir, cannot understand me; — your intellectual vision is too limited. And I, — I will not understand you.

'Won't you, by jingo! Then your vision shall be limited, as far as two uncommon black eyes can limit it. But come, Robinson, if you don't want to quarrel, I don't.'

'As for quarrelling,' said Robinson, 'it is the work of children. Come, Brisket, will you jump with me into yonder river? The first that reaches the further side, let him have her!' And he pointed up Bishopsgate Street towards the Thames.

'Perhaps you can swim?' said Brisket.

'Not a stroke!' said Robinson.

'Then what a jolly pair of fools we should be!'

'Ah-h-h-h! That's the way to try a man's metal!'

'If you talk to me about metal, young man, I'll drop into you. You've been a-sending all manner of messages to me about a barrel of gunpowder and that sort of thing, and it's my mind that you're a little out of your own. Now I ain't going to have anything to do with gunpowder, nor yet with the river. It's a nasty place is the river; and when I want a wash I shan't go there.'

'"Dreadfully staring through muddy impurity!"' said Robinson.

'Impurity enough,' continued the other; 'and I won't have anything to do with it. Now, I'll tell you what. Will you give me your word, as a man, never to have nothing more to say to Maryanne Brown?'

'Never again to speak to her?'

'Not, except in the way of respect, when she's Mrs Brisket.'

'Never again to clasp her hand in mine?'

'Not by no means. And if you want me to remain quiet, you'd a deal better stow that kind of thing. I'll tell you what it is — I'm beginning to see my way with old Brown.'

'Et tu, Brute?' said Robinson, clasping his hands together.

'I'm beginning to see my way with old Brown,' continued Brisket; 'and, to tell you the truth at once, I don't mean to be interfered with.'

'Has — my partner — promised — her hand to you?'

'Yes, he has; and five hundred pounds with it.'

'And she —?'

'Oh, she's all right. There isn't any doubt about she. I've just come from she, as you call her. Now that I see my way, she and I is to be one.'

'And where's the money to come from, Mr Brisket?'

'The father'll stand the money — in course.'

'I don't know where he'll get it, then; certainly not out of the capital of our business, Mr Brisket. And since you are so keen about seeing your way, Mr Brisket, I advise you to be quite sure that you do see it.'

'That's my business, young man; I've never been bit yet, and I don't know as I'm going to begin now. I never moves till I see my way. They as does is sure to tumble.'

'Well; see your way,' said Robinson. 'See it as far as your natural lights will enable you to look. It's nothing to me.'

'Ah, but I must hear you say that you renounce her.'

'Renounce her, false harpy! Ay, with all my heart.'

'But I won't have her called out of her name.'

'She is false.'

'Hold your tongue, or I'll drop into you. They're all more or less false, no doubt; but I won't have you say so of her. And since you're so ready about the renouncing, suppose you put it on paper — "I renounce my right to the hand and heart of Maryanne Brown." You've got pen and ink there; — just put it down.'

'It shall not need,' said Robinson.

'Oh, but it does need. It'll put an end to a world of trouble and make her see that the thing is all settled. It can't be any sorrow to you, because you say she's a false harpy.'

'Nevertheless, I love her.'

'So do I love her; and as I'm beginning to see my way, why, of course, I mean to have her. We can't both marry her; can we?'

'No; not both,' said Robinson. 'Certainly not both.'

'Then you just write as I bid you,' said Brisket.

'Bid me, sir!'

'Well, — ask you; if that will make it easier.'

'And what if I don't?'

'Why, I shall drop into you. That's all about it. There's the pen, ink, and paper; you'd better do it.'

Not at first did Robinson write those fatal words by which he gave up all his right to her he loved; but before that interview was ended the

97

words were written. 'What matters it?' he said, at last, just as Brisket had actually risen from his seat to put his vile threat into execution. 'Has not she renounced me?'

'Yes,' said Brisket, 'she has done that certainly.'

'Had she been true to me,' continued Robinson, 'to do her a pleasure I would have stood up before you till you had beaten me into the likeness of one of your own carcases.'

'That's what I should have done, too.'

'But now; — why should I suffer now?'

'No, indeed; why should you?'

'I would thrash you if I could, for the pure pleasure.'

'No doubt; no doubt.'

'But it stands to reason that I can't. God, when He gave me power of mind, gave you power of body.'

'And a little common sense along with it, my friend. I'm generally able to see my way, big as I look. Come; what's the good of arguing. You're quick at writing, I know, and there's the paper.'

Then George Robinson did write. The words were as follows; — 'I renounce the hand and heart of Maryanne Brown. I renounce them for ever. — George Robinson.'

On the night of that day, while the hammers were still ringing by gaslight in the unfinished shop; while Brown and Jones were still busy with the goods, and Mrs Jones was measuring out to the shop-girls yards of Magenta ribbon, short by an inch, Robinson again walked down to the bridge. 'The bleak wind of March makes me tremble and shiver,' said he to himself — 'but, "Not the dark arch or the black flowing river."'

'Come, young man, move on,' said a policeman to him. And he did move on.

'But for that man I should have done it then,' he whispered, in his solitude, as he went to bed.

CHAPTER IX

SHOWING HOW MR ROBINSON WAS
EMPLOYED ON THE OPENING DAY

'Et tu, Brute?' were the words with which Mr Brown was greeted at six o'clock in the morning on that eventful day, when, at early dawn, he met his young partner at Magenta House. He had never studied the history of Caesar's death, but he understood the reproach as well as any Roman ever did.

'It was your own doing, George,' he said. 'When she was swore at in that way, and when you went away and left her —.'

'It was she went away and left me.'

'"Father," said she when she came back. "I shall put myself under the protection of Mr William Brisket." What was I to do then? And when he came himself, ten minutes afterwards, what was I to say to him? A father is a father, George; and one's children is one's children.'

'And they are to be married?'

'Not quite at once, George.'

'No. The mercenary slaughterer will reject that fair hand at last, unless it comes to him weighted

100

with a money-bag. From whence are to come those five hundred pounds without which William Brisket will not allow your daughter to warm herself at his hearthstone?'

'As Jones has got the partnership, George, Maryanne's husband should have something.'

'Ah, yes! It is I, then, — I, as one of the partners of this house, who am to bestow a dowry upon her who has injured me, and make happy the avarice of my rival! Since the mimic stage first represented the actions of humanity, no such fate as that has ever been exhibited as the lot of man. Be it so. Bring hither the cheque-book. That hand that was base enough to renounce her shall, with the same pen, write the order for the money.'

'No, George, no,' said Mr Brown. 'I never meant to do that. Let him have it — out of the profits.'

'Ha!'

'I said in a month, — if things went well. Of course, I meant, — well enough.'

'But they'll lead you such a life as never man passed yet. Maryanne, you know, can be bitter; very bitter.'

'I must bear it, George. I've been a-bearing a long while, and I'm partly used to it. But, George, it isn't a pleasure to me. It isn't a pleasure to a poor old father to be nagged at by his daughters from his very breakfast down to his very supper. And they comes to me sometimes in bed, nagging at me worse than ever.'

'My heart has often bled for you, Mr Brown.'

'I know it has, George; and that's why I've loved you and trusted you. And now you won't quarrel with me, will you, though I have a little thrown you over like?'

What was Robinson to say? Of course he forgave him. It was in his nature to forgive; and he would even have forgiven Maryanne at that moment, had she come to him and asked him. But she was asleep in her bed, dreaming, perchance, of that big Philistine whom she had chosen as her future lord. A young David, however, might even yet arise, who should smite that huge giant with a stone between the eyes.

Then did Mr Brown communicate to his partner those arrangements as to grouping which his younger daughter had suggested for the opening of the house. When Robinson first heard that Maryanne intended to be there, he declared his intention of standing by her side, though he would not deign even to look her in the face. 'She shall see that she has no power over me, to make me quail,' he said. And then he was told that Brisket also would be there; Maryanne had begged the favour of him, and he had unwillingly consented. 'It is hard to bear,' said Robinson, 'very hard. But it shall be borne. I do not remember ever to have heard of the like.'

'He won't come often, George, you may be sure.'

'That I should have planned these glories for him! Well, well; be it so. What is the pageantry to me? It has been merely done to catch the butterflies, and of these he is surely the largest. I will sit alone above, and work there with my brain for the service of the firm, while you below are satisfying the eyes of the crowd.'

And so it had been, as was told in that chapter which was devoted to the opening day of the house. Robinson had sat alone in the very room in which he had encountered Brisket, and had barely left his seat for one moment when the first rush of the public into the shop had made his heart leap within him. There the braying of the horn in the street, and the clatter of the armed horsemen on the pavement, and the jokes of the young boys, and the angry threatenings of the policemen, reached his ears. 'It is well,' said he; 'the ball has been set a-rolling, and the work that has been well begun is already half completed. When once the steps of the unthinking crowd have habituated themselves to move hitherward, they will continue to come with the constancy of the tide, which ever rolls itself on the same strand.' And then he tasked himself to think how that tide should be made always to flow, — never to ebb. 'They must be brought here,' said he, 'ever by new allurements. When once they come, it is only in accordance with the laws of human nature that they should leave their money behind them.' Upon that, he prepared the words for another card, in which he begged his friends, the public of the city, to come to Magenta House, as friends should come. They were invited to see, and not to buy. The firm did not care that purchases should be made thus early in their career. Their great desire was that the arrangements of the establishment should be witnessed before any considerable portion of the immense stock had been moved for the purpose of retail sale. And then the West End public were especially requested to inspect the furs which were being collected for the anticipated sale of the next winter. It was as he wrote these words that he heard that demand for the African monkey muff, and heard also Mr Jones's discreet answer. 'Yes,' said he to himself; 'before we have done, ships shall come to us from all coasts; real ships. From Tyre and Sidon, they shall come; from Ophir and Tarshish, from the East and from the West, and from the balmy southern islands. How sweet will it be to be named among the Merchant Princes of this great commercial nation!' But he felt that Brown and Jones would never be Merchant Princes, and he already looked forward to the day when he would be able to emancipate himself from such thraldom.

It has been already said that a considerable amount of business was done over the counter on the first day, but that the sum of money taken was not as great as had been hoped. That this was caused by Mr Brown's injudicious mode of going to work, there could be no doubt. He had filled the shelves of the shop with cheap articles for which he had paid, and had hesitated in giving orders for heavy amounts to the wholesale houses. Such orders had of course been given, and in some cases had been given in vain; but quite enough of them had been honoured to show what might have been done, had there been no hesitation. 'As a man of capital, I must object,' he had said to Mr Robinson, only a week before the house was opened. 'I wish I could make you understand that you have no capital.' 'I would I could divest you of the idea and the money too,' said Robinson. But it was all of no use. A domestic fowl that has passed all its days at a barn-door can never soar on the eagle's wing. Now Mr Brown was the domestic fowl, while the eagle's pinion belonged to his youngest partner. By whom in that firm the kite was personified, shall not here be stated.

Brisket on that day soon left the shop; but as Maryanne Brown remained there, Robinson did not descend among the throng. There was no private door to the house, and therefore he was forced to walk out between the counters when he went to his dinner. On that occasion, he passed close by Miss Brown, and met that young lady's eye without quailing. She looked full upon him; and then, turning her face round to her sister, tittered with an air of scorn.

'I think he's been very badly used,' said Sarah Jane.

'And who has he got to blame but his own want of spirit?' said the other. This was spoken in the open shop, and many of the young men and women heard it. Robinson, however, merely walked on, raising his hat, and saluting the daughters of the senior partner. But it must be acknowledged that such remarks as that greatly aggravated the misery of his position.

It was on the evening of that day, when he was about to leave the establishment for the night, that he heard a gentle creeping step on the stairs, and presently Mrs Jones presented herself in the room in which he was sitting. Now if there was any human fellow-creature on the face of this earth whom George Robinson had brought himself to hate, that human fellow-creature was Sarah Jane Jones. Jones himself he despised, but his feeling towards Mrs Jones was stronger than contempt. To him it was odious that she should be present in the house at all, and he had obtained from her father a direct promise that she should not be allowed to come behind the counters after this their opening day.

'George,' she said, coming up to him. 'I have come upstairs because I wish to have a few words with you private.'

'Will you take a chair?' said he, placing one for her. One is bound to be courteous to a lady, even though that lady be a harpy.

'George,' she again began, — she had never called him 'George' before, and he felt himself sorely tempted to tell her that his name was Mr Robinson. 'George, I've brought myself to look upon you quite as a brother-in-law, you know.'

'Have you?' said he. 'Then you have done me an honour that does not belong to me, — and never will.'

'Now don't say that, George. If you'll only bring yourself to show a little more spirit to Maryanne, all will be right yet.'

What was she that she should talk to him about spirit? In these days there was no subject which was more painful to him than that of personal courage. He was well aware that he was no coward. He felt within himself an impulse that would have carried him through any danger of which the result would not have been ridiculous. He could have led a forlorn hope, or rescued female weakness from the fangs of devouring flames. But he had declined, — he acknowledged to himself that he had declined, — to be mauled by the hands of an angry butcher, who was twice his size. 'One has to keep one's own path in the world,' he had said to himself; 'but nevertheless, one avoids a chimney-sweeper. Should I have gained anything had I allowed that huge monster to hammer at me?' So he had argued. But, though he had thus argued, he had been angry with himself, and now he could not bear to be told that he had lacked spirit.

'That is my affair,' he replied to her. 'But those about me will find that I do not lack spirit when I find fitting occasion to use it.'

'No; I'm sure they won't. And now's the time, George. You're not going to let that fellow Brisket run off with Maryanne from before your eyes.'

'He's at liberty to run anywhere for me.'

'Now, look here, George. I know you're fond of her.'

'No. I was once; but I've torn her from my heart.'

'That's nonsense, George. The fact is, the more she gives herself airs and makes herself scarce and stiff to you, the more precious you think her.' Ignorant as the woman was of almost everything, she did know something of human nature.

'I shall never trouble myself about her again,' said he.

'Oh, yes, you will; and make her Mrs Robinson before you've done. Now, look here, George; that fellow Brisket won't have her, unless he gets the money.'

'It's nothing to me,' said Robinson.

'And where's the money to come from, if not out of the house? Now, you and Jones has your rights as partners, and I do hope you and he won't let the old man make off with the capital of the firm in that way. If he gives Brisket five hundred pounds, — and there isn't much more left —'

'I'll tell you what, Mrs Jones; — he may give Brisket five thousand pounds as far as I am concerned. Whatever Mr Brown may do in that way, I shan't interfere to prevent him.'

'You shan't!'

'It's his own money, and, as far as George Robinson is concerned —'

'His own money, and he in partnership with Jones! Not a penny of it is his own, and so I'll make them understand. As for you, you are the softest —'

'Never mind me, Mrs Jones.'

'No; I never will mind you again. Well, to be sure! And you'd stand by and see the money given away in that way to enable the man you hate to take away the girl you love! Well, I never —. They did say you was faint-hearted, but I never thought to see the like of that in a thing that called itself a man.' And so saying, she took herself off.

It cannot be,
But I am pigeon-livered, and lack gall,
To make oppression bitter,

said Robinson, rising from his seat, and slapping his forehead with his hand; and then he stalked backwards and forwards through the small room, driven almost to madness by the misery of his position. 'I am not splenetic and rash,' he said; 'yet have I something in me dangerous. I loved Ophelia. Forty thousand Briskets could not, with all their quantities of love, make up my sum.'

At this time Mr Brown still lived at the house in Smithfield. It was intended that he should move to Bishopsgate Street as soon as the upper rooms could be made ready for him, but the works had hitherto been confined to the shop. On this, the night of the opening day, he intended to give a little supper to his partners; and Robinson, having promised to join it, felt himself bound to keep his word. 'Brisket will not be there?' he asked, as he walked across Finsbury

Square with the old man. 'Certainly not,' said Mr Brown; 'I never thought of asking him.' And yet, when they reached the house, Brisket was already seated by the fire, superintending the toasting of the cheese, as though he were one of the family. 'It's not my doing, George; indeed, it's not,' whispered Mr Brown, as they entered the sitting-room of the family.

That supper-party was terrible to Robinson, but he bore it all without flinching. Jones and his wife were there, and so also, of course, was Maryanne. Her he had seen at the moment of his entry, sitting by with well-pleased face, while her huge lover put butter and ale into the frying-pan. 'Why, Sarah Jane,' she said, 'I declare he's quite a man cook. How useful he would be about a house!'

'Oh, uncommon,' said Sarah Jane. 'And you mean to try before long, don't you, Mr Brisket?'

'You must ask Maryanne about that,' said he, raising his great red face from the fire, and putting on the airs and graces of a thriving lover.

'Don't ask me anything,' said Maryanne, 'for I won't answer anything. It's nothing to me what he means to try.'

'Oh, ain't it, though,' said Brisket. And then they all sat down to supper. It may be imagined with what ease Robinson listened to conversation such as this, and with what appetite he took his seat at that table.

'Mr Robinson, may I give you a little of this cheese?' said Maryanne. What a story such a question told of the heartlessness, audacity, and iron nerves of her who asked it! What power, and at the same time what cruelty, there must have been within that laced bodice, when she could bring herself to make such an offer!

'By all means,' said Robinson, with equal courage. The morsel was then put upon his plate, and he swallowed it. 'I would he had poisoned it,' said he to himself. 'With what delight would I then partake of the dish, so that he and she partook of it with me!'

The misery of that supper-party will never be forgotten. Had Brisket been Adonis himself, he could not have been treated with softer courtesies by those two harpies; and yet, not an hour ago, Sarah Jane Jones had been endeavouring to raise a conspiracy against his hopes. What an ass will a man allow himself to become under such circumstances! There sat the big butcher, smirking and smiling, ever and again dipping his unlovely lips into a steaming beaker of brandy-and-water, regarding himself as triumphant in the courts of Venus. But that false woman who sat at his side would have sold him piecemeal for money, as he would have sold the carcase of a sheep.

'You do not drink, George,' said Mr Brown.

'It does not need,' said Robinson; and then he took his hat and went his way.

On that night he swore to himself that he would abandon her for ever, and devote himself to commerce and the Muses. It was then that he composed the opening lines of a poem which may yet make his name famous wherever the English language is spoken: —

The golden-eyed son of the Morning rushed
  down the wind like a trumpet,
His azure locks adorning with emeralds fresh
  from the ocean.

CHAPTER X

SHOWING HOW THE FIRM
INVENTED A NEW SHIRT

It has already been said that those four men in
armour, on the production of whom Robinson
had especially prided himself, were dispensed
with after the first fortnight. This, no doubt, was
brought about through the parsimony of Mr
Brown, but in doing so he was aided by a fortuitous circumstance. One of the horses trampled on a child near the Bank, and then the
police and press interfered. At first the partners
were very unhappy about the child, for it was reported to them that the poor little fellow would
die. Mr Brown went to see it, and ascertained
that the mother knew how to make the most of
the occurrence; — and so, after a day or two, did
the firm. The Jupiter daily newspaper took the
matter up, and lashed out vigorously at what it
was pleased to call the wickedness as well as ab-
surdity of such a system of advertising; but as the
little boy was not killed, nor indeed seriously
hurt, the firm was able to make capital out of the
Jupiter, by sending a daily bulletin from Magenta

113

House as to the state of the child's health. For a week the newspapers inserted these, and allowed the firm to explain that they supplied nourishing food, and paid the doctor's bill; but at the end of the week the editor declined any further correspondence. Mr Brown then discontinued his visits; but the child's fortune had been made by gifts from a generous public, and the whole thing had acted as an excellent unpaid advertisement. Now, it is well understood by all trades that any unpaid advertisement is worth twenty that have cost money.

In this way the men in armour were put down, but they will be long remembered by the world of Bishopsgate Street. That they cost money is certain. 'Whatever we do,' said Mr Brown, 'don't let's have any more horses. You see, George, they're always eating!' He could not understand that it was nothing, though the horses had eaten gilded oats, so long as there were golden returns.

The men in armour, however, were put down, as also was the car of Fame. One horse only was left in the service of the firm, and this was an ancient creature that had for many years belonged to the butter establishment in Smithfield. By this animal a light but large wooden frame was dragged about, painted Magenta on its four sides, and bearing on its various fronts different notices as to the business of the house. A boy stood uncomfortably in the centre, driving the slow brute by means of reins which were inserted through the apertures of two of the letters; through another letter above there was a third hole for his eyes, and, shut up in this prison, he was enjoined to keep moving throughout the day. This he did at the slowest possible pace, and thus he earned five shillings a week. The arrangement was one made entirely by Mr Brown, who himself struck the bargain with the boy's father. Mr Robinson was much ashamed of this affair, declaring that it would be better to abstain altogether from advertising in that line than to do it in so ignoble a manner; but Mr Brown would not give way, and the magenta box was dragged about the streets till it was altogether shattered and in pieces.

Stockings was the article in which, above all others, Mr Brown was desirous of placing his confidence. 'George,' said he, 'all the world wears stockings; but those who require African monkey muffs are in comparison few in number. I know Legg and Loosefit of the Poultry, and I'll purchase a stock.' He went to Legg and Loosefit and did purchase a stock, absolutely laying out a hundred pounds of ready money for hosiery, and getting as much more on credit. Stockings is an article on which considerable genius might be displayed by any house intending to do stockings, and nothing else; but taken up in this small way by such a firm as that of 81, Bishopsgate Street, it was simply embarrassing. 'Now you can say something true in your advertisements,' said Mr Brown, with an air of triumph, when the invoice of the goods arrived.

'True!' said Robinson. He would not, however,

sneer at his partner, so he retreated to his own room, and went to work. 'Stockings!' said he to himself. 'There is no room for ambition in it! But the word "Hose" does not sound amiss.' And then he prepared that small book, with silk magenta covers and silvery leaves, which he called *The New Miracle!*

'The whole world wants stockings,' he began, not disdaining to take his very words from Mr Brown —' and Brown, Jones, and Robinson are prepared to supply the whole world with the stockings which they want. The following is a list of some of the goods which are at present being removed from the river to the premises at Magenta House, in Bishopsgate Street. B., J., and R. affix the usual trade price of the article, and the price at which they are able to offer them to the public.

'One hundred and twenty baskets of ladies' Spanish hose, — usual price, 1s. 3d.; sold by B., J., and R. at $9^{31}/_{44}d$.'

'Baskets!' said Mr Brown, when he read the little book.

'It's all right,' said Robinson. 'I have been at the trouble to learn the trade language.'

'Four hundred dozen white cotton hose, — usual price, 1s. $0^{11}/_{42}d$.; sold by B., J., and R. at $7^{11}/_{44}d$.

'Eight stack of China and pearl silk hose, — usual price, 3*s.*; sold by B., J., and R. for 1*s.* 9^{31}⁄$_{44}$*d.*

'Fifteen hundred dozen of Balbriggan, — usual price, 1*s.* 6*d.*; sold by B., J., and R. for 10^{11}⁄$_{42}$*d.*'

It may not, perhaps, be necessary to continue the whole list here; but as it was read aloud to Mr Brown, he sat aghast with astonishment. 'George!' said he, at last, 'I don't like it. It makes me quite afeared. It does indeed.'

'And why do you not like it?' said Robinson, quietly laying down the manuscript, and putting his hand upon it. 'Does it want vigour?'

'No; it does not want vigour.'

'Does it fail to be attractive? Is it common-place?'

'It is not that I mean,' said Mr Brown. 'But —'

'Is it not simple? The articles are merely named, with their prices.'

'But, George, we haven't got 'em. We couldn't hold such a quantity. And if we had them, we should be ruined to sell them at such prices as that. I did want to do a genuine trade in stockings.'

'And so you shall, sir. But how will you begin unless you attract your customers?'

'You have put your prices altogether too low,' said Jones. 'It stands to reason you can't sell them for the money. You shouldn't have put the prices at all; — it hampers one dreadful. You don't know what it is to stand down there among 'em all, and tell 'em that the cheap things haven't come.

'Say that they've all been sold,' said Robinson.

'It's just the same,' argued Jones. 'I declare last Saturday night I didn't think my life was safe in the crowd.'

'And who brought that crowd to the house?' demanded Robinson. 'Who has filled the shop below with such a throng of anxious purchasers?'

'But, George,' said Mr Brown, 'I should like to have one of these bills true, if only that one might show it as a sample when the people talk to one.'

'True!' said Robinson, again. 'You wish that it should be true! In the first place, did you ever see an advertisement that contained the truth? If it were as true as heaven, would any one believe it? Was it ever supposed that any man believed an advertisement? Sit down and write the truth, and see what it will be! The statement will show itself of such a nature that you will not dare to publish it. There is the paper, and there the pen. Take them, and see what you can make of it.'

'I do think that somebody should be made to believe it,' said Jones.

'You do!' and Robinson, as he spoke, turned angrily at the other. 'Did you ever believe an advertisement?' Jones, in self-defence, protested that he never had. 'And why should others be more simple than you? No man, — no woman believes them. They are not lies; for it is not intended that they should obtain credit. I should despise the man who attempted to base his advertisements on a system of facts, as I would the builder who lays his foundation upon the sand. The groundwork of advertising is romance. It is poetry in its very essence. Is Hamlet true?'

'I really do not know,' said Mr Brown.

'There is no man, to my thinking, so false,' continued Robinson, 'as he who in trade professes to be true. He deceives, or endeavours to do so. I do not. No one will believe that we have fifteen hundred dozen of Balbriggan.'

'Nobody will,' said Mr Brown.

'But yet that statement will have its effect. It will produce custom, and bring grist to our mill without any dishonesty on our part. Advertisements are profitable, not because they are believed, but because they are attractive. Once understand that, and you will cease to ask for truth.' Then he turned himself again to his work and finished his task without further interruption.

'You shall sell your stockings, Mr Brown,' he said to the senior member of the firm, about three days after that.

'Indeed, I hope so.'

'Look here, sir!' and then he took Mr Brown to the window. There stood eight stalwart porters, divided into two parties of four each, and on their shoulders they bore erect, supported on painted frames, an enormous pair of gilded, embroidered brocaded, begartered wooden stockings. On the massive calves of these was set forth a statement of the usual kind, declaring that 'Brown, Jones, and Robinson, of 81, Bishopsgate Street, had just received 40,000 pairs of best French silk ladies' hose direct from Lyons.'

'And now look at the men's legs,' said Robinson. Mr Brown did look, and perceived that they were dressed in magenta-coloured knee-breeches, with magenta-coloured stockings. They were gorgeous in their attire, and at this moment they were starting from the door in different directions. 'Perhaps you will tell me that that is not true?'

'I will say nothing about it for the future,' said Mr Brown.

'It is not true,' continued Robinson; 'but it is a work of fiction, in which I take leave to think that elegance and originality are combined.'

'We ought to do something special in shirts,' said Jones, a few days after this. 'We could get a few dozen from Hodges, in King Street, and call them Eureka.'

'Couldn't we have a shirt of our own?' said Mr Robinson. 'Couldn't you invent a shirt, Mr Jones?' Jones, as Robinson looked him full in the face, ran his fingers through his scented hair, and said that he would consult his wife. Before the day was over, however, the following notice was already in type: —

MANNED IN A STATE OF BLISS
BROWN, JONES, AND ROBINSON have

sincere pleasure in presenting to the Fashionable World their new KATAKAIRION SHIRT, in which they have thoroughly overcome the difficulties, hitherto found to be insurmountable, of adjusting the bodies of the Nobility and Gentry to an article which shall be at the same time elegant, comfortable, lasting, and cheap.

B., J., and R.'s KATAKAIRION SHIRT, and their Katakairion Shirt alone, is acknowledged to unite these qualities.

Six Shirts for 39s. 9d.

The Katakairion shirt is specially recommended to Officers going to India and elsewhere, while it is at the same time eminently adapted for the Home Consumption.

'I think I would have considered it a little more, before I committed myself,' said Jones.

'Ah, yes; you would have consulted your wife; as I have not got one, I must depend on my own wits.'

'And are not likely to have one either,' said Jones.

'Young men, young men, said Mr Brown, raising his hands impressively, 'if as Christians you cannot agree, at any rate you are bound to do so as partners. What is it that the Psalmist says, "Let dogs delight, to bark and bite —."'

The notice as to the Katakairion shirt was printed on that day, as originally drawn out by Robinson, and very widely circulated on the two

121

or three following mornings. A brisk demand ensued, and it was found that Hodges, the wholesale manufacturer, of King Street, was able to supply the firm with an article which, when sold at 39s. 6d., left a comfortable profit.

'I told you that we ought to do something special in shirts,' said Jones, as though the whole merit of the transaction were his own.

Gloves was another article to which considerable attention was given; —

BROWN, JONES, AND ROBINSON have made special arrangements with the glove manufacturers of Worcestershire, and are now enabled to offer to the public English-sewn Worcester gloves, made of French kid, at a price altogether out of the reach of any other house in the trade.

'B., J., and R. boldly defy competition.

When that notice was put up in front of the house, none of the firm expected that any one would believe in their arrangement with the Worcestershire glove-makers. They had no such hope, and no such wish. What gloves they sold, they got from the wholesale houses in St Paul's Churchyard, quite indifferent as to the county in which they were sewn, or the kingdom from which they came. Nevertheless, the plan answered, and a trade in gloves was created.

But perhaps the pretty little dialogues which were circulated about the town, did more than anything else to make the house generally known to mothers and their families.

'Mamma, mamma, I have seen such a beautiful sight!'

one of them began.

'My dearest daughter, what was it?'
'I was walking home through the City, with my kind cousin Augustus, and he took me to that wonderfully handsome and extraordinarily large new shop, just opened by those enterprising men, Brown, Jones, and Robinson, at No. 81, Bishopsgate Street. They call it "Nine Times Nine, or Magenta House."'
'My dearest daughter, you may well call it wonderful. It is the wonder of the age. Brown, Jones, and Robinson sell everything; but not only that, — they sell everything good; and not only that — they sell everything cheap. Whenever your wants induce you to make purchases, you may always be sure of receiving full value for your money at the house of Brown, Jones, and Robinson.'

In this way, by efforts such as these, which were never allowed to flag for a single hour, — by a continued series of original composition which, as regards variety and striking incidents, was, perhaps, never surpassed, — a great and stirring trade was established within six months of the opening day. By this time Mr Brown had learned to be silent on the subject of advertising, and had been brought to confess, more than once, that the subject was beyond his comprehension.

'I am an old man, George,' he said once, 'and all this seems to be new.'

'If it be not new, it is nothing,' answered Robinson.

'I don't understand it,' continued the old man; 'I don't pretend to understand it; I only hope that it's right.'

The conduct which Jones was disposed to pursue gave much more trouble. He was willing enough to allow Robinson to have his own way, and to advertise in any shape or manner, but he was desirous of himself doing the same thing. It need hardly be pointed out here that this was a branch of trade for which he was peculiarly unsuited, and that his productions would be stale, inadequate, and unattractive. Nevertheless, he persevered, and it was only by direct interference at the printer's, that the publication of documents was prevented which would have been fatal to the interests of the firm.

'Do I meddle with you in the shop?' Robinson would say to him.

'You haven't the personal advantages which are required for meeting the public,' Jones would answer.

'Nor have you the mental advantages without which original composition is impossible.'

In spite of all these difficulties a considerable trade was established within six months, and the shop was usually crowded. As a drawback to this, the bills at the printer's and at the stationer's had become very heavy, and Robinson was afraid to disclose their amount to his senior partner. But nevertheless he persevered. 'Faint heart never won fair lady,' he repeated to himself, over and over again, — the fair lady for whom his heart sighed being at this time Commercial Success.

Vestigia Nulla Retrorsum. That should be the motto of the house. He failed, however, altogether in making it intelligible to Mr Brown.

CHAPTER XI

JOHNSON OF MANCHESTER

It was about eight months after the business had been opened that a circumstance took place which gave to the firm a reputation, which for some few days was absolutely metropolitan. The affair was at first fortuitous, but advantage was very promptly taken of all that occurred; no chance was allowed to pass by unimproved; and there was, perhaps, as much genuine talent displayed in the matter as though the whole had been designed from the beginning. The transaction was the more important as it once more brought Mr Robinson and Maryanne Brown together, and very nearly effected a union between them. It was not, however, written in the book that such a marriage should ever be celebrated, and the renewal of love which for a time gave such pleasure to the young lady's father, had no other effect than that of making them in their subsequent quarrels more bitter than ever to each other.

It was about midwinter when the circumstances now about to be narrated took place. Mr Brown had gone down to the neighbourhood of Manchester for the purpose of making certain bona fide purchases of coloured prints, and had there come to terms with a dealer. At this time there was a strike among the factories, and the goods became somewhat more scarce in the market, and, therefore, a trifle dearer than was ordinarily the case. From this arose the fact that the agreement made with Mr Brown was not kept by the Lancashire house, and that the firm in Bishopsgate was really subjected to a certain amount of commercial ill-treatment.

'It is a cruel shame,' said Mr Brown — 'a very cruel shame; when a party in trade has undertaken a transaction with another party, no consideration should hinder that party from being as good as his word. A tradesman's word should be his bond.' This purchase down among the factories had been his own special work, and he had been proud of it. He was, moreover, a man who could ill tolerate any ill-usage from others. 'Can't we do anything to 'em, George? Can't we make 'em bankrupts?'

'If we could, what good would that do us?' said Robinson. 'We must put up with it.'

'I'd bring an action against them,' said Jones.

'And spend thirty or forty pounds with the lawyers,' said Robinson. 'No; we will not be such fools as that. But we might advertise the injury.'

'Advertise the injury,' said Mr Brown, with his eyes wide open. By this time he had begun to understand that the depth of his partner's finesse was not to be fathomed by his own unaided intelligence.

'And spend as much money in that as with the lawyers,' said Jones.

'Probably more,' said Robinson, very calmly. 'We promised the public in our last week's circular that we should have these goods.'

'Of course we did,' said Mr Brown; 'and now the public will be deceived!' And he lifted up his hands in horror at the thought.

'We'll advertise it,' said Robinson again; and then for some short space he sat with his head resting on his hands. 'Yes, we'll advertise it. Leave me for awhile, that I may compose the notices.'

Mr Brown, after gazing at him for a moment with a countenance on which wonder and admiration were strongly written, touched his other partner on the arm, and led him from the room.

The following day was Saturday, which at Magenta House was always the busiest day of the week. At about four o'clock in the afternoon the shop would become thronged, and from that hour up to ten at night nearly as much money was taken as during all the week besides. On that Saturday at about noon the following words were to be read at each of the large sheets of glass in the front of the house. They were printed, of course, on magenta paper, and the corners and margins were tastefully decorated: —

Brown, Jones, and Robinson, having been greatly deceived by Johnson of Manchester, are not able to submit to the public the 40,000 new specimens of English prints, as they had engaged to do, on this day. But they beg to assure their customers and the public in general that they will shortly do so, however tremendous may be the sacrifice.

'But it was Staleybridge,' said Mr Brown, 'and the man's name was Pawkins.'

'And you would have me put up "Pawkins of Staleybridge," and thus render the firm liable to an indictment for libel? Are not Pawkins and Johnson all the same to the public?'

'But there is sure to be some Johnson at Manchester.

'There are probably ten, and therefore no man can say that he is meant. I ascertained that there were three before I ventured on the name.'

On that afternoon some trifling sensation was created in Bishopsgate Street, and a few loungers were always on the pavement reading the notice. Robinson went out from time to time, and heard men as they passed talking of Johnson of Manchester. 'It will do,' said he. 'You will see that it will do. By seven o'clock on next Saturday evening I will have the shop so crowded that women who are in shall be unable to get out again.'

That notice remained up on Saturday evening, and till twelve on Monday, at which hour it was replaced by the following: —

> Johnson of Manchester has proved himself utterly unable to meet his engagement. The public of the metropolis, however, may feel quite confident that Brown, Jones, and Robinson will not allow any provincial manufacturer to practise such dishonesty on the City with impunity.

The concourse of persons outside then became much greater, and an audible hum of voices not unfrequently reached the ears of those within. During this trying week Mr Jones, it must be acknowledged, did not play his part badly. It had come home to him in some manner that this peculiar period was of vital importance to the house, and on each day he came down to business dressed in his very best. It was pleasant to see him as he stood at the door, shining with bear's grease, loaded with gilt chains, glittering with rings, with the lappets of his coat thrown back so as to show his filled shirt and satin waistcoat. There he stood, rubbing his hands and looking out upon the people as though he scorned to notice them. As regards intellect, mind, apprehension, there was nothing to be found in the personal appearance of Jones, but he certainly possessed an amount of animal good looks which had its weight with weak-minded females.

The second notice was considered sufficient to attract notice on Monday and Tuesday. On the latter day it became manifest that the conduct of Johnson of Manchester had grown to be matter of public interest, and the firm was aware that persons from a distance were congregating in Bishopsgate Street, in order that they might see with their own eyes the notices at Magenta House.

Early on the Wednesday, the third of the series appeared. It was very short, and ran as follows: —

'Johnson of Manchester is off!'
'The police are on his track!'

This exciting piece of news was greedily welcomed by the walking public, and a real crowd had congregated on the pavement by noon. A little after that time, while Mr Brown was still at dinner with his daughter upstairs, a policeman called and begged to see some member of the firm. Jones, whose timidity was overwhelming, immediately sent for Mr Brown; and he, also embarrassed, knocked at the door of Mr Robinson's little room, and asked for counsel.

'The Peelers are here, George,' he said. 'I knew there'd be a row.

'I hope so,' said Robinson; 'I most sincerely hope so.'

As he stood up to answer his senior partner he saw that Miss Brown was standing behind her father, and he resolved that, as regarded this occasion, he would not be taunted with want of spirit.

'But what shall I say to the man?' asked Mr Brown.

'Give him a shilling and a glass of spirits; beg him to keep the people quiet outside, and promise him cold beef and beer at three o'clock. If he runs rusty, send for me.' And then, having thus instructed the head of the house, he again seated himself before his writing materials at the table.

'Mr Robinson,' said a soft voice, speaking to him through the doorway, as soon as the ponderous step of the old man was heard descending the stairs.

'Yes; I am here,' said he.

'I don't know whether I may open the door,' said she; 'for I would not for worlds intrude upon your studies.'

He knew that she was a Harpy. He knew that her soft words would only bring him to new grief. But yet he could not help himself. Strong, in so much else, he was utterly weak in her hands. She was a Harpy who would claw out his heart and feed upon it, without one tender feeling of her own. He had learned to read her character, and to know her for what she was. But yet he could not help himself.

'There will be no intrusion,' he said. 'In half an hour from this time, I go with this copy to the printer's. Till then I am at rest.'

'At rest!' said she: 'How sweet it must be to rest after labours such as yours! Though you and I are two, Mr Robinson, who was once one, still I hear

132

of you, and — sometimes think of you.'

'I am surprised that you should turn your thoughts to anything so insignificant,' he replied.

'Ah! that is so like you. You are so scornful, and so proud, — and never so proud as when pretending to be humble. I sometimes think that it is better that you and I are two, because you are so proud. What could a poor girl like me have done to satisfy you?'

False and cruel that she was! 'Tis thus that the basilisk charms the poor bird that falls a victim into its jaws.

'It is better that we should have parted,' said he. 'Though I still love you with my whole heart, I know that it is better.'

'Oh, Mr Robinson!'

'And I would that your nuptials with that man in Aldersgate Street were already celebrated.'

'Oh, you cruel, heartless man!'

'For then I should be able to rest. If you were once another's, I should then know —'

'You would know what, Mr Robinson?'

'That you could never be mine. Maryanne!'

'Sir!'

'If you would not have me disgrace myself for ever by my folly, leave me now.'

'Disgrace yourself! I'm sure you'll never do that. "Whatever happens George Robinson will always act the gentleman," I have said of you, times after times, both to father and to William Brisket. "So he will!" father has answered. And then William Brisket has said —; I don't know

133

whether I ought to tell you what he said. But what he said was this — "If you're so fond of the fellow, why don't you have him?"'

All this was false, and Robinson knew that it was false. No such conversation had ever passed. Nevertheless, the pulses of his heart were stirred.

'Tell me this,' said he. 'Are you his promised wife?'

'Laws, Mr Robinson!'

'Answer me honestly, if you can. Is that man to be your husband? If it be so it will be well for him, and well for you, but, above all, it will be well for me, that we should part. And if it be so, why have you come hither to torment me?'

'To torment you, George!'

"Yes; to torment me!' And then he rose suddenly from his feet, and advanced with rapid step and fierce gesture towards the astonished girl. 'Think you that love such as mine is no torment? Think you that I have no heart, no feeling; that this passion which tears me in pieces can exist without throwing a cloud upon my life? With you, as I know too well, all is calm and tranquil. Your bosom boils with no ferment. It has never boiled. It will never boil. It can never boil. It is better for you so. You will marry that man, whose house is good, and whose furniture has been paid for. From his shop will come to you your daily meals, — and you will be happy. Man wants but little here below, nor wants that little long. Adieu.'

'Oh, George, are you going so?'

'Yes; I am going. Why should I stay? Did I not

with my own hand in this room renounce you?'

'Yes; you did, George. You did renounce me, and that's what's killing me. So it is, — killing me.' Then she threw herself in a chair and buried her face in her handkerchief.

'Would that we could all die,' he said, 'and that everything should end. But now I go to the printer's. Adieu, Maryanne.'

'But we shall see each other occasionally, — as friends?'

'To what purpose? No; certainly not as friends. To me such a trial would be beyond my strength.' And then he seized the copy from the table, and taking his hat from the peg, he hurried out of the room.

'As William is so stiff about the money, I don't know whether it wouldn't be best after all,' said she, as she took herself back to her father's apartments.

Mr Brown, when he met the policeman, found that that excellent officer was open to reason, and that when properly addressed he did not actually insist on the withdrawal of the notice from the window. 'Every man's house is his castle, you know,' said Mr Brown. To this the policeman demurred, suggesting that the law quoted did not refer to crowded thoroughfares. But when invited to a collation at three o'clock, he remarked that he might as well abstain from action till that hour, and that he would in the meantime confine his beat to the close vicinity of Magenta House. A friendly arrangement grew out of this, which for awhile was convenient to both parties, and two policemen remained in the front of the house, and occasionally entered the premises in search of refreshment.

After breakfast on the Thursday the fourth notice was put up: —

The public of London will be glad to learn that Brown, Jones, and Robinson have recovered the greatest part of their paper which was in the hands of Johnson of Manchester. Bills to the amount of fifteen thousand pounds are, however, still missing.

It was immediately after this that the second policeman was considered to be essentially necessary. The whole house, including the young men and women of the shop, were animated with an enthusiasm which spread itself even to the light porter of the establishment. The conduct of Johnson, and his probable fate, were discussed aloud among those who believed in him, while they who were incredulous communicated their want of faith to each other in whispers. Mr Brown was smiling, affable, and happy; and Jones arrived on the Friday morning with a new set of torquoise studs in his shirt. Why men and women should have come to the house for gloves, stockings, and ribbons, because Johnson of Manchester was said to have run away, it may be difficult to explain. But such undoubtedly was the fact, and the sales during that week were so great, as to make it seem that actual commercial prosperity was at hand.

'If we could only keep up the ball!' said Robinson.

'Couldn't we change it to Tomkins of Leeds next week?' suggested Jones.

'I rather fear that the joke might be thought stale,' replied Robinson, with a good-natured smile. 'There is nothing so fickle as the taste of the public. The most popular author of the day can never count on favour for the next six months.' And he bethought himself that, great as he was at the present moment, he also might be eclipsed, and perhaps forgotten, before the posters which he was then preparing had been torn down or become soiled.

On the Friday no less than four letters appeared in the daily Jupiter, all dated from Manchester, all signed by men of the name of Johnson, and all denying that the writer of that special letter had had any dealings whatever with Brown, Jones, and Robinson, of Bishopsgate Street, London. There was "Johnson Brothers," "Johnson and Co," "Alfred Johnson and Son," and "Johnson and Johnson;" and in one of those letters a suggestion was made that B., J., and R., of London, should state plainly who was the special Johnson that had gone off with the paper belonging to their house.

'I know we shall be detected,' said Mr Brown, upon whose feelings these letters did not act favourably.

'There is nothing to detect,' said Robinson; 'but I will write a letter to the editor.'

This he did, stating that for reasons which must be quite obvious to the commercial reading public, it would be very unwise in the present state of affairs to give any detailed description of that Mr Johnson who had been named; but that B., J., and R. were very happy to be able to certify that that Mr Johnson who had failed in his engagements to them was connected neither with Johnson Brothers, or Johnson and Co.; nor with Alfred Johnson and Son, or Johnson and Johnson. This also acted as an advertisement, and no doubt brought grist to the mill.

On the evening of that same Friday a small note in a scented envelope was found by Robinson on his table when he returned upstairs from the shop. Well did he know the handwriting, and often in earlier days had he opened such notes with mixed feelings of joy and triumph. All those past letters had been kept by him, and were now lying under lock and key in his desk, tied together with green silk, ready to be returned when the absolute fact of that other marriage should have become a certainty. He half made up his mind to return the present missive unopened. He knew that good could not arise from a renewed correspondence. Nevertheless, he tore asunder the envelope, and the words which met his eyes were as follows: —

Miss Brown's compliments to Mr Robinson, and will Mr Robinson tea with us in papa's room on Saturday, at six o'clock? There will be nobody else but Mr and Mrs Poppins, that used to be Miss Twizzle. Papa, perhaps, will have to go back to the shop when he's done tea. Miss Brown hopes Mr Robinson will remember old days, and not make himself scornful.

'Scornful!' said he. 'Ha! ha! Yes; I scorn her; — I do scorn her. But still I love her.' Then he sat down and accepted the invitation.

Mr Robinson presents his compliments to Miss Brown, and will do himself the honour of accepting her kind invitation for to-morrow evening. Mr Robinson begs to assure Miss Brown that he would have great pleasure in meeting any of Miss Brown's friends whom she might choose to ask.

'Psha!' said Maryanne, when she read it. 'It would serve him right to ask Bill. And I would, too, only —.' Only it would hardly have answered her purpose, she might have said, had she spoken out her mind freely.

In the meantime the interest as to Johnson of Manchester was reaching its climax. At ten o'clock on Saturday morning each division of the window was nearly covered by an enormous bill, on which in very large letters it was stated that —

'Johnson of Manchester has been taken.'

From that till twelve the shop was inundated by persons who were bent on learning what was the appearance and likeness of Johnson. Photographers came to inquire in what gaol he was at present held, and a man who casts heads in plaster of Paris was very intent upon seeing him. No information could, of course, be given by the men and women behind the counters. Among them there was at present raging a violent discussion as to the existence or non-existence of Johnson. It was pleasant to hear Jones repeating the circumstances to the senior partner. 'Mr Brown, there's Miss Glassbrook gone over to the anti-Johnsonites. I think we ought to give her a month's notice.' To those who inquired of Mr Brown himself, he merely lifted up his hands and shook his head. Jones professed that he believed the man to be in the underground cells of Newgate.

The bill respecting Johnson's capture remained up for two hours, and then it was exchanged for another; —

Johnson has escaped, but no expense shall be spared in his recapture.

At four in the afternoon the public was informed as follows; —

Johnson has got off, and sailed for America.

And then there was one other, which closed the

play late on Saturday evening —

Brown, Jones, and Robinson beg to assure the public that they shall be put out of all suspense early on Monday morning.

'And what shall we really say to them on Monday?' asked Mr Jones.

'Nothing at all,' replied Mr Robinson. 'The thing will be dead by that time. If they call, say that he's in Canada.'

'And won't there be any more about it?'

'Nothing, I should think. We, however, have gained our object. The house will be remembered, and so will the name of Brown, Jones, and Robinson.

And it was so. When the Monday morning came the windows were without special notices, and the world walked by in silence, as though Johnson of Manchester had never existed. Some few eager inquirers called at the shop, but they were answered easily; and before the afternoon the name had almost died away behind the counters. 'I knew I was right,' said Miss Glassbrook, and Mr Jones heard her say so.

In and about the shop Johnson of Manchester was heard of no more, but in Mr Brown's own family there was still a certain interest attached to the name. How it came about that this was so, shall be told in the next chapter.

CHAPTER XII
SAMSON AND DELILAH

In the commercial world of London there was
one man who was really anxious to know what
were the actual facts of the case with reference to
Johnson of Manchester. This was Mr William
Brisket, whose mind at this time was perplexed
by grievous doubts. He was called to act in a case
of great emergency, and was by no means sure
that he saw his way. It had been hinted to him by
Miss Brown, on the one side, that it behoved her
to look to herself, and take her pigs to market
without any more shilly-shallying, — by which
expression the fair girl had intended to signify
that it would suit her now to name her wedding-
day. And he had been informed by Mr Brown, on
the other side, that that sum of five hundred
pounds should be now forthcoming; — or, if not
actually the money, Mr Brown's promissory note
at six months should be handed to him, dated
from the day of his marriage with Maryanne.

Under these circumstances, he did not see his
way. That the house in Bishopsgate Street was

doing a large business he did not doubt. He visited the place often, and usually found the shop crowded. But he did doubt whether that business was very lucrative. It might be that the whole thing was a bubble, and that it would be burst before that bill should have been honoured. In such case, he would have saddled himself with an empty-handed wife, and would decidedly not have seen his way. In this emergency he went to Jones and asked his advice. Jones told him confidentially that, though the bill of the firm for five thousand pounds would be as good as paper from the Bank of England, the bill of Mr Brown himself as an individual would be worth nothing.

Although Mr Brisket had gone to Jones as a friend, there had been some very sharp words between them before they separated. Brisket knew well enough that all the ready money at the command of the firm had belonged to Mr Brown, and he now took upon himself to say that Maryanne had a right to her share. Jones replied that there was no longer anything to share, and that Maryanne's future husband must wait for her fortune till her father could pay it out of his income. 'I couldn't see my way like that; not at all,' said Brisket. And then there had been high words between them.

It was at this time that the first act of Johnson of Manchester's little comedy was being played, and people in Mr Brisket's world were beginning to talk about the matter. 'They must be doing a deal of trade,' said one. 'Believe me, it is all flash and sham,' said another. 'I happen to know that old Brown did go down to Manchester and see Johnson there,' said the first. 'There is no such person at all,' said the second. So this went on till Mr Brisket resolved that his immediate matrimony should depend on the reality of Johnson's existence. If it should appear that Johnson, with all his paper, was a false meteor; that no one had deceived the metropolitan public; that no one had been taken and had then escaped, he would tell Miss Brown that he did not see his way. The light of his intelligence told him that promissory notes from such a source, even though signed by all the firm, would be illusory. If, on the other hand, Johnson of Manchester had been taken, then, he thought, he might accept the bill — and wife.

'Maryanne,' he said to the young lady on that day on which she had afterwards had her interview with Robinson, 'what's all this about Johnson of Manchester?'

'I know nothing about your Johnsons, nor yet about your Manchesters,' said Miss Brown, standing with her back to her lover. At this time she was waxing wroth with him, and had learned to hate his voice, when he would tell her that he had not yet seen his way.

'That's all very well, Maryanne; but I must know something before I go on.'

'Who wants you to go on? Not I, I'm sure; nor anybody belonging to me. If I do hate anything, it's them mercenary ways. There's one who really loves me, who'd be above asking for a shilling, if I'd only put out my hand to him.'

'If you say that again, Maryanne, I'll punch his head.'

'You're always talking of punching people's heads; but I don't see you do so much. I should-n't wonder if you don't want to punch my head some of these days.'

'Maryanne, I never riz a hand to a woman yet.'

'And you'd better not, as far as I'm concerned, — not as long as the pokers and tongs are about.' And then there was silence between them for awhile.

'Maryanne,' he began again, 'can't you find out about this Johnson?'

'No; I can't,' said she.

'You'd better.'

'Then I won't,' said she.

'I'll tell you what it is, then, Maryanne. I don't see my way the least in life about this money.'

'Drat your way! Who cares about your way?'

'That's all very fine, Maryanne; but I care. I'm a man as is as good as my word, and always was. I defy Brown, Jones, and Robinson to say that I'm off, carrying anybody's paper. And as for paper, it's a thing as I knows nothing about, and never wish. When a man comes to paper, it seems to me there's a very thin wall betwixt him and the gut-ter. When I buys a score of sheep or so, I pays for them down; and when I sells a leg of mutton, I ex-pects no less myself. I don't owe a shilling to no one, and don't mean; and the less that any one owes me, the better I like it. But Maryanne, when a man trades in that way, a man must see his way. If he goes about in the dark, or with his eyes shut, he's safe to get a fall. Now about this five hundred pound; if I could only see my way —'

As to the good sense of Mr Brisket's remarks, there was no difference of opinion between him and his intended wife. Miss Brown would at that time have been quite contented to enter into partnership for life on those terms. And though these memoirs are written with the express view of advocating a theory of trade founded on quite a different basis, nevertheless, it may be admitted that Mr Brisket's view of commerce has its charms, presuming that a man has the where-withal. But such a view is apt to lose its charms in female eyes if it be insisted on too often, or too violently. Maryanne had long since given in her adhesion to Mr Brisket's theory; but now, weary with repetition of the lesson, she was disposed to rebel.

'Now, William Brisket,' she said, 'just listen to me. If you talk to me again about seeing your way, you may go and see it by yourself. I'm not so badly off that I'm going to have myself twitted at in that way. If you don't like me, you can do the other thing. And this I will say, when a gentleman has spoken his mind free to a lady, and a lady has given her answer free back to him, it's a very mean thing for a gentleman to be say-ing so much about money after that. Of course, a girl has got herself to look to; and if I take up with you, why, of course, I have to say, "Stand off," to any other young man as may wish to keep me company. Now, there's one as shall be nameless that wouldn't demean himself to say a word about money.'

'Because he ain't got none himself, as I take it.'

'He's a partner in a first-rate commercial firm. And I'll tell you what, William Brisket, I'll not hear a word said against him, and I'll not be put upon myself. So now I wishes you good morning.' And so she left him.

Brisket, when he was alone, scratched his head, and thought wistfully of his love. 'I should like to see my way,' said he. 'I always did like to see my way. And as for that old man's bit of paper —' Then he relapsed once again into silence.

It was within an hour of all this that Maryanne had followed her father to George Robinson's room. She had declared her utter indifference as to Johnson of Manchester; but yet it might, perhaps, be as well that she should learn the truth. From her father she had tried to get it, but he had succeeded in keeping her in the dark. To Jones it would be impossible that she should apply; but from Robinson she might succeed in obtaining his secret. She had heard, no doubt, of Samson and Delilah, and thought she knew the way to the strong man's locks. And might it not be well for her to forget that other Samson, and once more to trust herself to her father's partners? When she weighed the two young tradesmen one against the other, balancing their claims with such judgment as she possessed, she doubted much as to her choice. She thought that she might be happy with either: — but then it was necessary that the other dear charmer should be away. As to Robinson, he would marry her, she knew, at once, without any stipulations. As to Brisket, — if Brisket should be her ultimate choice, — it would be necessary that she should either worry her father out of the money, or else cheat her lover into the belief that the money would be forthcoming. Having taken all these circumstances into consideration, she invited Mr Robinson to tea.

Mr Brown was there, of course, and so also were Mr and Mrs Poppins. When Robinson entered, they were already at the tea-table, and the great demerits of Johnson of Manchester were under discussion.

'Now Mr Robinson will tell us everything,' said Mrs Poppins. 'It's about Johnson, you know. Where has he gone to, Mr Robinson?' But Robinson professed that he did not know.

'He knows well enough,' said Maryanne, 'only he's so close. Now do tell us.'

'He'll tell *you* anything *you* choose to ask him,' said Mrs Poppins.

'Tell me anything! Not him, indeed. What does he care for me?'

'I'm sure he would if he only knew what you were saying before he came into the room.'

'Now don't, Polly!'

'Oh, but I shall! because it's better he should know.'

'Now, Polly, if you don't hold your tongue, I'll be angry! Mr Robinson is nothing to me, and never will be, I'm sure. Only if he'd do me the favour, as a friend, to tell us about Mr Johnson, I'd take it kind of him.'

In the meantime Mr Brown and his young married guest were discussing things commercial on their own side of the room, and Poppins, also, was not without a hope that he might learn the secret. Poppins had rather despised the firm at first, as not a few others had done, distrusting all their earlier assurances as to trade bargains, and having been even unmoved by the men in armour. But the great affair of Johnson of Manchester had overcome even his doubts, and he began to feel that it was a privilege to be noticed by the senior partner in a house which could play such a game as that. It was not that Poppins believed in Johnson, or that he thought that 15,000*l.* of paper had at any time been missing. But, nevertheless, the proceeding had affected his mind favourably with reference to Brown, Jones, and Robinson, and brought it about that he now respected them, — and, perhaps, feared them a little, though he had not respected or feared them heretofore. Had he been the possessor of a wholesale house of business, he would not now have dared to refuse them goods on credit, though he would have done so before Johnson of Manchester had become known to the world. It may therefore be surmised that George Robinson had been right, and that he had understood the ways of British trade when he composed the Johnsonian drama.

'Indeed, I'd rather not, Mr Poppins,' said Mr Brown. 'Secrets in trade should be secrets. And though Mr Johnson has done us a deal of mischief, we don't want to expose him.'

'But you've been exposing him ever so long,' pleaded Poppins.

'Now Poppins,' said that gentleman's wife, 'don't you be troubling Mr Brown. He's got other things to think of than answering your questions. I should like to know myself, I own, because all the town's talking about it. And it does seem odd to me that Maryanne shouldn't know.'

'I don't, then,' said Maryanne. 'And I do think when a lady asks a gentleman, the least thing a gentleman can do is to tell. But I shan't ask no more, — not of Mr Robinson. I was thinking —. But never mind, Polly. Perhaps it's best as it is.'

'Would you have me betray my trust?' said Robinson. 'Would you esteem me the more because I had deceived my partners? If you think that I am to earn your love in that way, you know but little of George Robinson.' Then he got up, preparing to leave the room, for his feelings were too many for him.

'Stop, George, stop,' said Mr Brown.

'Let him go,' said Maryanne.

'If he goes away now I shall think him as hard as Adam,' said Mrs Poppins.

'There's three to one again him,' said Mr

Poppins to himself. 'What chance can he have?' Mr Poppins may probably have gone through some such phase of life himself.

'Let him go,' said Maryanne again. 'I wish he would. And then let him never show himself here again.'

'George Robinson, my son, my son!' exclaimed the old man.

It must be understood that Robinson had heard all this, though he had left the room. Indeed, it may be surmised that had he been out of hearing the words would not have been spoken. He heard them, for he was still standing immediately beyond the door, and was irresolute whether he would depart or whether he would return.

'George Robinson, my son, my son!' exclaimed the old man again.

'He shall come back!' said Mrs Poppins, following him out of the door. 'He shall come back, though I have to carry him myself.'

'Polly,' said Maryanne, 'if you so much as whisper a word to ask him, I'll never speak to you the longest day you have to live.'

But the threat was thrown away upon Mrs Poppins, and, under her auspices, Robinson was brought back into the room. 'Maryanne,' said he, 'will you renounce William Brisket?'

'Laws, George!' said she.

'Of course she will,' said Mrs Poppins, 'and all the pomps and vanities besides.'

'My son, my son!' said old Brown, lifting up

both his hands. 'My daughter, my daughter! My children, my children!' And then he joined their hands together and blessed them.

He blessed them, and then went down into the shop. But before the evening was over, Delilah had shorn Samson of his locks. 'And so there wasn't any Johnson after all,' said she.

But Robinson, as he returned home, walked again upon roses.

CHAPTER XIII
THE WISDOM OF POPPINS

George Robinson again walked upon roses, and for a while felt that he had accomplished bliss. What has the world to offer equal to the joy of gratified love? What triumph is there so triumphant as that achieved by valour over beauty?

> Take the goods the gods provide you.
> The lovely Thais sits beside you.

Was not that the happiest moment in Alexander's life. Was it not the climax of all his glories, and the sweetest drop which Fortune poured into his cup? George Robinson now felt himself to be a second Alexander. Beside him the lovely Thais was seated evening after evening; and he, with no measured stint, took the goods the gods provided. He would think of the night of that supper in Smithfield, when the big Brisket sat next to his love, half hidden by her spreading flounces, and would remember how, in his spleen, he had likened his rival to an ox prepared for the sacrifice with garlands. 'Poor ignorant beast of the field!' he had said, apostrophizing the unconscious Brisket, 'how little knowest thou how ill those flowers become thee, or for what purpose thou art thus caressed! They will take from thee thy hide, thy fatness, all that thou hast, and divide thy carcase among them. And yet thou thinkest thyself happy! Poor foolish beast of the field!' Now that ox had escaped from the toils, and a stag of the forest had been caught by his antlers, and was bound for the altar. He knew all this, and yet he walked upon roses and was happy. 'Sufficient for the day is the evil thereof,' he said to himself. 'The lovely Thais sits beside me. Shall I not take the goods the gods provide me?'

The lovely Thais sat beside him evening after evening for nearly two months, up in Mr Brown's parlour, but as yet nothing had been decided as to the day of their marriage. Sometimes Mr and Mrs Poppins would be there smiling, happy, and confidential; and sometimes Mr and Mrs Jones careworn, greedy, and suspicious. On those latter evenings the hours would all be spent in discussing the profits of the shop and the fair division of the spoils. On this subject Mrs Jones would be very bitter, and even the lovely Thais would have an opinion of her own which seemed to be anything but agreeable to her father.

'Maryanne,' her lover said to her one evening, when words had been rather high among them, 'if you want your days to be long in the land, you must honour your father and mother.'

'I don't want my days to be long, if we're never to come to an understanding,' she answered. 'And I've got no mother, as you know well, or you wouldn't treat me so.'

'You must understand, father,' said Sarah Jane, 'that things shan't go on like this. Jones shall have his rights, though he don't seem half man enough to stand up for them. What's the meaning of partnership, if nobody's to know where the money goes to?'

'I've worked like a horse,' said Jones. 'I'm never out of that place from morning to night, — not so much as to get a pint of beer. And, as far as I can see, I was better off when I was at Scrimble and Grutts. I did get my salary regular.'

Mr Brown was at this time in tears, and as he wept he lifted up hands. 'My children, my children!' said he.

'That's all very well, father,' said Maryanne. 'But whimpering won't keep anybody's pot a-boiling. I'm sick of this sort of thing, and, to tell the truth, I think it quite time to see some sort of a house over my head.'

'Would that I could seat you in marble halls! said George Robinson.

'Oh, bother!' said Maryanne. 'That sort of a thing is very good in a play, but business should be business.' It must always be acknowledged, in favour of Mr Brown's youngest daughter, that her views were practical, and not overstrained by romance.

During these two or three months a considerable intimacy sprang up between Mr Poppins and George Robinson. It was not that there was any similarity in their characters, for in most respects they were essentially unlike each other. But, perhaps, this very difference led to their friendship. How often may it be observed in the fields that a high-bred, quick-paced horse will choose some lowly donkey for his close companionship, although other horses of equal birth and speed be in the same pasture! Poppins was a young man of an easy nature and soft temper, who was content to let things pass by him unquestioned, so long as they passed quietly. Live and let live, were words that were often on his lips; — by which he intended to signify that he would overlook the peccadilloes of other people, as long as other people overlooked his own. When the lady who became afterwards Mrs Poppins had once called him a rascal, he had not with loud voice asserted the injustices of the appellation, but had satisfied himself with explaining to her that, even were it so, he was still fit for her society. He possessed a practical philosophy of his own, by which he was able to steer his course in life. He was not, perhaps, prepared to give much to others, but neither did he expect that much should be given to him. There was no ardent generosity in his temperament; but then, also, there was no malice or grasping avarice. If in one respect he differed much from our Mr Robinson, so also in another respect did he differ equally from our Mr Jones. He was at this time a counting-house clerk in a large wharfinger's establishment, and had married on a salary of eighty pounds a year. 'I tell you what it is, Robinson,' said he, about this time: 'I don't understand this business of yours.'

'No,' said Robinson; 'perhaps not. A business like ours is not easily understood.'

'You don't seem to me to divide any profits.'

'In an affair of such magnitude the profits cannot be adjusted every day, nor yet every month.'

'But a man wants his bread and cheese every day. Now, there's old Brown. He's a deal sharper than I took him for.'

'Mr Brown, for a commercial man of the old school, possesses considerable intelligence,' said Robinson. Throughout all these memoirs, it may be observed that Mr Robinson always speaks with respect of Mr Brown.

'Very considerable indeed,' said Poppins. 'He seems to me to nobble everything. Perhaps that was the old school. The young school ain't so very different in that respect; — only, perhaps, there isn't so much for them to nobble.'

'A regular division of our profits has been arranged for in our deed of partnership,' said Robinson.

'That's uncommon nice, and very judicious,' said Poppins.

'It was thought to be so by our law advisers,' said Robinson.

'But yet, you see, old Brown nobbles the

money. Now, if ever I goes into partnership, I shall bargain to have the till for my share. You never get near the till, do you?'

'I attend to quite another branch of the business,' said Robinson.

'Then you're wrong. There's no branch of the business equal to the ready money branch. Old Brown has lots of ready money always by him now-a-days.'

It certainly was the case that the cash received day by day over the counter was taken by Mr Brown from the drawers and deposited by him in the safe. The payments into the bank were made three times a week, and the checks were all drawn by Mr Brown. None of these had ever been drawn except on behalf of the business; but then the payments into the bank had by no means tallied with the cash taken; and latterly, — for the last month or so, — the statements of the daily cash taken had been very promiscuous. Some payments had, of course, been made both to Jones and Robinson for their own expenses, but the payments made by Mr Brown to himself had probably greatly exceeded these. He had a vague idea that he was supreme in money matters, because he had introduced 'capital' into the firm. George Robinson had found it absolutely impossible to join himself in any league with Jones, so that hitherto Mr Brown had been able to carry out his own theory. The motto, *Divide et impera,* was probably unknown to Mr Brown in those words, but he had undoubtedly been acting on the wisdom which is conveyed in that doctrine.

Jones and his wife were preparing themselves for war, and it was plain to see that a storm of battle would soon be raging. Robinson also was fully alive to the perils of his position, and anxious as he was to remain on good terms with Mr Brown, was aware that it would be necessary for him to come to some understanding. In his difficulty he had dropped some hints to his friend Poppins, not exactly explaining the source of his embarrassment, but saying enough to make that gentleman understand the way in which the firm was going on.

'I suppose you're in earnest about that girl,' said Poppins. Poppins had an offhand, irreverent way of speaking, especially on subjects which from their nature demanded delicacy, that was frequently shocking to Robinson.

'If you mean Miss Brown,' said Robinson, in a tone of voice that was intended to convey a rebuke, 'I certainly am in earnest. My intention is that she shall become Mrs Robinson.'

'But when?'

'As soon as prudence will permit and the lady will consent. Miss Brown has never been used to hardship. For myself, I should little care what privations I might be called on to bear, but I could hardly endure to see her in want.'

'My advice to you is this. If you mean to marry her, do it at once. If you and she together can't manage the old man, you can't be worth your salt. If you can do that, then you can throw Jones overboard.'

'I am not in the least afraid of Jones.'

'Perhaps not; but still you'd better mind your P's and Q's. It seems to me that you and he and the young women are at sixes and sevens, and that's the reason why old Brown is able to nobble the money.'

'I certainly should be happier,' said Robinson, 'if I were married, and things were settled.'

'As to marriage,' said Poppins, 'my opinion is this; if a man has to do it, he might as well do it at once. They're always pecking at you; and a fellow feels that if he's in for it, what's the good of his fighting it out?'

'I should never marry except for love,' said Robinson.

'Nor I neither,' said Poppins. 'That is, I couldn't bring myself to put up with a hideous old hag, because she'd money. I should always be wanting to throttle her. But as long as they're young, and soft, and fresh, one can always love 'em; — at least I can.'

'I never loved but one,' said Robinson.

'There was a good many of them used to be pretty much the same to me. They was all very well; but as to breaking my heart about them, — why, it's a thing that I never understood.'

'Do you know, Poppins, what I did twice, — ay, thrice, — in those dark days?'

'What; when Brisket was after her?'

'Yes; when she used to say that she loved another. Thrice did I go down to the river bank, intending to terminate this wretched existence.'

'Did you now?'

'I swear to you that I did. But Providence, who foresaw the happiness that is in store for me, withheld me from the leap.'

'Polly once took up with a sergeant, and I can't say I liked it.'

'And what did you do?'

'I got uncommon drunk, and then I knocked the daylight out of him. We've been the best of friends ever since. But about marrying; — if a man is to do it, he'd better do it. It depends a good deal on the young woman, of course, and whether she's comfortable in her mind. Some women ain't comfortable, and then there's the devil to pay. You don't get enough to eat, and nothing to drink; and if ever you leave your pipe out of your pocket, she smashes it. I've know'd 'em of that sort, and a man had better have the rheumatism constant.'

'I don't think Maryanne is like that.'

'Well; I can't say. Polly isn't. She's not over good, by no means, and would a deal sooner sit in a arm-chair and have her victuals and beer brought to her, than she'd break her back by working too hard. She'd like to be always a-junketing, and that's what she's best for, — as is the case with many of 'em.'

'I've seen her as sportive as a young fawn at the Hall of Harmony.'

'But she ain't a young fawn any longer; and as

for harmony, it's my idea that the less of harmony a young woman has the better. It makes 'em give themselves airs, and think as how their ten fingers were made to put into yellow gloves, and that a young man hasn't nothing to do but to stand treat, and whirl 'em about till he ain't able to stand. A game's all very well, but bread and cheese is a deal better.'

'I love to see beauty enjoying itself gracefully. My idea of a woman is incompatible with the hard work of the world. I would fain do that myself, so that she should ever be lovely.'

'But she won't be lovely a bit the more. She'll grow old all the same, and take to drink very like. When she's got a red nose and a pimply face, and a sharp tongue, you'd be glad enough to see her at the wash-tub then. I remember an old song as my father used to sing, but my mother couldn't endure to hear it.

Woman takes delight in abundance of
    pleasure,
But a man's life is to labour and toil.

That's about the truth of it, and that's what comes of your Halls of Harmony.

'You would like woman to be a household drudge.'

'So I would, — only drudge don't sound well. Call her a ministering angel instead, and it comes to the same thing. They both of 'em means much of a muchness; — getting up your linen decent, and seeing that you have a bit of something hot when you come home late. Well, good-night, old fellow. I shall have my hair combed if I stay much longer. Take my advice, and as you mean to do it, do it at once. And don't let the old 'un nobble all the money. Live and let live. That's fair play all over.' And so Mr Poppins took his leave.

Had anybody suggested to George Robinson that he should go to Poppins for advice as to his course of life, George Robinson would have scorned the suggestion. He knew very well the great difference between him and his humble friend, both as regarded worldly position and intellectual attainments. But, nevertheless, there was a strain of wisdom in Poppins' remarks which, though it appertained wholly to matters of low import, he did not disdain to use. It was true that Maryanne Brown still frequented the Hall of Harmony, and went there quite as often without her betrothed as with him. It was true that Mr Brown had adopted a habit of using the money of the firm, without rendering a fair account of the purpose to which he applied it. The Hall of Harmony might not be the best preparation for domestic duties, nor Mr Brown's method of applying the funds the best specific for commercial success. He would look to both these things, and see that some reform were made. Indeed, he would reform them both entirely by insisting on a division of the profits, and by taking Maryanne to his own bosom. Great ideas filled his mind. If any undue opposition were made to his wishes when expressed, he would leave the firm, break up the business, and carry his now well-known genius for commercial enterprise to some other concern in which he might be treated with a juster appreciation of his merits.

'Not that I will ever leave thee, Maryanne,' he said to himself, as he resolved these things in his mind.

CHAPTER XIV

MISTRESS MORONY

It was about ten days after the conversation recorded in the last chapter between Mr Robinson and Mr Poppins that an affair was brought about through the imprudence and dishonesty of Mr Jones, which for some time prevented that settlement of matters on which Mr Robinson had resolved. During those ten days he had been occupied in bringing his resolution to a fixed point; and then, when the day and hour had come in which he intended to act, that event occurred which, disgraceful as it is to the annals of the Firm, must now be told.

There are certain small tricks of trade, well known to the lower class of houses in that business to which Brown, Jones, and Robinson had devoted themselves, which for a time may no doubt be profitable, but which are very apt to bring disgrace and ruin upon those who practise them. To such tricks as these Mr Jones was wedded, and by none of the arguments which he used in favour of a high moral tone of commerce could Robinson prevail upon his partner to abandon them. Nothing could exceed the obstinacy and blindness of Mr Jones during these discussions. When it was explained to him that the conduct he was pursuing was hardly removed, — nay, it was not removed, — from common swindling, he would reply that it was quite as honest as Mr Robinson's advertisements. He would quote especially those Katakairion shirts which were obtained from Hodges, and of which the sale of 39s. 6d. the half-dozen had by dint of a wide circulation of notices become considerable. 'If that isn't swindling, I don't know what is,' said Jones.

'Do you know what Katakairion means?' said Robinson.

'No; I don't,' said Jones. 'And I don't want to know.'

'Katakairion means "fitting,"' said Robinson; 'and the purchaser has only to take care that the shirt he buys does fit, and then it is Katakairion.'

'But we didn't invent them.'

'We invented the price and the name, and that's as much as anybody does. But that is not all. It's a well-understood maxim in trade, that a man may advertise whatever he chooses. We advertise to attract notice, not to state facts. But it's a mean thing to pass off a false article over the counter. If you will ticket your goods, you should sell them according to the ticket.'

At first, the other partners had not objected to this ticketing, as the practice is now common, and there is at first sight an apparent honesty about it which has its seduction. A lady seeing 21s. 7d. marked on a mantle in the window, is able to contemplate the desired piece of goods and to compare it, in silent leisure, with her finances. She can use all her power of eye, but, as a compensation to the shopkeeper, is debarred from the power of touch; and then, having satisfied herself as to the value of the thing inspected, she can go in and buy without delay or trouble to the vendor. But it has been found by practice that so true are the eyes of ladies that it is useless to expose in shop-windows articles which are not good of their kind, and cheap at the price named. To attract customers in this way, real bargains must be exhibited; and when this is done, ladies take advantage of the unwary tradesman, and unintended sacrifices are made. George Robinson soon perceived this, and suggested that the ticketing should be abandoned. Jones, however, persevered, observing that he knew how to remedy the evil inherent in the system. Hence difficulties arose, and, ultimately, disgrace which was very injurious to the Firm, and went near to break the heart of Mr Brown.

According to Jones's plan, the articles ticketed in the window were not, under any circumstances, to be sold. The shopmen, indeed, were forbidden to remove them from their positions under any entreaties or threats from the customers. The customer was to be at first informed, with all the blandishment at the shopman's command, that the goods furnished within the shop were exact counterparts of those exposed. Then the shopman was to argue that the arrangements of the window could not be disturbed. And should a persistent purchaser after that insist on a supposed legal right, to buy the very thing ticketed, Mr Jones was to be called; in which case Mr Jones would inform the persistent purchaser that she was regarded as unreasonable, violent, and disagreeable; and that, under such circumstances, her custom was not wanted by Brown, Jones, and Robinson. The disappointed female would generally leave the shop with some loud remarks as to swindling, dishonesty, and pettifogging, to which Mr Jones could turn a deaf ear. But sometimes worse than this would ensue; ladies would insist on their rights; scrambles would occur in order that possession of the article might be obtained; the assistants in the shop would not always take part with Mr Jones; and, as has been before said, serious difficulties would arise.

There can be no doubt that Jones was very wrong. He usually was wrong. His ideas of trade were mean, limited, and altogether inappropriate to business on a large scale. But, nevertheless, we cannot pass on to the narration of a circumstance as it did occur, without expressing our strong abhorrence of those ladies who are desirous of purchasing cheap goods to the manifest injury of the tradesmen from whom they buy them. The ticketing of goods at prices below their value is not to our taste, but the purchasing of such goods is less so. The lady who will take advantage of a tradesman, that she may fill her house with linen, or cover her back with finery, at his cost, and in a manner which her own means would not fairly permit, is, in our estimation, — a robber. It is often necessary that tradesmen should advertise tremendous sacrifices. It is sometimes necessary that they should actually make such sacrifices. Brown, Jones, and Robinson have during their career been driven to such a necessity. They have smiled upon their female customers, using their sweetest blandishments, while those female customers have abstracted their goods at prices almost nominal. Brown, Jones, and Robinson, in forcing such sales, have been coerced by the necessary laws of trade; but while smiling with all their blandishments, they have known that the ladies on whom they have smiled have been — robbers.

Why is it that commercial honesty has so seldom charms for women? A woman who would give away the last shawl from her back will insist on smuggling her gloves through the Custom-house! Who can make a widow understand that she should not communicate with her boy in the colonies under the dishonest cover of a newspaper? Is not the passion for cheap purchases altogether a female mania? And yet every cheap purchase, — every purchase made at a rate so cheap as to deny the vendor his fair profit is, in truth, a dishonesty; — a dishonesty to which the purchaser is indirectly a party. Would that women could be taught to hate bargains! How much less useless trash would there be in our houses, and how much fewer tremendous sacrifices in our shops!

Brown, Jones, and Robinson, when they had been established some six or eight months, had managed to procure from a house in the silk trade a few black silk mantles of a very superior description. The lot had been a remnant, and had been obtained with sundry other goods at a low figure. But, nevertheless, the proper price at which the house could afford to sell them would exceed the mark of general purchasers in Bishopsgate Street. These came into Mr Jones' hands, and he immediately resolved to use them for the purposes of the window. Some half-dozen of them were very tastefully arranged upon racks, and were marked at prices which were very tempting to ladies of discernment. In the middle of one window there was a copious mantle, of silk so thick that it stood almost alone, very full in its dimensions, and admirable in its fashion. This mantle, which would not have been dearly bought for 3*l*. 10*s*. or 4*l*., was unjudiciously ticketed at 38*s*. 11$\frac{11}{42}$*d*. 'It will bring dozens of women to the shop,' said Jones, 'and we have an article of the same shape and colour, which we can do at that price uncommonly well.' Whether or no the mantle had brought dozens of women into the shop, cannot now be said, but it certainly brought one there whom Brown, Jones, and

Robinson will long remember.

Mrs Morony was an Irishwoman who, as she assured the magistrates in Worship Street, had lived in the very highest circles in Limerick, and had come from a princely stock in the neighbouring county of Glare. She was a full-sized lady, not without a certain amount of good looks, though at the period of her intended purchase in Bishopsgate Street, she must have been nearer fifty than forty. Her face was florid, if not red, her arms were thick and powerful, her eyes were bright, but, as seen by Brown, Jones, and Robinson, not pleasant to the view, and she always carried with her an air of undaunted resolution. When she entered the shop, she was accompanied by a thin, acrid, unmarried female friend, whose feminine charms by no means equalled her own. She might be of about the same age, but she had more of the air and manner of advanced years. Her nose was long, narrow and red; her eyes were set very near together; she was tall and skimpy in all her proportions; and her name was Miss Biles. Of the name and station of Mrs Morony, or of Miss Biles, nothing was of course known when they entered the shop; but with all these circumstances, B., J., and R. were afterwards made acquainted.

'I believe I'll just look at that pelisse, if you plaze,' said Mrs Morony, addressing herself to a young man who stood near to the window in which the mantle was displayed.

'Certainly, ma'am,' said the man. 'If you'll step

this way, I'll show you the article.'

'I see the article there,' said Mrs Morony, poking at it with her parasol. Standing where she did she was just able to touch it in this way. 'That's the one I mane, with the price; — how much was it, Miss Biles?'

'One, eighteen, eleven and halfpenny,' said Miss Biles, who had learned the figures by heart before she ventured to enter the shop.

'If you'll do me the favour to step this way I'll show you the same article,' said the man, who was now aware that it was his first duty to get the ladies away from that neighbourhood.

But Mrs Morony did not move. 'It's the one there that I'm asking ye for,' said she, pointing again, and pointing this time with the hooked end of her parasol. 'I'll throuble ye, young man, to show me the article with the ticket.'

'The identical pelisse, if you please, sir,' said Miss Biles, 'which you there advertise as for sale at one, eighteen, eleven and a halfpenny.' And then she pressed her lips together, and looked at the shopman with such vehemence that her two eyes seemed to grow into one.

The poor man knew that he was in a difficulty, and cast his eyes across the shop for assistance. Jones, who in his own branch was ever on the watch, — and let praise for that diligence be duly given to him, — had seen from the first what was in the wind. From the moment in which the stout lady had raised her parasol he felt that a battle was imminent; but he had thought it prudent to abstain awhile from the combat himself. He hovered near, however, as personal protection might be needed on behalf of the favourite ornament of his window.

'I'll throuble you, if you plaze, sir, to raich me that pelisse,' said Mrs Morony.

'We never disturb our window,' said the man, 'but we keep the same article in the shop.'

'Don't you be took in by that, Mrs Morony,' said Miss Biles.

'I don't mane,' said Mrs Morony. 'I shall insist, sir —'

Now was the moment in which, as Jones felt, the interference of the general himself was necessary. Mrs Morony was in the act of turning herself well round towards the window, so as to make herself sure of her prey when she should resolve on grasping it. Miss Biles had already her purse in her hand, ready to pay the legal claim. It was clear to be seen that the enemy was of no mean skill and of great valour. The intimidation of Mrs Morony might be regarded as a feat beyond the power of man. Her florid countenance had already become more than ordinarily rubicund, and her nostrils were breathing anger.

'Ma'am,' said Mr Jones, stepping up and ineffectually attempting to interpose himself between her and the low barrier which protected the goods exposed to view, 'the young man has already told you that we cannot disarrange the window. It is not our habit to do so. If you will do me the honour to walk to a chair, he shall show you any articles which you may desire to inspect.'

'Don't you be done,' whispered Miss Biles.

'I don't mane, if I know it,' said Mrs Morony, standing her ground manfully. 'I don't desire to inspect anything, — only that pelisse.'

'I am sorry that we cannot gratify you,' said Mr Jones.

'But you must gratify me. It's for sale, and the money's on it.'

'You shall have the same article at the same price;' and Mr Jones, as he spoke, endeavoured to press the lady out of her position. 'But positively you cannot have that. We never break through our rules.'

'Chaiting the public is the chief of your rules, I'm thinking,' said Mrs Morony; 'but you'll not find it so aisy to chait me. Pay them the money down on the counter, Miss Biles, dear.' And so saying she thrust forth her parasol, and succeeded in her attempt to dislodge the prey. Knowing well where to strike her blow and obtain a hold, she dragged forth the mantle, and almost got it into her left hand. But Jones could not stand by and see his firm thus robbed. Dreadful as was his foe in spirit, size and strength, his manliness was too great for this. So he also dashed forward, and was the first to grasp the silk.

'Are you going to rob the shop?' said he.

'Is it rob?' said Mrs Morony. 'By the powers, thin, ye're the biggest blag-guard my eyes have seen since I've been in London, and that's saying a long word. Is it rob to me? I'll tell you what it is, young man, — av you don't let your fingers off this pelisse that I've purchased, I'll have you before the magisthrates for stailing it. Have you paid the money down, dear?'

Miss Biles was busy counting out the cash, but no one was at hand to take it from her. It was clear that the two confederates had prepared themselves at all points for the contest, having, no doubt, more than once inspected the article from the outside, — for Miss Biles had the exact sum ready, done to the odd halfpenny. 'There,' said she, appealing to the young man who was nearest to her, 'one, eighteen, eleven, and a halfpenny.' But the young man was deaf to the charmer, even though she charmed with ready money. 'May I trouble you to see that the cash is right.' But the young man would not be troubled.

'You'd a deal better leave it go, ma'am,' said Jones, 'or I shall be obliged to send for the police.'

'Is it the police? Faith, thin, and I think you'd better send! Give me my mantilla, I say. It's bought and paid for at your own price.'

By this time there was a crowd in the shop, and Jones, in his anxiety to defend the establishment, had closed with Mrs Morony, and was, as it were, wrestling with her. His effort, no doubt, had been to disengage her hand from the unfortunate mantle; but in doing so, he was led into some slight personal violence towards the lady. And now Miss Biles, having deposited her money, attacked him from behind, declaring that her friend would be murdered.

'Come, hands off. A woman's a woman always!' said one of the crowd who had gathered round them.

'What does the man mean by hauling a female about that way?' said another.

'The poor crathur's nigh murthered wid him intirely,' said a countrywoman from the street.

'If she's brought the thingumbob at your own price, why don't you give it her?' asked a fourth.

'I'll be hanged if she shall have it!' said Jones, panting for breath. He was by no means deficient in spirit on such an occasion as this.

'And it's my belief you will be hanged,' said Miss Biles, who was still working away at his back.

The scene was one which was not creditable to the shop of English tradesmen in the nineteenth century. The young men and girls had come round from behind the counter, but they made no attempt to separate the combatants. Mr Jones was not loved among them, and the chance of war seemed to run very much in favour of the lady. One discreet youth had gone out in quest of a policeman, but he was not successful in his search till he had walked half a mile from the door. Mr Jones was at last nearly smothered in the encounter, for the great weight and ample drapery of Mrs Morony were beginning to tell upon him. When she got his back against the counter, it was as though a feather bed was upon him. In the meantime the unfortunate mantle had fared badly between them, and was now not worth the purchase-money which, but ten minutes since, had been so eagerly tendered for it.

Things were in this state when Mr Brown slowly descended into the arena, while George Robinson, standing at the distant doorway in the back, looked on with blushing cheeks. One of the girls had explained to Mr Brown what was the state of affairs, and he immediately attempted to throw oil on the troubled waters.

'Wherefore all this noise?' he said, raising both his hands as he advanced slowly to the spot. 'Mr Jones, I implore you to desist!' But Mr Jones was wedged down upon the counter, and could not desist.

'Madam, what can I do for you?' And he addressed himself to the back of Mrs Morony, which was still convulsed violently by her efforts to pummel Mr Jones.

'I believe he's well nigh killed her; I believe he has,' said Miss Biles.

Then, at last, the discreet youth returned with three policemen, and the fight was at an end. That the victory was with Mrs Morony nobody could doubt. She held in her hand all but the smallest fragment of the mantle, — the price of which, however, Miss Biles had been careful to repocket, — and showed no sign of exhaustion, whereas Jones was speechless. But, nevertheless, she was in tears, and appealed loudly to the police and to the crowd as to her wrongs.

'I'm fairly murthered with him, thin, so I am, — the baist, the villain, the swindhler. What am I to do at all, and my things all desthroyed? Look at this, thin!' and she held up the cause of war. 'Did mortial man iver see the like of that? And I'm beaten black and blue wid him, — so I am.' And then she sobbed violently.

'So you are, Mrs Morony,' said Miss Biles. 'He to call himself a man indeed, and to go to strike a woman!'

'It's thrue for you, dear,' continued Mrs Morony. 'Policemen, mind, I give him in charge. You're all witnesses, I give that man in charge.'

Mr Jones, also, was very eager to secure the intervention of the police, — much more so than was Mr Brown, who was only anxious that everybody should retire. Mr Jones could never be made to understand that he had in any way been wrong. 'A firm needn't sell an article unless it pleases,' he argued to the magistrate. 'A firm is bound to make good its promises, sir,' replied the gentleman in Worship Street. 'And no respectable firm would for a moment hesitate to do so.' And then he made some remarks of a very severe nature.

Mr Brown did all that he could to prevent the affair from becoming public. He attempted to bribe Mrs Morony by presenting her with the torn mantle; but she accepted the gift, and then preferred her complaint. He bribed the policemen, also; but, nevertheless, the matter got into the newspaper reports. The daily Jupiter, of course, took it up, — for what does it not take up in its solicitude for poor British human nature? — and tore Brown, Jones, and Robinson to pieces in a leading article. No punishment could be inflicted on the firm, for, as the magistrate said, no offence could be proved. The lady, also, had certainly been wrong to help herself. But the whole affair was damaging in the extreme to Magenta House, and gave a terrible check to that rapid trade which had already sprang up under the influence of an extended system of advertising.

CHAPTER XV
MISS BROWN NAMES THE DAY

George Robinson had been in the very act of
coming to an understanding with Mr Brown as
to the proceeds of the business, when he was interrupted by that terrible affair of Mrs Morony.
For some days after that the whole establishment
was engaged in thinking, talking, and giving evi-
dence about the matter, and it was all that the
firm could do to keep the retail trade going
across the counter. Some of the young men and
women gave notice, and went away; and others
became so indifferent that it was necessary to get
rid of them. For a week it was doubtful whether
it would be possible to keep the house open, and
during that week Mr Brown was so paralyzed by
his feelings that he was unable to give any assistance. He sat upstairs moaning, accompanied
generally by his two daughters; and he sent a
medical certificate to Worship Street, testifying
his inability to appear before the magistrate.
From what transpired afterwards we may say that
the magistrate would have treated him more

leniently than did the young women. They were aware that whatever money yet remained was in his keeping; and now, as at the time of their mother's death, it seemed fitting to them that a division should be made of the spoils.

'George,' he said one evening to his junior partner, 'I'd like to be laid decent in Kensal Green! I know it will come to that soon.'

Robinson hereupon reminded him that care had killed a cat; and promised him all manner of commercial greatness if he could only rouse himself to his work. 'The career of a merchant prince is still open to you,' said Robinson, enthusiastically.

'Not along with Maryanne and Sarah Jane, George!'

'Sarah Jane is a married woman, and sits at another man's hearth. Why do you allow her to trouble you?'

'She is my child, George. A man can't deny himself to his child. At least I could not. And I don't want to be a merchant prince. If I could only have a little place of my own, that was my own; and where they wouldn't always be nagging after money when they come to see me.'

Poor Mr Brown! He was asking from the fairies that for which we are all asking, — for which men have ever asked. He merely desired the comforts of the world, without its cares. He wanted his small farm, of a few acres, as Horace wanted it, and Cincinnatus, and thousands of statesmen, soldiers, and merchants, from their days down to ours; his small farm, on which, however, the sun must always shine, and where no weeds should flourish. Poor Mr Brown! Such little farms for the comforts of old age can only be attained by long and unwearied cultivation during the years of youth and manhood.

It was on one occasion such as this, not very long after the affair of Mrs Morony, that Robinson pressed very eagerly upon Mr Brown the special necessity which demanded from the firm at the present moment more than ordinary efforts in the way of advertisement.

'Jones has given us a great blow,' said Robinson.

'I fear he has,' said Mr Brown.

'And now, if we do not put our best foot forward it will be all up with us. If we flag now, people will see that we are down. But if we go on with audacity, all those reports will die away, and we shall again trick our beams, and flame once more in the morning sky.'

It may be presumed that Mr Brown did not exactly follow the quotation, but the eloquence of Robinson had its desired effect. Mr Brown did at last produce a sum of five hundred pounds, with which printers, stationers, and advertising agents were paid or partially paid, and Robinson again went to work.

'It's the last,' said Mr Brown, with a low moan, 'and would have been Maryanne's!'

Robinson, when he heard this, was much struck by the old man's enduring courage. How had he been able to preserve this sum from the young woman's hands, pressed as he had been by her and by Brisket? Of this Robinson said nothing, but he did venture to allude to the fact that the money must, in fact, belong to the firm.

This is here mentioned, chiefly as showing the reason why Robinson did not for awhile renew the business on which he was engaged when Mrs Morony's presence in the shop was announced. He felt that no private matter should be allowed for a time to interfere with his renewed exertions; and he also felt that as Mr Brown had responded to his entreaties in that matter of the five hundred pounds, it would not become him to attack the old man again immediately. For three months he applied himself solely to business; and then, when affairs had partially been restored under his guidance, he again resolved, under the further instigation of Poppins, to put things at once on a proper footing.

'So you ain't spliced yet,' said Poppins.

'No, not yet.'

'Nor won't be, — not to Maryanne Brown. There was my wife at Brisket's, in Aldersgate Street, yesterday, and we all know what that means.'

'What does it mean?' demanded Robinson, scowling fearfully. 'Would you hint to me that she is false?'

'False! No! she's not false that I know of. She's ready enough to have you, if you can put yourself right with the old man. But if you can't, — why, of course, she's not to wait till her hair's grey. She and Polly are as thick as thieves, and so Polly has been to Aldersgate Street. Polly says that the Jones's are getting their money regularly out of the till.'

'Wait till her hair be grey!' said Robinson, when he was left to himself. 'Do I wish her to wait? Would I not stand with her at the altar to-morrow, though my last half-crown should go to the greedy priest who joined us? And she has sent her friend to Aldersgate Street, — to my rival! There must, at any rate, be an end of this!'

Late on that evening, when his work was over, he took a glass of hot brandy-and-water at the 'Four Swans,' and then he waited upon Mr Brown. He luckily found the senior partner alone. 'Mr Brown,' said he, 'I've come to have a little private conversation.'

'Private, George! Well, I'm all alone. Maryanne is with Mrs Poppins, I think.'

With Mrs Poppins! Yes; and where might she not be with Mrs Poppins? Robinson felt that he had it within him at that moment to start off for Aldersgate Street. 'But first to business,' said he, as he remembered the special object for which he had come.

'For the present it is well that she should be away,' he said. 'Mr Brown, the time has now come at which it is absolutely necessary that I should know where I am.'

'Where you are, George?'

'Yes; on what ground I stand. Who I am before

the world, and what interest I represent. Is it the fact that I am the junior partner in the house of Brown, Jones, and Robinson?'

'Why, George, of course you are.'

'And is it the fact that by the deed of partnership drawn up between us, I am entitled to receive one quarter of the proceeds of the business?'

'No, George, no; not proceeds.'

'What then?'

'Profits, George; one quarter of the profits.'

'And what is my share for the year now over?'

'You have lived, George; you must always remember that. It is a great thing in itself even to live out of a trade in these days. You have lived; you must acknowledge that.'

'Mr Brown, I am not a greedy man, nor a suspicious man, nor an idle man, nor a man of pleasure. But I am a man in love.'

'And she shall be yours, George.'

'Ay, sir, that is easily said. She shall be mine, and in order that she may be mine, I must request to know what is accurately the state of our account?'

'George,' said Mr Brown in a piteous accent, 'you and I have always been friends.'

'But there are those who will do much for their enemies out of fear, though they will do nothing for their friends out of love. Jones has a regular income out of the business.'

'Only forty shillings or so on every Saturday night; nothing more, on my honour. And then they've babbies, you know, and they must live.'

'By the terms of our partnership I am entitled to as much as he.'

'But then, George, suppose that nobody is entitled to nothing! Suppose there is no profits. We all must live, you know, but then it's only hand to mouth; is it?'

How terrible was this statement as to the affairs of the firm, coming, as it did, from the senior partner, who not more than twelve months since entered the business with a sum of four thousand pounds in hard cash! Robinson, whose natural spirit in such matters was sanguine and buoyant, felt that even he was depressed. Had four thousand pounds gone, and was there no profit? He knew well that the stock on hand would not even pay the debts that were due. The shop had always been full, and the men and women at the counter had always been busy. The books had nominally been kept by himself; but who can keep the books of a concern, if he be left in ignorance as to the outgoings and incomings?

'That comes of attempting to do business on a basis of capital!' he said in a voice of anger.

'It comes of advertising, George. It comes of little silver books, and big wooden stockings, and men in armour, and cats-carrion shirts; that's what it's come from, George.'

'Never,' said Robinson, rising from his chair with energetic action. 'Never. You may as well tell me that the needle does not point to the pole, that the planets have not their appointed courses, that the swelling river does not run to the sea. There are facts as to which the world has ceased to dispute, and this is one of them. Advertise, advertise, advertise! It may be that we have fallen short in our duty; but the performance of a duty can never do an injury.' In reply to this, old Brown merely shook his head. 'Do you know what Barlywig has spent on his physic; Barlywig's Medean Potion? Forty thousand a-year for the last ten years, and now Barlywig is worth; — I don't know what Barlywig is worth; but I know he is in Parliament.'

'We haven't stuff to go on like that, George.' In answer to this, Robinson knew not what to urge, but he did know that his system was right.

At this moment the door opened, and Maryanne Brown entered the room. 'Father,' she said, as soon as her foot was over the threshold of the door; but then seeing that Mr Brown was not alone, she stopped herself. There was an angry spot on her cheeks, and it was manifest from the tone of her voice that she was about to address her father in anger. 'Oh, George; so you are there, are you? I suppose you came, because you knew I was out.'

'I came, Maryanne,' said he, putting out his hand to her, 'I came — to settle our wedding day.'

'My children, my children!' said Mr Brown.

'That's all very fine,' said Maryanne; 'but I've heard so much about wedding days, that I'm sick of it, and don't mean to have none.'

'What; you will never be a bride?'

'No; I won't. What's the use?'

'You shall be my bride; — to-morrow if you will.'

'I'll tell you what it is, George Robinson; my belief of you is, that you are that soft, a man might steal away your toes without your feet missing 'em.'

'You have stolen away my heart, and my body is all the lighter.'

'It's light enough; there's no doubt of that, and so is your head. Your heels too were, once, but you've given up that.'

'Yes, Maryanne. When a man commences the stern realities of life, that must be abandoned. But now I am anxious to commence a reality which is not stern, — that reality which is for me to soften all the hardness of this hardworking world. Maryanne, when shall be our wedding day?'

For a while the fair beauty was coy, and would give no decisive answer; but at length under the united pressure of her father and lover, a day was named. A day was named, and Mr Brown's consent to that day was obtained; but this arrangement was not made till he had undertaken to give up the rooms in which he at present lived, and to go into lodgings in the neighbourhood.

'George,' said she, in a confidential whisper, before the evening was over, 'if you don't manage about the cash now, and have it all your own way, you must be soft.' Under the influence of gratified love, he promised her that he would manage it.

'Bless you, my children, bless you,' said Mr Brown, as they parted for the night. 'Bless you, and may your loves be lasting, and your children obedient.'

CHAPTER XVI

SHOWING HOW ROBINSON WALKED UPON ROSES

'Will it ever be said of me when my history is told that I spent forty thousand pounds a-year in advertising a single article? Would that it might be told that I had spent ten times forty thousand.' It was thus that Robinson had once spoken to his friend Poppins, while some remnant of that five hundred pounds was still in his hands.

'But what good does it do? It don't make anything.'

'But it sells them, Poppins.'

'Everybody wears a shirt, and no one wears more than one at a time. I don't see that it does any good.'

'It is a magnificent trade in itself. Would that I had a monopoly of all the walls in London! The very arches of the bridges must be worth ten thousand a-year. The omnibuses are invaluable; the cabs are a mine of wealth; and the railway stations throughout England would give a revenue for an emperor. Poppins, my dear fellow. I fancy that you have hardly looked into the depths of it.'

'Perhaps not,' said Poppins. 'Some objects to them that they're all lies. It isn't that I mind. As far as I can see, everything is mostly lies. The very worst article our people can get for sale, they call "middlings;" the real middlings are "very superior," and so on. They're all lies; but they don't cost anything, and all the world knows what they mean. Bad things must be bought and sold, and if we said our things was bad, nobody would buy them. But I can't understand throwing away so much money and getting nothing.'

Poppins possessed a glimmering of light, but it was only a glimmering. He could understand that a man should not call his own goods middling; but he could not understand that a man is only carrying out the same principle in an advanced degree, when he proclaims with a hundred thousand voices in a hundred thousand places, that the article which he desires to sell is the best of its kind that the world has yet produced. He merely asserts with his loudest voice that his middlings are not middlings. A little man can see that he must not cry stinking fish against himself; but it requires a great man to understand that in order to abstain effectually from so suicidal a proclamation, he must declare with all the voice of his lungs, that his fish are that moment hardly out of the ocean. 'It's the poetry of euphemism,' Robinson once said to Poppins; — but he might as well have talked Greek to him.

Robinson often complained that no one understood him; but he forgot that it is the fate of great men generally to work alone, and to be not comprehended. The higher a man raises his head, the more necessary is it that he should learn to lean only on his own strength, and to walk his path without even the assistance of sympathy. The greedy Jones had friends. Poppins with his easy epicurean laisser aller, — he had friends. The decent Brown, who would so fain be comfortable, had friends. But for Robinson, there was no one on whose shoulder he could rest his head, and from whose heart and voice he could receive sympathy and encouragement.

From one congenial soul, — from one soul that he had hoped to find congenial, — he did look for solace; but even here he was disappointed. It has been told that Maryanne Brown did at last consent to name the day. This occurred in May, and the day named was in August. Robinson was very anxious to fix it at an earlier period, and the good-natured girl would have consented to arrange everything within a fortnight. 'What's the use of shilly-shallying?' said she to her father. 'If it is to be done, let it be done at once. I'm so knocked about among you, I hardly know where I am.' But Mr Brown would not consent. Mr Brown was very feeble, but yet he was very obstinate. It would often seem that he was beaten away from his purpose, and yet he would hang on it with more tenacity than that of a stronger man. 'Town is empty in August, George, and then you can be spared for a run to Margate for two or three days.'

'Oh, we don't want any nonsense, said Maryanne; 'do we, George?'

'All I want is your own self,' said Robinson.

'Then you won't mind going into lodgings for a few months,' said Brown.

Robinson would have put up with an attic, had she he loved consented to spread her bridal couch so humbly; but Maryanne declared with resolution that she would not marry till she saw herself in possession of the rooms over the shop.

'There'll be room for us all for awhile,' said old Brown.

'I think we might manage,' said George.

'I know a trick worth two of that,' said the lady. 'Who's to make pa go when once we begin in that way? As I mean to end, so I'll begin. And as for you, George, there's no end to your softness. You're that green, that the very cows would eat you.' Was it not well said by Mr Robinson in his preface to these memoirs, that the poor old commercial Lear, whose name stood at the head of the firm, was cursed with a Goneril, — and with a Regan?

But nothing would induce Mr Brown to leave his home, or to say that he would leave his home, before the middle of August, and thus the happy day was postponed till that time.

'There's many a slip 'twixt the cup and the lip,' said Poppins, when he was told. 'Do you take care that she and Polly ain't off to Aldersgate Street together.'

'Poppins, I wouldn't be cursed with your idea

of human nature, — not for a free use of all the stations on the North Western. Go to Aldersgate Street now that she is my affianced bride!'

'That's gammon,' said Poppins. 'When once she's married she'll go straight enough. I believe that of her, for she knows which side her bread's buttered. But till the splice is made she's a right to please herself; that's the way she looks at it.'

'And will it not please her to become mine?'

'It's about the same with 'em all,' continued Poppins. 'My Polly would have been at Hong Kong with the Buffs by this time, if I hadn't knocked the daylight out of that sergeant.' And Poppins, from the tone in which he spoke of his own deeds, seemed to look back upon his feat of valour with less satisfaction than it had given him at the moment. Polly was his own certainly; but the comfort of his small menage was somewhat disturbed by his increasing family.

But to return. Robinson, as we have said, looked in vain to his future partner in life for a full appreciation of his own views as to commerce. 'It's all very well, I daresay,' said she; 'but one should feel one's way.'

'When you launch your ship into the sea,' he replied, 'you do not want to feel your way. You know that the waves will bear her up, and you send her forth boldly. As wood will float upon water, so will commerce float on the ocean streams of advertisement.'

'But if you run aground in the mud, where are you then? Do you take care, George, or your boat'll be water-logged.'

It was during some of these conversations that Delilah cut another lock of hair from Samson's head, and induced him to confess that he had obtained that sum of five hundred pounds from her father, and spent it among those who prepared for him his advertisements. 'No!' said she, jumping up from her seat. 'Then he had it after all?'

'Yes; he certainly had it.'

'Well, that passes. And after all he said!'

A glimmering of the truth struck coldly upon Robinson's heart. She had endeavoured to get from her father this sum and had failed. She had failed, and the old man had sworn to her that he had it not. But for what purpose had she so eagerly demanded it? 'Maryanne,' he said, 'if you love another more fondly than you love me —'

'Don't bother about love, George, now. And so you got it out of him and sent it all flying after the rest. I didn't think you were that powerful.'

'The money, Maryanne, belonged to the firm.'

'Gracious knows who it belongs to now. But, laws; — when I think of all that he said, it's quite dreadful. One can't believe a word that comes out of his mouth.'

Robinson also thought that it was quite dreadful when he reflected on all that she must have said before she had given up the task as hopeless. Then, too, an idea came upon him of what he might have to endure when he and she should be one bone and one flesh. How charming was she to the eyes! how luxuriously attractive, when in her softer moments she would laugh, and smile, and joke at the winged hours as they passed! But already was he almost afraid of her voice, and already did he dread the fiercer glances of her eyes. Was he wise in this that he was doing? Had he not one bride in commerce, a bride that would never scold; and would it not be well for him to trust his happiness to her alone? So he argued within his own breast. But nevertheless, Love was still the lord of all.

'And the money's all gone?' said Maryanne.

'Indeed it is. Would I had as many thousands to send after it.'

'It was like your folly, George, not to keep a little of it by you, knowing how comfortable it would have been for us at the beginning.'

'But, my darling, it belonged to the firm.'

'The firm! Ain't they all helping themselves hand over hand, except you? There was Sarah Jane in the shop behind the counter all yesterday afternoon. Now, I tell you what it is; if she's to come in I won't stand it. She's not there for nothing, and she with children at home. No wonder she can keep a nursemaid, if that's where she spends her time. If you would go down more into the shop, George, and write less of them little books in verse, it would be better for us all.'

And so the time passed on towards August, and the fifteenth of that month still remained fixed as the happy day. Robinson spent some portion of this time in establishing a method of advertisement, which he flattered himself was altogether new; but it must be admitted in these pages that his means for carrying it out were not sufficient. In accordance with this project it would have been necessary to secure the co-operation of all the tailors' foremen in London, and this could not be done without a douceur to the men. His idea was, that for a period of a month in the heart of the London season, no new coat should be sent home to any gentleman without containing in the pocket one of those alluring little silver books, put out by Brown, Jones, and Robinson.

'The thing is, to get them opened and looked at,' said Robinson. 'Now, I put it to you, Poppins, whether you wouldn't open a book like that if you found that somebody had put it into your tail coat.'

'Well, I should open it.'

'You would be more or less than mortal did you not? If it's thrown into your cab, you throw it out. If a man hands it to you in the street, you drop it. If it comes by post, you throw it into the waste-paper basket. But I'll defy the sternest or the idlest man not to open the leaves of such a work as that when he first takes it out of his new dress-coat. Surprise will make him do so. Why should his tailor send him the book of B., J., and R.? There must be something in it. The name of B., J., and R., becomes fixed in his memory, and then the work is done. If the tailors had been true to me, I might have defied the world.' But the tailors were not true to him.

During all this time nothing was heard of Brisket. It could not be doubted that Brisket, busy among his bullocks in Aldersgate Street, knew well what was passing among the Browns in Bishopsgate Street. Once or twice it occurred to Robinson that the young women, Maryanne namely and Mrs Poppins, expected some intervention from the butcher. Was it possible that Mr Brisket might be expected to entertain less mercenary ideas when he found that his prize was really to be carried off by another? But whatever may have been the expectations of the ladies, Brisket made no sign. He hadn't seen his way, and therefore he had retired from the path of love.

But Brisket, even though he did not see his way, was open to female seduction. Why it was, that at this eventful period of Robinson's existence Mrs Poppins should have turned against him? Why his old friend, Polly Twizzle, should have gone over to his rival, Robinson never knew. It may have been because, in his humble way, Poppins himself stood firmly by his friend; for such often is the nature of women. Be that as it may, Mrs Poppins, who is now again his fast friend, was then his enemy.

'We shall have to go to this wedding of George's,' Poppins said to his wife, when the first week in August had already passed. 'I suppose old Pikes 'ill give me a morning.' Old Pikes was a partner in the house to which Poppins was attached.

'I shan't buy my bonnet yet awhile,' said Mrs Poppins.

'And why not, Polly?'

'For reasons that I know of.'

'But what reasons?'

'You men are always half blind, and t'other half stupid. Don't you see that she's not going to have him?'

'She must be pretty sharp changing her mind, then. Here's Tuesday already, and next Tuesday is to be the day.'

'Then it won't be next Tuesday; nor yet any Tuesday this month. Brisket's after her again.'

'I don't believe it, Polly.'

'Then disbelieve it. I was with him yesterday, and I'll tell you who was there before me; — only don't you go to Robinson and say I said so.'

'If I can't make sport, I shan't spoil none,' said Poppins.

'Well, Jones was there. Jones was with Brisket, and Jones told him that if he'd come forward now he should have a hundred down, and a promise from the firm for the rest of it.'

'Then Jones is a scoundrel.'

'I don't know about that,' said Mrs Poppins. 'Maryanne is his wife's sister, and he's bound to do the best he can by her. Brisket is a deal steadier than Georgy Robinson, and won't have to look for his bread so soon, I'm thinking.'

'He hasn't half the brains,' said Poppins.

'Brains is like soft words; they won't butter no parsnips.'

'And you've been with Brisket?' said the husband.

'Yes; why not? Brisket and I was always friends. I'm not going to quarrel with Brisket because Georgy Robinson is afraid of him. I knew how it would be with Robinson when he didn't stand up to Brisket that night at the Hall of Harmony. What's a man worth if he won't stand up for his young woman? If you hadn't stood up for me I wouldn't have had you.' And so ended that conversation.

'A hundred pounds down?' said Brisket to Jones the next day.

'Yes, and our bill for the remainder.'

'The cash on the nail.'

'Paid into your hand,' said Jones.

'I think I should see my way,' said Brisket; 'at any rate I'll come up on Saturday.'

'Much better say to-morrow, or Friday.'

'Can't. It's little Gogham Fair on Friday; and I always kills on Thursday.'

'Saturday will be very late.'

'There'll be time enough if you've got the money ready. You've spoken to old Brown, I suppose. I'll be up as soon after six on Saturday evening as I can come. If Maryanne wants to see me, she'll find me here. It won't be the first time.'

Thus was it that among his enemies the happiness of Robinson's life was destroyed. Against Brisket he breathes not a word. The course was open to both of them; and if Brisket was the best horse, why, let him win!

But in what words would it be right to depict the conduct of Jones?

CHAPTER XVII

A TEA-PARTY IN BISHOPSGATE STREET

If it shall appear to those who read these memoirs that there was much in the conduct of Mr Brown which deserves censure, let them also remember how much there was in his position which demands pity. In this short narrative it has been our purpose to set forth the commercial doings of the house of Brown, Jones, and Robinson, rather than the domestic life of the partners, and, therefore, it has been impossible to tell of all the trials through which Mr Brown passed with his children. But those trials were very severe, and if Mr Brown was on certain points untrue to the young partner who trusted him, allowances for such untruth must be made. He was untrue; but there is one man, who, looking back upon his conduct, knows how to forgive it.

The scenes upstairs at Magenta House during that first week in August had been very terrible. Mr Brown, in his anxiety to see his daughter settled, had undoubtedly pledged himself to abandon the rooms in which he lived, and to take lodgings elsewhere. To this promised self-sacrifice Maryanne was resolved to keep him bound; and when some hesitation appeared on his part, she swore to him that nothing should induce her to become Mrs Robinson till he had packed his things and was gone. Mr Brown had a heart to feel, and at this moment he could have told how much sharper than a serpent's tooth is a child's ingratitude!

But he would have gone; he would have left the house, although he had begun to comprehend that in leaving it he must probably lose much of his authority over the money taken in the shop; he would, however, have done so, had not Mrs Jones come down upon him with the whole force of her tongue, and the full violence of her malice. When Robinson should have become one with Maryanne Brown, and should also have become the resident partner, then would the influence of Mrs Jones in that establishment have been brought to a speedy close.

The reader shall not be troubled with those frightful quarrels in which each of the family was pitted against the others. Sarah Jane declared to her father, in terms which no child should have used to her parent, that he must be an idiot and doting if he allowed his youngest daughter and her lover to oust him from his house and from all share in the management of the business. Brown then appealed piteously to Maryanne, and begged that he might be allowed to occupy a small closet as his bed-room. But Maryanne was inexorable. He had undertaken to go, and unless he did go she would never omit to din into his ears this breach of his direct promise to her. Maryanne became almost great in her anger, as with voice raised so as to drown her sister's weaker tones, she poured forth her own story of her own wrongs.

'It has been so from the beginning,' she said. 'When I first knew Brisket, it was not for any love I had for the man, but because mother took him up. Mother promised him money; and then I said I'd marry him, — not because I cared for him, but because he was respectable and all right. And then mother hadn't the money when the pinch came, and, of course, Brisket wasn't going to be put upon; — why should he? So I took up with Robinson, and you knew it, father.'

'I did, Maryanne; I did.'

'Of course you did. I wasn't going to make a fool of myself for no man. I have got myself to look to; and if I don't do it myself, they who is about me won't do it for me.'

'Your old father would do anything for you.'

'Father, I hate words! What I want is deeds. Well, then; — Robinson came here and was your partner, and meanwhile I thought it was all right. And who was it interfered? Why, you did. When Brisket went to you, you promised him the money: and then he went and upset Robinson. And we had that supper in Smithfield, and Robinson was off and I was to be Mrs Brisket out of hand. But then, again, the money wasn't there.'

'I couldn't make the money, Maryanne.'

'Father, it's a shame for you to tell such falsehoods before your own daughters.'

'Oh, Maryanne! you wicked girl!' said Sarah Jane.

'If I'm wicked, there's two of us so, Sarah Jane! You had the money, and you gave it to Robinson for them notices of his. I know all about it now! And then what could you expect of Brisket? Of course he was off. There was no fal-lal about love, and all that, with him. He wanted a woman to look after his house; but he wanted something with her. And I wanted a roof over my head; — which I'm not likely to have, the way you're going on.'

'While I have a morsel, you shall have half.'

'And when you haven't a morsel, how will it be then? Of course when I saw all this, I felt myself put upon. There was Jones getting his money out of the shop!'

'Well, miss,' said Sarah Jane; 'and isn't he a partner?'

'You ain't a partner, and I don't know what business you have there. But every one was helping themselves except me. I was going to the wall. I have always been going to the wall. Well; when Brisket was off, I took up with Robinson again. I always liked him the best, only I never thought of my own likings. I wasn't that selfish. I took up with Robinson again; but I wasn't going to be any man's wife, if he couldn't put a roof over my head. Well, father, you know what was said then, and now you're going back from it.'

'I suppose you'd better have Mr Brisket,' said the old man, after a pause.

'Will you give Brisket those five hundred pounds?' And then those embassies to Aldersgate Street were made by Mrs Poppins and by Mr Jones. During this time Maryanne, having spoken her mind freely, remained silent and sullen. That her father would not go out on the appointed day, she knew. That she would not marry Robinson unless he did, she knew also. She did not like Brisket; but, as she had said, she was not so selfish as to let that stand in the way. If it was to be Brisket, let it be Brisket. Only let something be done.

Only let something be done. It certainly was not a matter of surprise that she should demand so much. It must be acknowledged that all connected with the firm and family began to feel that the house of Brown, Jones, and Robinson, had not succeeded in establishing itself on a sound basis. Mr Brown was despondent, and often unwell. The Jones's were actuated by no ambition to raise themselves to the position of British merchants, but by a greedy desire to get what little might be gotten in the scramble. Robinson still kept his shoulder to the collar, but he did so with but little hope. He had made a fatal mistake in leaguing himself with uncongenial partners, and began to feel that this mistake must be expiated by the ruin of his present venture. Under such circumstances Maryanne Brown was not unreasonable in desiring that something should be done. She had now given a tacit consent to that plan for bringing back Brisket, and consequently her brother-in-law went at once to work.

It must be acknowledged that the time was short. When Brisket, with such easy indifference, postponed his visit to Bishopsgate Street till the Saturday, giving to Gogham Market and the slaughtering of his beasts a preference to the renewal of his love, he regarded the task before him as a light one. But it must be supposed that it was no light task to Miss Brown. On the Tuesday following that Saturday, she would, if she were true to her word, join herself in wedlock to George Robinson. She now purposed to be untrue to her word; but it must be presumed that she had some misgivings at the heart when she thought of the task before her.

On the Thursday and the Friday she managed to avoid Robinson. On the Saturday morning they met in her father's room for a minute, and when he attempted to exercise a privilege to which his near approaching nuptials certainly entitled him, she repulsed him sullenly: 'Oh, come; none of that.' 'I shall require the more on Tuesday,' he replied, with his ordinary good-humour. She spoke nothing further to him then, but left the room and went away to her friend Mrs Poppins.

Robinson belonged to a political debating club, which met on every Saturday evening at the 'Goose and Gridiron' in one of the lanes behind the church in Fleet Street. It was, therefore, considered that the new compact might be made in Bishopsgate Street on that evening without any danger of interruption from him. But at the hour of dinner on that day, a word was whispered into his ear by Poppins. 'I don't suppose you care about it,' said he, 'but there's going to be some sort of doing at the old man's this evening.'

'What doing?'

'It's all right, I suppose; but Brisket is going to be there. It's just a farewell call, I suppose.'

'Brisket with my love!' said Robinson. 'Then will I be there also.'

'Don't forget that you've got to chaw up old Crowdy on the paper question. What will the Geese do if you're not there?' The club in question was ordinarily called the Goose Club, and the members were in common parlance called 'The Geese'.

'I will be there also,' said Robinson. 'But if I should be late, you will tell the Geese why it is so.'

'They all know you are going to be married,' said Poppins. And then they parted.

The hour at which the parliament of the Geese assembled was, as a rule, a quarter before eight in the evening, so that the debate might absolutely begin at eight. Seven was the hour for tea in Bishopsgate Street, but on the present occasion Brisket was asked for half-past seven, so that Robinson's absence might be counted on as a certainty. At half-past seven to the moment

Brisket was there, and the greeting between him and Maryanne was not of a passionate nature.

'Well, old girl, here I am again,' he said, as he swung his burly body into the room.

'I see you,' she said, as she half reluctantly gave him her hand. 'But remember, it wasn't me who sent for you. I'd just as lief you stayed away.' And then they went to business.

Both Jones and his wife were there; and it may perhaps be said, that if Maryanne Brown had any sincerity of feeling at her heart, it was one of hatred for her brother-in-law. But now, this new change in her fortunes was being brought about by his interference, and he was, as it were, acting as her guardian. This was very bitter to her, and she sat on one side in sullen silence, and to all appearances paid no heed to what was being said.

The minds of them all were so intent on the business part of the transaction that the banquet was allowed to remain untouched till all the preliminaries were settled. There was the tea left to draw till it should be as bitter as Maryanne's temper, and the sally luns were becoming as cold as Sarah Jane's heart. Mr Brown did, in some half-bashful manner, make an attempt at performing the duties of a host. 'My dears, won't Mr Brisket have his dish of tea now it's here?' But 'my dears' were deaf to the hint. Maryanne still sat sullen in the corner, and Sarah Jones stood bolt upright, with ears erect, ready to listen, ready to speak, ready to interfere with violence should the moment come when anything was to be gained on her side by doing so.

They went to the work in hand, with very little of the preamble of courtesy. Yes; Brisket marry her on the terms proposed by Jones. He could see his way if he had a hundred pounds down, and the bill of the Firm at three months for the remaining sum.

'Not three months, Brisket; six months,' suggested Brown. But in this matter Brisket was quite firm, and Mr Brown gave way.

But, as all of them knew, the heat of the battle would concern the names which were to be written on the bill. Brisket demanded that the bill should be from the firm. Jones held that as a majority of the firm were willing that this should be so, Mr Brown was legally entitled to make the bill payable at the bank out of the funds of the house. In this absurd opinion he was supported violently by his wife. Brisket, of course, gave no opinion on the subject. It was not for him to interfere among the partners. All he said was, that the bill of the firm had been promised to him, and that he shouldn't see his way with anything else. Mr Brown hesitated, — pondering painfully over the deed he was called upon to do. He knew that he was being asked to rob the man he loved; — but he knew also, that if he did not do so, he must go forth from his home. And then, when he might be in want of comfort, the child for whose sake he should do so would turn from him without love or pity.

'Jones and me would do it together,' said Mr Brown.

'Jones won't do nothing of the kind.' said Jones's careful wife.

'It would be no good if he did,' said Brisket. 'And, I'll tell you what it is, I'm not going to be made a fool of; I must know how its to be at once, or I'm off.' And he put out his hand as though to take up his hat.

'What fools you are!' said Maryanne, speaking from her chair in the corner. 'There's not one of you knows George Robinson. Ask him to give his name to the bill, and he'll do it instantly.'

'Who is it wants the name of George Robinson?' said the voice of that injured man, as at the moment he entered the room. 'George Robinson is here.' And then he looked round upon the assembled councillors, and his eyes rested at last with mingled scorn and sorrow upon the face of Maryanne Brown; — with mingled scorn and sorrow, but not with anger. 'George Robinson is here; who wants his name? — and why?'

'Will you take a cup of tea, George?' said Mr Brown, as soon as he was able to overcome his first dismay.

'Maryanne,' said Robinson, 'why is that man here?' and he pointed to Brisket.

'Ask them,' said Maryanne, and she turned her face away from him, in towards the wall.

'Mr Brown, why is he here? Why is your

daughter's former lover here on the eve of her marriage with me?'

'I will answer that question, if you please,' said Jones, stepping up.

'You!' And Robinson, looking at him from head to foot, silenced him with his look. 'You answer me! From you I will take no answer in this matter. With you I will hold no parley on this subject. I have spoken to two whom I loved, and they have given me no reply. There is one here whom I do not love and he shall answer me. Mr Brisket, though I have not loved you, I have believed you to be an honest man. Why are you here?'

'To see if we can agree about my marrying that young woman,' said Brisket, nodding at her with his head, while he still kept his hands in his trousers' pockets.

'Ah! Is it so? There she is, Mr Brisket; and now, for the third time, I shall go out from your presence, renouncing her charms in your favour. When first I did so at the dancing-room, I was afraid of your brute strength, because the crowd was looking on and I knew you could carry out your unmanly threat. And when I wrote that paper the second time, you had again threatened me, and I was again afraid. My heart was high on other matters, and why should I have sacrificed myself? Now I renounce her again; but I am not afraid, — for my heart is high on nothing.'

'George, George!' said Maryanne, jumping from her seat. 'Leave him, leave him, and I'll promise —' And then she seized hold of his arm. For the moment some touch of a woman's feeling had reached her heart. At that instant she perhaps recognized, — if only for the instant, that true love is worth more than comfort, worth more than well assured rations of bread and meat, and a secure roof. For that once she felt rather than understood that an honest heart is better than a strong arm. But it was too late.

'No,' said he, 'I'll have no promise from you; — your words are false. I've humbled myself as the dust beneath your feet, because I loved you, — and, therefore, you have treated me as the dust. The man who will crawl to a woman will ever be so treated.'

'You are about right there, old fellow,' said Brisket.

'Leave me, I say.' For still she held his arm. She still held his arm, for she saw by his eye what he intended, though no one else had seen.

'You have twitted me with my cowardice,' he said; 'but you shall see that I am no coward. He is the coward!' and he pointed with his finger to Brisket. 'He is the coward, for he will undergo no risk.' And then, without further notice, George Robinson flew at the butcher's throat.

It was very clear that Brisket himself had suspected no such attack, for till the moment at which he felt Robinson's fingers about his cravat, he had still stood with his hands in the pockets of his trousers. He was very strong, and when his thoughts were well made up to the idea of a fight, could in his own way be quick enough with his fists; but otherwise he was slow in action, nor was he in any way passionate.

'Halloo,' he said, striving to extricate himself, and hardly able to articulate, as the handkerchief tightened itself about his neck. 'Ugh-h-h.' And getting his arm round Robinson's ribs he tried to squeeze his assailant till he should drop his hold.

'I will have his tongue from his mouth,' shouted Robinson, and as he spoke, he gave another twist to the handkerchief.

'Oh, laws,' said Mrs Jones. 'The poor man will be choked,' and she laid hold of the tail of Robinson's coat, pulling at it with all her strength.

'Don't, don't,' said Mr Brown. 'George, George, you shall have her; indeed you shall, — only leave him.'

Maryanne the while looked on, as ladies of yore did look on when knights slaughtered each other for their smiles. And perhaps of yore the hearts of those who did look on were as cold and callous as was hers. For one moment of enthusiasm she had thought she loved, but now again she was indifferent. It might be settled as well this way as any other.

At length Brisket succeeded in actually forcing his weak assailant from him, Mrs Jones the while lending him considerable assistance; and then he raised his heavy fist. Robinson was there opposite to him, helpless and exhausted, just within his reach; and he raised his heavy fist to strike him down.

He raised his fist, and then he let it fall. 'No,' said he; 'I'm blowed if I'll hit you. You're better stuff than I thought you was. And now look here, young man; there she is. If she'll say that she'll have you, I'll walk out, and I won't come across you or she any more.'

Maryanne, when she heard this, raised her face and looked steadily at Robinson. If, however, she had any hope, that hope was fruitless.

'I have renounced her twice,' said he, 'and now I renounce her again. It is not now from fear. Mr Brown, you have my authority for accepting that bill in the name of the Firm.' Then he left the room and went forth into the street.

CHAPTER XVIII

AN EVENING AT THE 'GOOSE AND GRIDIRON'

Those political debaters who met together weekly at the 'Goose and Gridiron' were certainly open to the insinuation that they copied the practices of another debating society, which held its sittings farther west. In some respects they did so, and were perhaps even servile in their imitation. They divided themselves into parties, of which each had an ostensible leader. But then there was always some ambitious but hardly trustworthy member who endeavoured to gather round him a third party which might become dominant by trimming between the other two; and he again would find the ground cut from beneath his feet by new aspirants. The members never called each other by their own names, but addressed each always as 'The worthy Goose,' speaking at such moments with the utmost courtesy. This would still be done, though the speaker were using all his energy to show that that other Goose was in every sense unworthy. They had a perpetual chairman, for whom they affected the most unbounded respect. He was generally called 'The Grand,' his full title being 'The Most Worthy Grand Goose;' and members on their legs, when they wished to address the meeting with special eloquence, and were about to speak words which they thought peculiarly fit for public attention, would generally begin by thus invoking him. 'Most Worthy Grand,' they would say. But this when done by others than well accustomed speakers, was considered as a work either of arrogance or of ignorance. This great officer was much loved among them, and familiarly he was called 'My Grand.' Though there was an immensity of talk at these meetings, men speaking sometimes by the half hour whose silence the club would have been willing to purchase almost at any price, there were not above four established orators. There were four orators, of each of whom it was said that he copied the manner and tone of some great speaker in that other society. There was our friend Robinson, who in the elegance of his words, and the brilliancy of his ideas, far surpassed any other Goose. His words were irresistible, and his power in that assembly unequalled. But yet, as many said, it was power working only for evil. The liberal party to which he had joined himself did not dare to stand without him; but yet, if the whispers that got abroad were true, they would only too gladly have dispensed with him. He was terrible as a friend; but then he could be more terrible as a foe.

Then there was Crowdy, — Crowdy, whose high-flown ideas hardly tallied with the stern realities of his life. Crowdy was the leader of those who had once held firmly by Protection. Crowdy had been staunchly true to his party since he had a party, though it had been said of him that the adventures of Crowdy in search of a party had been very long and very various. There had been no Goose with a bitterer tongue than Crowdy; but now in these days a spirit of quiescence had fallen on him; and though he spoke as often as ever, he did not wield so deadly a tomahawk.

Then there was the burly Buggins, than whom no Goose had a more fluent use of his vernacular. He was not polished as Robinson, nor had he ever possessed the exquisite keenness of Crowdy. But in speaking he always hit the nail on the head, and carried his hearers with him by the energy and perspicuity of his argument. But by degrees the world of the Goose and Gridiron had learned that Buggins talked of things which he did not understand, and which he had not studied. His facts would not bear the light. Words fell from his mouth sweeter than honey; but sweet as they were they were of no avail. It was pleasant to hear Buggins talk, but men knew that it was useless.

But perhaps the most remarkable Goose in that assembly, as decidedly he was the most popular, was old Pan. He traced his birth to the mighty blood of the great Pancabinets, whose noble name he still proudly bore. Every one liked old Pancabinet, and though he did not now possess, and never had possessed, those grand oratorical powers which distinguished so highly the worthy Geese above mentioned, no Goose ever rose upon his legs more sure of respectful attention. The sway which he bore in that assembly was very wonderful, for he was an old man, and there were there divers Geese of unruly spirit. Lately he had associated himself much with our friend Robinson, for which many blamed him. But old Pancabinet generally knew what he was about, and having recognized the tremendous power of the young merchant from Bishopsgate Street, was full sure that he could get on better with him than he could against him.

It was pleasant to see 'My Grand' as he sat in his big arm-chair, with his beer before him, and his long pipe in his mouth. A benign smile was ever on his face, and yet he showed himself plainly conscious that authority lived in his slightest word, and that he had but to nod to be obeyed. That pipe was constant in his hand, and was the weapon with which he signified his approbation of the speakers. When any great orator would arise and address him as Most Worthy Grand, he would lay his pipe for an instant on the table, and, crossing his hands on his ample waistcoat, would bow serenely to the Goose on his legs. Then, not allowing the spark to be extinguished on his tobacco, he would resume the clay, and spread out over his head and shoulders a long soft cloud of odorous smoke. But when any upstart so addressed him, — any Goose not entitled by character to use the sonorous phrase, — he would still retain his pipe, and simply wink his eye. It was said that this distinction quite equalled the difference between big type and little. Perhaps the qualification which was most valued among The Geese, and most specially valued by The Worthy Grand, was a knowledge of the Forms of the Room, as it was called. These rules or formulas, which had probably been gradually invented for the complication of things which had once been too simple, were so numerous that no Goose could remember them all who was not very constant in his attention, and endowed with an accurate memory. And in this respect they were no doubt useful; — that when young and unskilled Geese tried to monopolize the attention of the Room, they would be constantly checked and snubbed, and at last subdued and silenced, by some reference to a forgotten form. No Goose could hope to get through a lengthy speech without such interruption till he had made the Forms of the Room a long and painful study.

On the evening in question, — that same evening on which Robinson had endeavoured to tear out the tongue of Brisket, — the Geese were assembled before eight o'clock. A motion that had been made elsewhere for the repeal of the paper duties was to be discussed. It was known that the minds of many Geese were violently set against a measure which they presumed to be most deleterious to the country; but old Pan, under the rigorous instigation of Robinson, had given in his adhesion, and was prepared to vote for the measure, — and to talk for it also, should there be absolute necessity. Buggins also was on the same side, — for Buggins was by trade a radical. But it was felt by all that the debate would be nothing unless Robinson should be there to 'chaw up' Crowdy, as had been intimated to our friend by that worthy Goose the young Poppins.

But at eight o'clock and at a quarter past eight Robinson was not there. Crowdy, not wishing to lacerate his foe till that foe should be there to feel the wounds, sat silent in his usual seat. Pancabinet, who understood well the beauty of silence, would not begin the fray. Buggins was ever ready to talk, but he was cunning enough to know that a future opportunity might be more valuable than the present one. Then up jumped Poppins. Now Poppins was no orator, but he felt that as the friend of Robinson, he was bound to address the meeting on the present occasion. There were circumstances which should be explained. 'Most worthy Grand, —' he began, starting suddenly to his legs; whereupon the worthy Grand slightly drew back his head, still holding his pipe between his lips, and winked at the unhappy Poppins. 'As the friend of the absent Robinson —' he went on; but he was at once interrupted by loud cries of 'order' from every side of the Room. And, worse than that, the Grand frowned at him. There was no rule more established than that which forbade the name of any Goose to be mentioned. 'I beg the Grand's pardon,' continued Poppins; 'I mean the absent worthy Goose. As his friend I rise to say a few words. I know he feels the greatest interest about this measure, which has been brought forward in the House of C —' But again he was interrupted. 'Order, order, order,' was shouted at him by vociferous Geese on every side, and the Grand frowned at him twice. When the Grand had frowned at a member three times, that member was silenced for the night. In this matter the assembly at the 'Goose and Gridiron' had not copied their rule from any other Body. But it is worthy of consideration whether some other Body might not do well to copy theirs. 'I beg the Grand's pardon again,' said the unhappy Poppins; 'but I meant in another place.' Hereupon a worthy Goose got up and suggested that their numbers should be counted. Now there was a rule that no debate could be continued unless a dozen Geese were present; and a debate once closed, was closed for that night. When such a hint was given to the Grand, it became the Grand's duty to count his Geese, and in order to effect this in accordance with the constitution of the assembly, it was necessary that the servants should withdraw. Strangers also were sometimes present, and at such moments they were politely asked to retire. When the suggestion was made, the suggestor no doubt knew that the requisite number was not there, but it usually happened on such occasions that some hangers-on were at hand to replenish the room. A Goose or two might be eating bread and cheese in the little parlour, — for food could not be introduced into the debating-room; and a few of the younger Geese might often be found amusing themselves with the young lady at the bar. Word would be passed to them that the Grand was about to count, and indeed they would hear the tap of his tobacco-stopper on the table. Then there would be a rush among these hungry and amorous Geese, and so the number would be made up. That they called making a flock.

When the suggestion was given on the present occasion the Grand put down his tankard from his hand and proceeded to the performance of his duty. Turning the mouthpiece of his long pipe-clay out from him, he pointed it slowly to one after another, counting them as he so pointed. First he counted up old Pancabinet, and a slight twinkle might be seen in the eyes of the two old men as he did so. Then, turning his pipe round the room, he pointed at them all, and it was found that there were fifteen present. 'There is a flock, and the discreet and worthy Goose is in possession of the room,' he said, bowing to Poppins. And Poppins again began his speech.

It was but a blundering affair, as was too often the case with the speeches made there; and then when Poppins sat down, the great Crowdy rose slowly to his legs. We will not attempt to give the speech of this eloquent Goose at length, for the great Crowdy often made long speeches. It may suffice to say that having a good cause he made the best of it, and that he pitched into our poor Robinson most unmercifully, always declaring as he did so that as his friend the enterprising and worthy Goose was absent, his own mouth was effectually closed. It may be noted here that whenever a Goose was in commerce the epithet 'enterprising' was always used when he was mentioned; and if he held or ever had held a service of trust, as Poppins did, he was called the 'discreet' Goose. And then, just as Crowdy finished his speech, the swinging door of the room was opened, and Robinson himself started up to his accustomed place.

It was easy to see that both the inner man had been disturbed and the outer. His hair and clothes had been ruffled in the embrace with Brisket, and his heart had been ruffled in its encounter with Maryanne. He had come straight from Bishopsgate Street to the 'Goose and Gridiron;' and now when he walked up to his seat, all the Geese remained silent waiting for him to declare himself.

'Most Worthy Grand,' he began; and immediately the long pipe was laid upon the table and the hands of the Grand were crossed upon his bosom. 'A circumstance has occurred to-night, which unfits me for these debates.' 'No, no, no,' was shouted on one side; and 'hear, hear, hear' on the other; during which the Grand again bowed and then resumed his pipe.

'If the chamber will allow me to wander away from paper for a moment, and to open the sores of a bleeding heart —'

'Question, question,' was then called by a jealous voice.

'The enterprising and worthy Goose is perfectly in order,' said the burly Buggins. 'Many a good heart will bleed before long if this debate is to be choked and smothered by the cackle of the incapable.'

'I submit that the question before the chamber is the repeal of the paper duties,' said the jealous voice, 'and not the bleeding heart of the enterprising and worthy Goose.'

'The question before the cabinet is,' said My Grand, 'that the chamber considers that two millions a-year will be lost for ever by the repeal of the paper duties; but if the enterprising and worthy Goose have any personal remarks to make bearing on that subject, he will be in order.'

'It is a matter of privilege,' suggested Poppins.

'A personal explanation is always allowed,' said Robinson, indignantly; 'nor did I think that any member of this chamber would have had the baseness to stop my voice when —'

'Order — order — order!'

'I may have been wrong to say baseness in this chamber, however base the worthy Goose may be; and, therefore, with permission of our worthy Grand, I will substitute "hardihood."' Whereupon the worthy Grand again bowed. But still there were cries of question from the side of the room opposite to that on which Robinson sat.

Then old Pancabinet rose from his seat, and all voices were hushed.

'If I may be allowed to make a suggestion,' said he, 'I would say that the enterprising and worthy Goose should be heard on a matter personal to himself. It may very probably be that the privileges of this chamber are concerned; and I think I may say that any worthy Goose speaking on matters affecting privilege in this chamber is always heard with that attention which the interest of the subject demands.' After that there was no further interruption, and Robinson was allowed to open his bleeding heart.

'Most Worthy Grand,' he again began, and again the pipe was laid down, for Robinson was much honoured. 'I come here hot from a scene of domestic woe, which has robbed me of all political discretion, and made the paper duty to me an inscrutable mystery. The worthy Geese here assembled see before them a man who has been terribly injured; one in whose mangled breast Fate has fixed her sharpest dagger, and poisoned the blade before she fixed it.' 'No — no — no.' 'Hear — hear — hear.' 'Yes, my Grand; she poisoned the blade before she fixed it. On Tuesday next I had hoped —' and here his voice became inexpressibly soft and tender, 'on Tuesday next I had hoped to become one bone and one flesh with a fair girl whom I have loved for months; — fair indeed to the outer eye, as flesh and form can make her; but ah! how hideously foul within.

And I had hoped on this day se'nnight to have received the congratulations of this chamber. I need not say that it would have been the proudest moment of my life. But, my Grand, that has all passed away. Her conduct has been the conduct of a Harpy. She is a Regan. She is false, heartless, and cruel; and this night I have renounced her.'

Hereupon a small Goose, very venomous, but vehemently attached to the privileges of his chamber, gave notice of a motion that that false woman should be brought before the Most Worthy Grand, and heard at the bar of the 'Goose and Gridiron.' But another worthy Goose showed that the enterprising and worthy Goose had by his own showing renounced the lady himself, and that, therefore, there could have been no breach of the privilege of the chamber. The notice of motion was then withdrawn.

'O woman!' continued Robinson, 'how terrible is thy witchcraft, and how powerful are thy charms! Thou spakest, and Adam fell. Thou sangest, and Samson's strength was gone. The head of the last of the prophets was the reward of thy meretricious feet. 'Twas thy damnable eloquence that murdered the noble Duncan. 'Twas thy lascivious beauty that urged the slaughter of the noble Dane. As were Adam and Samson, so am I. As were Macbeth and the foul king in the play, so is my rival Brisket. Most worthy Grand, this chamber must hold me excused if I decline to-night to enter upon the subject of the paper duties.' Then Robinson left the chamber, and the discussion was immediately adjourned to that day se'nnight.

CHAPTER XIX
GEORGE ROBINSON'S MARRIAGE

Thus ended George Robinson's dream of love. Never again will he attempt that phase of life. Beauty to him in future shall be a thing on which the eye may rest with satisfaction, as it may on the sculptor's chiselled marble, or on the varied landscape. It shall be a thing to look at, — possibly to possess. But for the future George Robinson's heart shall be his own. George Robinson is now wedded, and he will admit of no second wife. On that same Tuesday which was to have seen him made the legal master of Maryanne's charms, he vowed to himself that Commerce should be his bride; and, as in the dead of night he stood on the top of the hill of Ludgate, he himself, as high-priest, performed the ceremony. 'Yes,' said he on that occasion, 'O goddess, here I devote myself to thy embraces, to thine and thine only. To live for thee shall satisfy both my heart and my ambition. If thou wilt be kind, no softer loveliness shall be desired by me. George Robinson has never been untrue to his vows, nor shalt thou, O my chosen one, find him so now. For thee will I labour, straining every nerve to satisfy thy wishes. Woman shall henceforward be to me a doll for the adornment of whose back it will be my business to sell costly ornaments. In no other light will I regard the loveliness of her form. O sweet Commerce, teach me thy lessons! Let me ever buy in the cheapest market and sell in the dearest. Let me know thy hidden ways, and if it be that I am destined for future greatness, and may choose the path by which it shall be reached, it is not great wealth at which I chiefly aim. Let it rather be said of me that I taught the modern world of trade the science of advertisement.'

Thus did he address his new celestial bride, and as he spoke a passing cloud rolled itself away from before the moon's face, and the great luminary of the night shone down upon his upturned face. 'I accept the omen,' said Robinson, with lightened heart; and from that moment his great hopes never again altogether failed him, though he was doomed to pass through scorching fires of commercial disappointment.

But it must not be supposed that he was able to throw off his passion for Maryanne Brown without a great inward struggle. Up to that moment, in which he found Brisket in Mr Brown's room, and, as he stood for a moment on the landing-place, heard that inquiry made as to the use of his name, he had believed that Maryanne would at last be true to him. Poppins, indeed, had hinted his suspicions, but in the way of prophecy Poppins was a Cassandra. Poppins saw a good deal with those twinkling eyes of his, but Robinson did not trust to the wisdom of Poppins. Up to that hour he had believed in Maryanne, and then in the short flash of an instant the truth had come upon him. She had again promised herself to Brisket, if Brisket would only take her. Let Brisket have her if he would. A minute's thought was sufficient to bring him to this resolve. But hours of scorching torment must be endured ere he could again enjoy the calm working of a sound mind in a sound body.

It has been told how in the ecstasy of his misery he poured out the sorrows of his bleeding heart before his brethren at the debating club. They, with that ready sympathy which they always evince for the success or failure of any celebrated brother, at once adjourned themselves; and Robinson walked out, followed at a distance by the faithful Poppins.

'George, old fellow!' said the latter, touching his friend on the shoulder, at the corner of Bridge Street.

'Leave me!' exclaimed Robinson. 'Do not pry into sorrows which you cannot understand. I would be alone with myself this night.'

'You'd be better if you'd come to the "Mitre," and smoke a pipe,' said Poppins.

'Pipe me no pipes,' said Robinson.

'Oh, come. You'd better quit that, and take it

easy. After all, isn't it better so, than you should find her out when it was too late? There's many would be glad to have your chance.'

'Man!' shouted Robinson, and as he did so he turned round upon his friend and seized him by the collar of his coat. 'I loved that woman. Forty thousand Poppinses could not, with all their quantity of love, make up my sum.'

'Very likely not,' said Poppins.

'Would'st thou drink up Esil? Would'st thou eat a crocodile?'

'Heaven forbid,' said Poppins.

'I'll do it. And if thou prate of mountains —'

'But I didn't.'

'No, Poppins, no. That's true. Though I should be Hamlet, yet art not thou Laërtes. But Poppins, thou art Horatio.'

'I'm Thomas Poppins, old fellow; and I mean to stick to you till I see you safe in bed.'

'Thou art Horatio, for I've found thee honest. There are more things in heaven and earth, Horatio, than are dreamed of in our philosophy.'

'Come, old fellow.'

'Poppins, give me that man that is not passion's slave, and I will wear him in my heart's core; ay, in my heart of hearts; — as I do thee.' And then, falling on Poppins' neck, George Robinson embraced him.

'You'll be better after that,' said Poppins. 'Come, let's have a little chat over a drop of something hot, and then we'll go to bed. I'll stand Sammy.'

'Something hot!' said Robinson. 'I tell you, Poppins, that everything is hot to me. Here, here I'm hot.' And then he struck his breast. 'And yet I'm very cold. 'Tis cold to be alone; cold to have lost one's all. Poppins, I've loved a harpy.'

'I believe you're about right there,' said Poppins.

'A harpy! Her nails will grow to talons, and on her feet are hoofs. Within she is horn all over. There's not a drop of blood about her heart. Oh, Poppins!'

'You're very well out of it, George. But yet I'm sorry for you. I am, indeed.'

'And now, good-night. This way is mine; yours there.'

'What! to the bridge? No; I'm blessed if you do; at any rate not alone.'

'Poppins, tell me this; was Hamlet mad, or did he feign so?'

'Faith, very likely the latter. Many do that now. There are better rations in Bedlam, than in any of the gaols; — let alone the workhouses.'

'Ay; go mad for rations! There's no feigning there, Poppins. The world is doing that. But, Poppins, Hamlet feigned; and so do I. Let the wind blow as it may, I know a hawk from a hand-saw. Therefore you need not fear me.'

'I don't; but I won't let you go on to that bridge alone. You'll be singing that song of a suicide, till you're as low as low. Come and drink a drop of something, and wish Brisket joy with his wife.'

'I will,' said Robinson. And so the two went to the 'Mitre;' and there, comforted by the truth and honesty of his friend, Robinson resolved that he would be weak no longer, but, returning at once to his work, would still struggle on to rescue the house of Brown, Jones, and Robinson from that bourne of bankruptcy to which it was being hurried by the incompetency of his partners.

The following day was Sunday, and he rose at twelve with a racking headache. He had promised to take a chop with his friend at two, and at that hour he presented himself, with difficulty, at Mrs Poppins's room. She was busy laying the cloth as he entered, but his friend was seated, half-dressed, unshorn, pale, and drooping, in an old ann-chair near the window.

'It's a shame for you, George Robinson,' said the lady, as he entered, 'so it is. Look at that, for a father of a family, — coming home at three o'clock in the morning, and not able to make his way upstairs till I went down and fetched him!'

'I told her that we were obliged to sit out the debate,' said Poppins, winking eagerly at his friend.

'Debate indeed! A parcel of geese as you call yourself! Only geese go to bed betimes, and never get beastly drunk as you was, Poppins.'

'I took a bit of stewed cheese, which always disagrees with me.'

'Stewed cheese never disagrees with you when I'm with you. I'll tell you what it is, Poppins; if you ain't at home and in bed by eleven o'clock next Saturday, I'll go down to the "Goose and Gridiron," and I'll have that old Grandy out of his chair. That's what I will. I suppose you're so bad you can't eat a bit of nothing?' In answer to which, Robinson said that he did not feel himself to be very hungry.

'It's a blessing to Maryanne to have lost you; that's what it is.'

'Stop, woman,' said Robinson.

'Don't you woman me any womans. I know what stuff you're made of. It's a blessing for her not to have to do with a man who comes home roaring drunk, like a dead log, at three o'clock in the morning.'

'Now, Polly, —' began poor Poppins.

'Oh, ah, Polly! Yes. Polly's very well. But it was a bad day for Polly when she first sat eyes on you. There was Sergeant MacNash never took a drop too much in his life. And you're worse than Robinson ten times. He's got no children at home, and no wife. If he kills hisself with tobacco and gin, nobody will be much the worse. I know one who's got well out of it, anyway. And now, if either of you are able to eat, you can come.'

Robinson did not much enjoy his afternoon, but the scenes, as they passed, served to reconcile him to that lonely life which must, henceforward, be his fate. What was there to enjoy in the fate of Poppins, and what in the proposed happiness of Brisket? Could not a man be sufficient for himself alone? Was there aught of pleasantness in that grinding tongue of his friend's wife? Should not one's own flesh, — the bone of one's bone, — bind up one's bruises, pouring in balm with a gentle hand? Poppins was wounded sorely about the head and stomach, and of what nature was the balm which his wife administered? He, Robinson, had longed for married bliss, but now he longed no longer.

On the following Monday and Tuesday he went silently about his work, speaking hardly a word to anybody. Mr Brown greeted him with an apologetic sigh, and Jones with a triumphant sneer; but he responded to neither of them. He once met Maryanne in the passage, and bowed to her with a low salute, but he did not speak to her. He did not speak to her, but he saw the colour in her cheek, and watched her downcast eye. He was still weak as water, and had she clung to him even then, he would even then have forgiven her! But she passed on, and, as she left the house, she slammed the door behind her.

A little incident happened on that day, which is mentioned to show that, even in his present frame of mind, Robinson was able to take advantage of the smallest incident on behalf of his firm. A slight crowd had been collected round the door in the afternoon, for there had been a quarrel between Mr Jones and one of the young men, in which loud words had reached the street, and a baby, which a woman held in her arms, had been somewhat pressed and hurt. As soon as the tidings reached Robinson's ears he was instantly at his desk, and before the trifling accident was two hours passed, the following bill was in the printer's hands; —

CAUTION TO MOTHERS! — MOTHERS, BEWARE!

Three suckling infants were yesterday pressed to death in their mothers' arms by the crowd which had congregated before the house of Brown, Jones, and Robinson, at Nine times Nine, Bishopsgate Street, in their attempts to be among the first purchasers of that wonderful lot of cheap but yet excellent flannels, which B., J., and R. have just imported. Such flannels, at such a price, were never before offered to the British public. The sale, at the figures quoted below, will continue for three days more.

Magenta House.

And then followed the list.

It had chanced that Mr Brown had picked up a lot of remnants from a wholesale house in Houndsditch, and the genius of Robinson immediately combined that fact with the little incident above mentioned.

CHAPTER XX

SHOWING HOW MR BRISKET
DIDN'T SEE HIS WAY

Then two months passed by, and the summer was over. Early in September Mr Brown had been taken ill, and he went to Margate for a fortnight with his unmarried daughter. This had been the means of keeping Brisket quiet for a while with reference to that sum of money which he was to receive, and had given a reason why the marriage with him should not be performed at once. On Mr Brown's return, the matter was discussed, and Brisket became impatient. But the middle of October had come before any steps were taken to which it will be necessary to allude in the annals of the firm.

At that time Brisket, on two successive days, was closeted with his proposed father-in-law, and it was evident to Robinson that after each of these interviews Mr Brown was left in an unhappy frame of mind. At this time the affairs of the shop were not absolutely ruinous, — or would not have been so had there been a proper watch kept on the cash taken over the counter.

The heaviest amounts due were to the stationer, printer, and advertising agents. This was wrong, for such people of course press for their money; and whatever hitch or stoppage there may be in trade, there should, at any rate, be no hitch or stoppage in the capability for advertising. For the goods disposed of by the house payments had been made, if not with absolute punctuality on every side, at any rate so fairly that some supply was always forthcoming. The account at the bank had always been low; and, though a few small bills had been discounted, nothing like a mercantile system of credit had been established. All this was wrong, and had already betrayed the fact that Brown, Jones, and Robinson were little people, trading in a little way. It is useless to conceal the fact now, and these memoirs would fail to render to commerce that service which is expected from them, were the truth on this matter kept back from the public. Brown, Jones, and Robinson had not soared upwards into the empyrean vault of commercial greatness on eagle's wings. There are bodies so ponderous in their nature, that for them no eagle's wings can be found. The firm had commenced their pecuniary transactions on a footing altogether weak and unsubstantial. They had shown their own timidity, and had confessed, by the nature of their fiscal transactions, that they knew themselves to be small. To their advertising agents they should never have been behindhand in their payments for one day; but they should have been bold in demanding credit from their bank, and should have given their orders to the wholesale houses without any of that hesitation or reserve which so clearly indicates feebleness of purpose.

But in spite of this acknowledged weakness, a brisk trade over the counter had been produced; and though the firm had never owned a large stock, an unremitting sale was maintained of small goods, such as ribbons, stockings, hand-kerchiefs, and cotton gloves. The Katakairion shirts also had been successful, and now there was a hope that, during the coming winter, something might be done in African monkey muffs. At that time, therefore, the bill of the house at three months, though not to be re-garded as a bank-note, was not absolutely waste paper. How far Brisket's eyes were open on this matter cannot now be said; but he still expressed himself willing to take one hundred pounds in cash, and the remainder of Maryanne's fortune in the bill of the firm at three months.

And then Mr Brisket made a third visit to Bishopsgate Street, On all these occasions he passed by the door of the little room in which Robinson sat, and well did his late rival know his ponderous step. His late rival; — for Brisket was now welcome to come and go. 'Mr Brown!' said he, on one occasion, 'I have come here to have a settlement about this thing at once.'

'I've been ill, Brisket; very ill, you know,' said Mr Brown, pleadingly, 'and I'm not strong now.'

'But that can't make no difference about the

money. Maryanne is willing, and me also. When Christmas is coming on, it's a busy time in our trade, and I can't be minding that sort of thing then. If you've got the cash ready, and that bit of paper, we'll have it off next week.'

'I've never spoken to him about the paper;' and Mr Brown, as he uttered these words, pointed down towards the room in which Robinson was sitting.,

'Then you'd better,' said Brisket. 'For I shan't come here again after to-day. I'll see it out now one way or the other, and so I've told Maryanne.'

Mr Brown's sigh, when he heard these words, was prolonged and deep. 'You heard what he said that night,' continued Brisket. 'You ask him. He's game for anything of that sort.'

All these words Robinson had overheard, for the doors of the two rooms were close together, and neither of them had been absolutely closed. Now was the moment in which it behoved him to act. No false delicacy as to the nature of the conversation between his partner and that partner's proposed son-in-law withheld him; but rising from his seat, he walked straight into the upper room.

'Here he is, by jingo,' said Brisket. 'Talk of the —'

'Speak of an angel and behold his wings,' said Robinson, with a faint smile. 'I come on a visit which might befit an angel. Mr Brown, I consent that your daughter's dowry shall be paid from the funds of the firm.'

But Mr Brown, instead of expressing his thankful gratitude, as was expected, winked at his partner. The dull Brisket did not perceive it; but Robinson at once knew that this act of munificence on his part was not at the moment pleasing to the lady's father.

'You're a trump,' said Brisket; 'and when we're settled at home like, Maryanne and I that is, I hope you'll let bygones be bygones, and come and take pot luck with us sometimes. If there's a tender bit of steak about the place it shall be sent to the kitchen fire when you show your face.'

'Brisket,' said Robinson, 'there's my hand. I've loved her. I don't deny it. But you're welcome to her. No woman shall ever sit at the hearth of George Robinson; — but at her hearth George Robinson will never sit.'

'You shall be as welcome as if you did,' said Brisket; 'and a man can't say no fairer.'

But in the meantime Mr Brown still continued to wink, and Robinson understood that his consent to that bill transaction was not in truth desired. 'Perhaps, Mr Brisket,' said he, 'as this is a matter of business I and my partner had better discuss it for a moment together. We can go down into my room, Mr Brown.'

'With all my heart,' said Brisket. 'But remember this, both of you: if I don't see my way before I leave the house, I don't come here any more. I know my way pretty well from Aldersgate Street, and I'm sick of the road. I've been true to my word all along, and I'll be true to the end. But if

I don't see my way before I leave this house, re-member I'm off.'

'You shouldn't have said that,' whispered Brown to his partner as soon as the two were to-gether.

'Why not?'

'The money won't be there at the end of three months, not if we pay them other things. And where's the hundred pounds of ready to come from?'

'That's your look-out.'

'I haven't got it, George. Jones has it, I know; but I can't get it out of him.'

'Jones got a hundred pounds! And where should Jones have gotten it?'

'I know we have been wrong, George; I know we have. But you can't wonder at me, George; can you? I did bring four thousand pounds into it; didn't I?'

'And now you haven't got a hundred pounds!'

'If I have it's as much as I can say. But Jones has it, and ever so much more. If Brisket will wait, we can frighten it out of Jones.'

'If I know anything of human nature,' said Robinson, 'Brisket will not wait.'

'He would, if you hadn't spoke to him that way. He'd say he wouldn't, and go away, and Maryanne would blow up; but I should have worked the money out of Jones at last, and then Brisket would have waited.'

When Mr Brown had made this disclosure, whispering all the time as he leaned his head and shoulder on Robinson's upright desk, they both remained silent for a while. 'We have been wrong,' he had said; 'I know we have.' And Robinson, as he heard the words, perceived that from the beginning to the end he had been a victim. No wonder that the business should not have answered, when such confessions as these were wrung from the senior partner! But the fact alleged by Mr Brown in his own excuse was allowed its due weight by Robinson, even at that moment. Mr Brown had possessed money, — money which might have made his old age comfortable and respectable in obscurity. It was not surprising that he should be anxious to keep in his own hand some small remnant of his own property. But as for Jones! What excuse could be made for Jones! Jones had been a thief; and worse than ordinary thieves, for his thefts were committed on his own friends.

'And he has got the money,' said Robinson.

'Oh, yes!' said Mr Brown, 'there's no doubt in life about that.'

'Then, by the heaven above us, he shall refund it to the firm from which he has stolen it,' shouted Robinson, striking the desk with his fist as he did so.

'Whish, George, whish; Brisket will hear you.'

'Who cares? I have been robbed on every side till I care for nothing! What is Brisket to me, or what is your daughter? What is anything?'

'But, George —'

'Is there no honesty left in the world, Mr

Brown? That there is no love I had already learned. Ah me, what an age is this in which we live! Deceit, deceit, deceit; — it is all deceit!'

'The heart of a man is very deceitful,' said Mr Brown. 'And a woman's especially.'

'Delilah would have been a true wife now-a-days. But never mind. That man is still there, and he must be answered. I have no hundred pounds to give him.'

'No, George; no; we're sure of that.'

'When this business is broken up, as broken up it soon will be —'

'Oh, George, don't say so.'

'Ay, but it will. Then I shall walk out from Magenta House with empty pockets and with clean hands.'

'But think of me, George. I had four thousand pounds when we began. Hadn't I, now?'

'I do think of you, and I forgive you. Now go up to Brisket, for he will want his answer. I can assist you no further. My name is still left to me, and of that you may avail yourself. But as for money, George Robinson has none.'

About half an hour after that, Mr Brisket again descended the stairs with his usual ponderous and slow step, and went forth into the street, shaking the dust from his feet as he did so. He was sore offended, and vowed in his heart that he would never enter that house again. He had pressed Mr Brown home about the money; and that gentleman had suggested to him, first, that it should be given to him on the day after the marriage, and then that it should be included in the bill. 'You offered to take it all in one bill before, you know,' said Mr Brown. Hereupon Brisket began to think that he did not see his way at all, and finally left the house in great anger.

He went direct from thence to Mrs Poppins' lodgings, where he knew that he would find Miss Brown. Poppins himself was, of course, at his work, and the two ladies were together.

'I've come to wish you good-by,' he said, as he walked into the room.

'Laws, Mr Brisket!' exclaimed Mrs Poppins.

'It's all up about this marriage, and so I thought it right to come and tell you. I began straightforward, and I mean to end straightforward.'

'You mean to say you're not going to have her,' said Mrs Poppins.

'Polly, don't make a fool of yourself,' said Maryanne. 'Do you think I want the man. Let him go.' And then he did go, and Miss Brown was left without a suitor.

CHAPTER XXI

MR BROWN IS TAKEN ILL

Brisket kept his word, and never entered Magenta House again, nor, as far as George Robinson is aware, has he seen any of the Brown family from that day on which he gave up his intended marriage to this present. For awhile Maryanne Brown protested that she was well satisfied that this should be so. She declared to Mrs Poppins that the man was mercenary, senseless, uninteresting, heavy, and brutal; — and though in the bosom of her own family she did not speak out with equal freedom, yet from time to time she dropped words to show that she was not breaking her heart for William Brisket. But this mood did not last long. Before winter had come round the bitterness of gall had risen within her heart, and when Christmas was there her frame of mind was comfortable neither to herself nor to her unfortunate father.

During this time the house still went on. Set a business going, and it is astonishing how long it will continue to move by the force of mere daily routine. People flocked in for shirts and stockings, and young women came there to seek their gloves and ribbons, although but little was done to attract them, either in the way of advertisement or of excellence of supply. Throughout this wretched month or two Robinson knew that failure was inevitable, and with this knowledge it was almost impossible that he should actively engage himself in his own peculiar branch of business. There was no confidence between the partners. Jones was conscious of what was coming and was more eager than ever to feather his own nest. But in these days Mr Brown displayed a terrible activity. He was constantly in the shop, and though it was evident to all eyes that care and sorrow were heaping upon his shoulders a burden which he could hardly bear, he watched his son-in-law with the eyes of an Argus. It was terrible to see him, and terrible, alas, to hear him; — for at this time he had no reserve before the men and women engaged behind the counters. At first there had been a pretence of great love and confidence, but this was now all over. It was known to all the staff that Mr Brown watched his son-in-law, and known also that the youngest partner had been treated with injustice by them both.

They in the shop, and even Jones himself, knew little of what in these days was going on upstairs. But Robinson knew, for his room was close to that in which Mr Brown and his daughter lived; and, moreover, in spite of the ill-feeling which could not but exist between him and Miss Brown, he passed many hours in that room with her father. The bitterness of gall had now risen within her breast, and she had begun to realize that truth which must be so terrible for a woman, that she had fallen to the ground between two stools. It is a truth terrible to a woman. There is no position in a man's life of the same aspect. A man may fail in business, and feel that no further chance of any real success can ever come in his way; or he may fail in love, and in the soreness of his heart may know that the pleasant rippling waters of that fountain are for him dried for ever. But with a woman the two things are joined together. Her battle must be fought all in one. Her success in life and her romance must go together, hand in hand. She is called upon to marry for love, and if she marry not for love, she disobeys the ordinance of nature and must pay the penalty. But at the same time all her material fortune depends upon the nature of that love. An industrious man may marry a silly fretful woman, and may be triumphant in his counting-house though he be bankrupt in his drawing-room. But a woman has but the one chance. She must choose her life's companion because she loves him; but she knows how great is the ruin if loving one who cannot win for her that worldly success which all in the world desire to win.

With Maryanne Brown these considerations had become frightfully momentous. She had in her way felt the desire for some romance in life, but she had felt more strongly still how needful it was that she should attain by her feminine charms a position which would put her above want. 'As long as I have a morsel, you shall have half of it,' her father had said to her more than once. And she had answered him with terrible harshness, 'But what am I to do when you have no longer a morsel to share with me? When you are ruined, or dead, where must I then look for support and shelter?' The words were harsh, and she was a very Regan to utter them. But, nevertheless, they were natural. It was manifest enough that her father would not provide for her, and for her there was nothing but Eve's lot of finding an Adam who would dig for her support. She was hard, coarse, — almost heartless; but it may perhaps be urged in her favour, that she was not wilfully dishonest. She had been promised to one man, and though she did not love him she would have married him, intending to do her duty. But to this he would not consent, except under certain money circumstances which she could not command. Then she learned to love another man, and him she would have married; but prudence told her that she should not do so until he had a home in which to place her. And thus she fell to the ground between two stools, and, falling, perceived that there was nothing before her on which her eye could rest with satisfaction.

There are women, very many women, who could bear this, if with sadness, still without bitterness. It is a lot which many women have to bear; but Maryanne Brown was one within whose bosom all feelings were turned to gall by the prospect of such a destiny. What had she done to deserve such degradation and misfortune? She would have been an honest wife to either husband! That it could be her own fault in any degree she did not for a moment admit. It was the fault of those around her, and she was not the woman to allow such a fault to pass unavenged.

'Father,' she would say, 'you will be in the workhouse before this new year is ended.'

'I hope not, my child.'

'Hope! What's the good of hoping? You will. And where am I to go then? Mother left a handsome fortune behind her, and this is what you've brought us to.'

'I've done everything for the best, Maryanne.'

'Why didn't you give that man the money when you had it? You'd have had a home then when you'd ruined yourself. Now you'll have no home; neither shall I.'

All this was very hard to be borne. 'She nags at me that dreadful, George,' he once said, as he sat in his old arm-chair, with his head hanging wearily on his chest, 'that I don't know where I am or what I'm doing. As for the workhouse, I almost wish I was there.'

She would go also to Poppins' lodgings, and there quarrel with her old friend Polly. It may be that at this time she did not receive all the respect that had been paid to her some months back, and this reverse was, to her proud spirit, unendurable. 'Polly,' she said, 'if you wish to turn your back upon me, you can do so. But I won't put up with your airs.'

'There's nobody turning their back upon you, only yourself,' Polly replied; 'but it's frightful to hear the way you're always a-grumbling; — as if other people hadn't had their ups and downs besides you.'

Robinson also was taught by the manner of his friend Poppins that he could not now expect to receive that high deference which was paid to him about the time that Johnson of Manchester had been in the ascendant. Those had been the halcyon days of the firm, and Robinson had then been happy. Men at that time would point him out as he passed, as one worthy of notice; his companions felt proud when he would join them; and they would hint to him, with a mysterious reverence that was very gratifying, their assurance that he was so deeply occupied as to make it impossible that he should give his time to the ordinary slow courtesies of life. All this was over now, and he felt that he was pulled down with rough hands from the high place which he had occupied.

'It's all very well,' Poppins would say to him, 'but the fact is, you're a-doing of nothing.'

'If fourteen hours a day —' began Robinson. But Poppins instantly stopped him.

'Fourteen hours' work a day is nothing, if you

don't do anything. A man may sweat hard digging holes and filling them up again. But what I say is, he does not do any good. You've been making out all those long stories about things that never existed, but what's the world the better for it; — that's what I want to know. When a man makes a pair of shoes —' And so he went on. Coming from such a man as Poppins, this was hard to be borne. But nevertheless Robinson did bear it. Men at the 'Goose and Gridiron' also would shoulder him now-a-days, rather than make way for him. Geese whose names had never been heard beyond the walls of that room would presume to occupy his place. And on one occasion, when he rose to address the chamber, the Grand omitted the courtesy that had ever been paid to him, and forgot to lay down his pipe. This also he bore without flinching.

It was about the middle of February when a catastrophe happened which was the immediate forerunner of the fall of the house. Robinson had been at his desk early in the morning, — for, though his efforts were now useless, he was always there; and had been struck with dismay by the loudness of Maryanne's tone as she rebuked her father. Then Mrs Jones had joined them, and the battle had raged still more furiously. The voice of the old man, too, was heard from time to time. When roused by suffering to anger he would forget to speak in his usual falsetto treble, and break out in a few natural words of rough impassioned wrath. At about ten, Mr Brown came down into Robinson's room, and, seating himself on a low chair, remained there for awhile without moving, and almost without speaking. 'Is she gone, George?' he asked at last.

'Which of them?' said Robinson.

'Sarah Jane. I'm not so used to her, and it's very bad.' Then Robinson looked out and said that Mrs Jones was gone. Whereupon Mr Brown returned to his own room.

Again and again throughout the day Robinson heard the voices; but he did not go up to the room. He never did go there now, unless specially called upon to do so by business. At about noon, however, there came a sudden silence, — a silence so sudden that he noticed it. And then he heard a quick step across the floor. It was nothing to him, and he did not move from his seat; but still he kept his ears open, and sat thoughtless of other matters, as though he expected that something was about to happen. The room above was perfectly still, and for a minute or two nothing was done. But then there came the fall of a quicker step across the room, and the door was opened, and Maryanne, descending the four stairs which led to his own closet, was with him in an instant. 'George,' she said, forgetting all propriety of demeanour, 'father's in a fit!'

It is not necessary that the scene which followed should be described with minuteness in these pages. Robinson, of course, went up to Mr Brown's room, and a doctor was soon there in attendance upon the sick man. He had been struck by paralysis, and thus for a time had been put beyond the reach of his daughters' anger. Sarah Jane was very soon there, but the wretched state in which the old man was lying quieted even her tongue. She did not dare to carry on the combat as she looked on the contorted features and motionless limbs of the poor wretch as he lay on his bed. On her mind came the conviction that this was partly her work, and that if she now spoke above her breath, those around her would accuse her of her cruelty. So she slunk about into corners, whispering now and again with her husband, and quickly took herself off, leaving the task of nursing the old man to the higher courage of her sister.

And Maryanne's courage sufficed for the work. Now that she had a task before her she did it; — as she would have done her household tasks had she become the wife of Brisket or of Robinson. To the former she would have been a good wife, for he would have required no softness. She would have been true to him, tending him and his children; — scolding them from morning to night, and laying not unfrequently a rough hand upon them. But for this Brisket would not have cared. He would have been satisfied, and all would have been well. It is a thousand pities that, in that matter, Brisket could not have seen his way.

And now that her woman's services were really needed, she gave them to her father readily. It cannot be said that she was a cheerful nurse. Had he been in a state in which cheerfulness would have relieved him, her words would have again been sharp and pointed. She was silent and sullen, thinking always of the bad days that were coming to her. But, nevertheless, she was attentive to him, — and during the time of his terrible necessity even good to him. It is so natural to women to be so, that I think even Regan would have nursed Lear had Lear's body become impotent instead of his mind. There she sat close to his bed, and there from time to time Robinson would visit her. In those days they always called each other George and Maryanne, and were courteous to each other, speaking solely of the poor old sick man, who was so near to them both. Of their former joint hopes, no word was spoken then; nor, at any rate as regards the lady, was there even a thought of love. As to Jones, he very rarely came there. He remained in the shop below; where the presence of some member of the firm was very necessary, for, in these days, the number of hands employed had become low.

'I suppose it's all up down there,' she said one day, and as she spoke she pointed towards the shop. At this time her father had regained his consciousness, and had recovered partially the use of his limbs. But even yet he could not speak so as to be understood, and was absolutely helpless. The door of his bedroom was open, and Robinson was sitting in the front room, to which it opened.

'I'm afraid so,' said he. 'There are creditors

who are pressing us; and now that they have been frightened about Mr Brown, we shall be sold up.'

'You mean the advertising people?'

'Yes; the stationer and printer, and one or two of the agents. The fact is, that the money, which should have satisfied them, has been frittered away uselessly.'

'It's gone at any rate,' said she. 'He hasn't got it,' and she pointed to her father.

'Nor have I,' said Robinson. 'I came into it empty-handed, and I shall go out as empty. No one shall say that I cared more for myself than for the firm. I've done my best, and we have failed. That's all.'

'I am not going to blame you, George. My look-out is bad enough, but I will not say that you did it. It is worse for a woman than for a man. And what am I to do with him?' And again she pointed towards the inner room. In answer to this Robinson said something as to the wind being tempered for the shorn lamb. 'As far as I can see,' she continued, 'the sheep is best off that knows how to keep its own wool. It's always such cold comfort as that one gets, when the world means to thrust one to the wall. It's only the sheep that lets themselves be shorn. The lions and the tigers know how to keep their own coats on their own backs. I believe the wind blows colder on poor naked wretches than it does on those as have their carriages to ride in. Providence is very good to them that know how to provide for themselves.'

'You are young,' said he, 'and beautiful —'

'Psha!'

'You will always find a home if you require one.'

'Yes; and sell myself! I'll tell you what it is, George Robinson; I wish to enter no man's home unless I can earn my meat there by my work. No man shall tell me that I am eating his bread for nothing. As for love, I don't believe in it. It's all very well for them as have nothing to do and nothing to think of, — for young ladies who get up at ten in the morning, and ride about with young gentlemen, and spend half their time before their looking-glasses. It's like those poetry books you're so fond of. But it's not meant for them as must earn their bread by their own sweat. You talk about love, but it's only madness for the like of you.'

'I shall talk about it no more.'

'You can't afford it, George; nor yet can't I. What a man wants in a wife is some one to see to his cooking and his clothes; and what a woman wants is a man who can put a house over her head. Of course, if she have something of her own, she'll have so much the better house. As for me, I've got nothing now.'

'That would have made no difference with me.' Robinson knew that he was wrong to say this, but he could not help it. He knew that he would be a madman if he again gave way to any feeling of tenderness for this girl, who could be so hard in her manner, so harsh in her speech, and whose temperament was so utterly unsuited to his own. But as she was hard and harsh, so was he in all respects the reverse. As she had told him over and over again, he was tender-hearted even to softness.

'No; it wouldn't,' she replied. 'And, therefore, with all your cleverness, you are little better than a fool. You have been working hard and living poor these two years back, and what better are you? When that old man was weak enough to give you the last of his money, you didn't keep a penny.'

'Not a penny,' said Robinson, with some feeling of pride at his heart.

'And what the better are you for that? Look at them Joneses; they have got money. When the crash comes, they won't have to walk out into the street. They'll start somewhere in a little way, and will do very well.'

'And would you have had me become a thief?'

'A thief! You needn't have been a thief. You needn't have taken it out of the drawers as some of them did. I couldn't do that myself. I've been sore tempted, but I could never bring myself to that.' Then she got up, and went to her father, and Robinson returned again to the figures that were before him.

'What am I to do with him?' she again said, when she returned. 'When he is able to move, and the house is taken away from us, what am I to do with him? He's been bad to me, but I won't leave him.'

'Neither will I leave him, Maryanne.'

'That's nonsense. You've got nothing, no more than he has; and he's not your flesh and blood. Where would you have been now, if we'd been married on that day.'

'I should have been nearer to him in blood, but not truer to him as a partner.'

'It's lucky for you that your sort of partnership needn't last for ever. You've got your hands and your brain, and at any rate you can work. But who can say what must become of us? Looking at it all through, George, I have been treated hard; — haven't I, now?'

He could only say that of such hard treatment none of it rested on his conscience. At such a moment as this he could not explain to her that had she herself been more willing to trust in others, more prone to believe in Providence, less hard and worldly, things would have been better with her. Even now, could she have relaxed into tenderness for half-an-hour, there was one at her elbow who would have taken her at once, with all that burden of a worn-out pauper parent, and have poured into her lap all the earnings of his life. But Maryanne Brown could not relax into tenderness, nor would she ever deign to pretend that she could do so.

The first day on which Mr Brown was able to come out into the sitting-room was the very day on which Brown, Jones, and Robinson were declared bankrupts. Craddock and Giles, the stationers of St Mary Axe, held bills of theirs, as to

260

which they would not, — or probably could not, — wait; and the City and West End Commercial and Agricultural Joint-Stock Bank refused to make any further advances. It was a sad day; but one, at least, of the partners felt relieved when the blow had absolutely fallen, and the management of the affairs of the shop was taken out of the hands of the firm.

'And will we be took to prison?' asked Mr Brown. They were almost the first articulate words which he had been heard to utter since the fit had fallen on him; and Robinson was quick to assure him that no such misfortune would befall him.

'They are not at all bitter against us,' said Robinson. They know we have done our best.'

'And what will they do with us?' again asked Mr Brown.

'We shall have a sale, and clear out everything, and pay a dividend; — and then the world will be open to us for further efforts.'

'The world will never be open to me again,' said Mr Brown. 'And if I had only have kept the money when I had it —'

'Mr Brown,' said Robinson, taking him by the hand, 'you are ill now, and seen through the sickly hue of weakness and infirmity, affairs look bad and distressing; but ere long you will regain your strength.'

'No, George, I shall never do that.'

On this day the business of the shop still went on, but the proceeds of such sales as were made were carried to the credit of the assignees. Mr Jones was there throughout the day, doing nothing, and hardly speaking to any one. He would walk slowly from the front of the shop to the back, and then returning would stand in the doorway, rubbing his hands one over the other. When any female of specially smart appearance entered the shop, he would hand to her a chair, and whisper a few words of oily courtesy; but to those behind the counter he did not speak a word. In the afternoon Mrs Jones made her appearance, and when she had been there a few minutes, was about to raise the counter door and go behind; but her husband took her almost roughly by the arm, and muttering something to her, caused her to leave the shop. 'Ah, I knew what such dishonest doings must come to,' she said, as she went her way. 'And, what's more, I know who's to blame.' And yet it was she and her husband who had brought this ruin on the firm.

'George,' said Mr Brown, that evening, 'I have intended for the best, — I have indeed.'

'Nobody blames you sir.'

'You blame me about Maryanne.'

'No, by heaven; not now.'

'And she blames me about the money; but I've meant it for the best; — I have indeed.'

All this occurred on a Saturday, and on that same evening Robinson attended at his debating club, for the express purpose of explaining to the members the state of his own firm. 'It shall never be thrown in my teeth,' said he, 'that I became a bankrupt and was ashamed to own it.' So he got up and made a speech, in which he stated that Brown, Jones, and Robinson had failed, but that he could not lay it to his own charge that he had been guilty of any omission or commission of which he had reason to be ashamed as a British merchant. This is mentioned here, in order that a fitting record may be made of the very high compliment which was paid to him on the occasion by old Pancabinet.

'Most worthy Grand,' said old Pan, and as he spoke he looked first at the chairman and then down the long table of the room, 'I am sure I may truly say that we have all of us heard the statement made by the enterprising and worthy Goose with sentiments of regret and pain; but I am equally sure that we have none of us heard it with any idea that either dishonour or disgrace can attach itself in the matter to the name of —' (Order, order, order.) 'Worthy Geese are a little too quick,' continued the veteran debater with a smile — 'to the name of — one whom we all so highly value.' (Hear, hear, hear.) And then old Pancabinet moved that the enterprising and worthy Goose was entitled to the full confidence of the chamber. Crowdy magnanimously seconded the motion, and the resolution, when carried, was communicated to Robinson by the worthy Grand. Having thanked them in a few words, which were almost inaudible from his emotion, he left the chamber, and immediately afterwards the meeting was adjourned.

CHAPTER XXII

WASTEFUL AND IMPETUOUS SALE

There is no position in life in which a man receives so much distinguished attention as when he is a bankrupt, — a bankrupt, that is, of celebrity. It seems as though he had then realized the legitimate ends of trade, and was brought forth in order that those men might do him honour with whom he had been good enough to have dealings on a large scale. Robinson was at first cowed when he was called upon to see men who were now becoming aware that they would not receive more than 2*s.* 9*d.* in the pound out of all the hundreds that were owed to them. But this feeling very soon wore off, and he found himself laughing and talking with Giles the stationer, and Burrows the printer, and Sloman the official assignee, as though a bankruptcy were an excellent joke; and as though he, as one of the bankrupts, had by far the best of it. These men were about to lose, or rather had lost, large sums of money; but, nevertheless, they took it all as a matter of course, and were perfectly good-humoured. No word of reproach fell from their lips, and when they asked George Robinson to give them the advantage of his recognized talents in drawing up the bills for the sale, they put it to him quite as a favour; and Sloman, the assignee, went so far as to suggest that he should be remunerated for his work.

'If I can only be of any service to you,' said Robinson modestly.

'Of the greatest service,' said Mr Giles. 'A tremendous sacrifice, you know, — enormous liabilities, — unreserved sale, — regardless of cost; and all that sort of thing.'

'Lord bless you!' said Mr Burrows. 'Do you think he doesn't understand how to do all that better than you can tell him? You'll draw out the headings of the posters; won't you, Mr Robinson?'

'And put the numbers and figures into the catalogue,' suggested Mr Sloman. The best way is to put 'em down at about cost price. We find we can generally do 'em at that, if we can only get the people to come sharp enough.' And then, as the evening had fallen upon them, at their labours, they adjourned to the 'Four Swans' opposite, and Robinson was treated to his supper at the expense of his victims.

On the next day the house was closed. This was done in order that the goods might be catalogued and prepared for the final sale. The shop would then be again opened for a week, and, after that, there would be an end of Brown, Jones and Robinson. In spite of the good-humour which was shown by those from whom ill-humour on such an occasion might have been expected, there was a melancholy about this which was inexpressible. It has been said that there is nothing so exciting in trade as a grand final sacrificial sale. But it is like the last act of a tragedy. It is very good while it lasts, but what is to come after it? Robinson, as he descended into the darkened shop, and walked about amidst the lumber that was being dragged forth from the shelves and drawers, felt that he was like Marius on the ruins of Carthage. Here had been the scene of his glory! And then he remembered with what ecstasy he had walked down the shop, when the crowd without were anxiously inquiring the fate of Johnson of Manchester. That had been a great triumph! But to what had such triumphs led him?

The men and women had gone away to their breakfast, and he was standing there alone, leaning against one of the counters; he heard a slight noise behind him, and, turning round, saw Mr Brown, who had crept down from his own room without assistance. It was the first time since his illness that he had left the floor on which he lived, and it had been intended that he should never go into the shop again. 'Oh, Mr Brown, is this prudent?' said he, going up to him that he might give him the assistance of his arm.

'I wished to see it all once more, George.'

'There it is, then. There isn't much to see.'

'But a deal to feel; isn't there, George? — a deal to feel! It did look very pretty that day we opened it, — very pretty. The colours seem to have got dirty now.

'Bright colours will become dull and dirty, Mr Brown. It's the way of the world. The brighter they are in their brightness, the more dull will they look when the tinsel and gloss are gone.'

'But we should have painted it again this spring, if we'd stopped here.'

'There are things, Mr Brown, which one cannot paint again.'

'Iron and wood you can, or anything of the like of that.'

'Yes, Mr Brown; you may repaint iron and wood; but who can restore the faded colours to broken hopes and a bankrupt ambition? You see these arches here which with so light a span bear the burden of the house above them. So was the span of my heart on that opening day. No weight of labour then seemed to be too much for me. The arches remain and will remain; but as for the human heart —'

'Don't, George, — don't. It will kill me if I see you down in the mouth.'

'These will be repainted,' continued Robinson, 'and other breasts will glow beneath them with hopes as high as those we felt when you and the others stood here to welcome the public. But what artist can ever repaint our aspirations? The soiled columns of these windows will be regilded, and all here will be bright and young again; but for man, when he loses his glory, there is no regilding. Come, Mr Brown, we will go upstairs. They will be here soon, and this is no place now for you.' Then he took him by the hand and led him tenderly to his apartment.

There is something inexpressibly melancholy in the idea of bankruptcy in trade; — unless, indeed, when it may have been produced by absolute fraud, and in such a form as to allow of the bankrupts going forth with their pockets full. But in an ordinary way, I know nothing more sad than the fate of men who have embarked all in a trade venture and have failed. It may be, and probably is, the fact, that in almost all such cases the failure is the fault of the bankrupts; but the fault is so generally hidden from their own eyes, that they cannot see the justice of their punishment; and is often so occult in its causes that the justice cannot be discerned by any without deep scrutiny. They who have struggled and lost all feel only that they have worked hard, and worked in vain; that they have thrown away their money and their energy; and that there is an end, now and for ever, to those sweet hopes of independence with which they embarked their small boats upon the wide ocean of commerce. The fate of such men is very sad. Of course we hear of bankrupts who come forth again with renewed glories, and who shine all the brighter in consequence of their temporary obscurity. These are the men who can manage to have themselves repainted and regilded; but their number is not great. One hears of such because they are in their way memorable; and one does not hear of the poor wretches who sink down out of the world — back behind counters, and to menial work in warehouses. Of ordinary bankrupts one hears nothing. They are generally men who, having saved a little with long patience, embark it all and lose it with rapid impotence. They come forward once in their lives with their little ventures, and then retire never more to be seen or noticed. Of all the shops that are opened year after year in London, not above a half remain in existence for a period of twelve months; and not a half ever afford a livelihood to those who open them. Is not that a matter which ought to fill one with melancholy? On the establishment of every new shop there are the same high hopes, — those very hopes with which Brown, Jones, and Robinson commenced their career. It is not that all expect to shine forth upon the world as merchant princes, but all do expect to live upon the fruit of their labour and to put by that which will make their old age respectable. Alas! alas! Of those who thus hope how much the larger proportion are doomed to disappointment. The little lots of goods that are bought and brought together with so much pride turn themselves into dust and rubbish. The gloss and gilding wear away, as they wear away also from the heart of the adventurer, and then the small aspirant sinks back into the mass of nothings from whom he had thought to rise. When one thinks of it, it is very sad; but the sadness is not confined to commerce. It is the same at the bar, with the army, and in the Church. We see only the few who rise above the waves, and know nothing of the many who are drowned beneath the waters.

Perhaps something of all this was in the heart of our friend Robinson as he placed himself at his desk in his little room. Now, for this next day or two he would still be somebody in the career of Magenta House. His services were wanted; and therefore, though he was ruined, men smiled on him. But how would it be with him when that sale should be over, and when he would be called upon to leave the premises and walk forth into the street? He was aware now, though he had never so thought of himself before, that in the short days of his prosperity he had taken much upon himself, as the member of a prosperous firm. It had never then occurred to him that he had given himself airs because he was Robinson, of the house in Bishopsgate Street; but now he bethought himself that he had perhaps done so. How would men treat him when he should no longer be the same Robinson? How had he condescended to Poppins! how had he domineered at the 'Goose and Gridiron!' how had he patronized those who served him in the shop? Men remember these things of themselves quite as quickly as others remember them. Robinson thought of all this now, and almost wished that those visits to Blackfriars Bridge had not been in vain.

But nevertheless it behoved him to work. He had promised that he would use his own peculiar skill for the benefit of the creditors, and therefore, shaking himself as it were out of his despondency, he buckled himself to his desk. 'It is a grand opportunity,' he said, as he thought of the task before him, 'but my work will be no longer for myself and partners.

The lofty rhyme I still must make,
    Though other hands shall touch the money.
So do the bees for others' sake
    Fill their waxen combs with honey.'

Then, when he had thus solaced himself with verse, he sat down to his work.

There was a mine of wealth before him from which to choose. A tradesman in preparing the ordinary advertisements of his business is obliged to remember the morrow. He must not risk everything on one cast of the die. He must be in some degree modest and circumspect, lest he shut himself out from all possibility of rising to a higher note on any future opportunity. But in preparing for a final sacrifice the artist may give the reins to his imagination, and plunge at once into all the luxuries of the superlative. But to this pleasure there was one drawback. The thing had been done so often that superlatives had lost their value, and it had come to pass that the strongest language sounded impotently in the palled ears of the public. What idea can, in its own nature, be more harrowing to the soul than that of a TREMENDOUS SACRIFICE? but what effect would arise now-a-days from advertising a sale under such a heading? Every little milliner about Tottenham Court Road has her 'Tremendous Sacrifice!' when she desires to rid her shelves of ends of ribbons and bits of soiled flowers. No; some other language than this must be devised. A phraseology not only startling but new must be invented in preparing the final sale of the house of Brown, Jones, and Robinson.

He threw himself back in his chair, and sat for awhile silent, with his finger fixed upon his brow. The first words were everything, and what should be the first words? At last, in a moment, they came to him, and he wrote as follows: —

RUIN! RUIN! RUIN!!!
WASTEFUL AND IMPETUOUS SALE

At Magenta House, 81, Bishopsgate Street, on March the 5th, and three following days, the Stock in Trade of the bankrupts, Brown, Jones, and Robinson, valued at 209,657*l.* 15*s.* 3*d.*, will be thrown broadcast before the public at the frightful reduction of 75 per Cent. on the cost price.

To acquire the impetus and force necessary for the realization of so vast a property, all goods are quoted for TRUE, HONEST, BONA-FIDE SALE at One-Quarter the Cost Price.

This is a Solemn Fact, and one which well merits the earnest attention of every mother of a family in England. The goods are of the first class. And as no attempt in trade has ever hitherto been made of equal magnitude to that of the bankrupts', it may with absolute truth be said that no such opportunity as this has ever yet been afforded to the public of supplying themselves with the richest articles of luxury at prices which are all but nominal. How will any lady hereafter forgive herself, who shall fail to profit by such an opportunity as this?

Such was the heading of his bills, and he read and re-read the words, not without a glow of pleasure. One can be in love with ruin so long as the excitement lasts. 'A Solemn Fact!' he repeated to himself; 'or shall I say a Glorious Fact? Glorious would do well for the public view of the matter; but as it touches the firm, Solemn, perhaps, is more appropriate. Mother of a Family! Shall I say, also, of every Father? I should like to include all; but then the fathers never come, and it would sound loaded.' Again he looked at the bill, again read it, and then proceeded to describe with great accuracy, on a fly-leaf, the dimensions of the paper to be used, the size of the different types, and the adaptation of various colours. 'That will do,' said he, 'I think that will do.'

But this which he had now done, though, perhaps, the most important part of his task, was by no means the most laborious. He had before him various catalogues of the goods, and it remained for him to affix the prices, to describe the qualities, and to put down the amount of each on hand. This was no light task, and he worked hard at it into the middle of the night. But long before that time came he had thrust away from him the inefficient lists with which he had been supplied, and trusted himself wholly to his imagination. So may be seen the inspired schoolmaster who has beneath his hands the wretched verses of a dull pupil. For awhile he attempts to reduce to reason and prosody the futile efforts of the scholar, but anon he lays aside in disgust the distasteful task, and turning his eyes upwards to the Muse who has ever been faithful, he dashes off a few genial lines of warm poetry. The happy juvenile, with wondering pen, copies the work, and the parent's heart rejoices over the prize which his child has won. So was it now with Robinson. What could he do with a poor gross of hose, numbered 7 to 10? or what with a score or two of middling kids? There were five dozen and nine left of the Katakairions. Was he to put down such numbers as those in his sacrificial catalogue? For awhile he kept these entries before him as a guide — as a guide which in some sort he might follow at a wide distance. But he found that it was impossible for him to be so guided, even at any distance, and at last he thrust the poor figures from him altogether and trampled them under his feet. 'Tablecloths, seven dozen and a half, different sizes.' That was the last item he read, and as he pushed it away, the following were the words which his fertile pen produced: —

The renowned flemish Treble Table Damasks, of argentine brightness and snow-like purity, with designs of absolute grandeur and artistic perfection of outline. To dine eight persons, worth 1*l*. 8*s*. 6*d*., for 7*s*. 3*d*.; to dine twelve, worth 1*l*. 18*s*. 6*d*., for 10*s*. 11^{11}⁄$_{42}$*d*.; to dine sixteen, worth 3*l*. 19*s*. 6*d*., for 19*s*. 9^{11}⁄$_{44}$*d*.; and so on, at the same rate, to any size which the epicurean habits of this convivial age can possibly require.

Space will not permit us here to give the bill entire, but after this fashion was it framed. And then the final note was as follows: —

N.B. — Many tons weight of First-Class Table Damasks and Sheetings, soiled but not otherwise impaired; also of Ribbons, Gloves, Hose, Shirts, Crinolines, Paletots, Mantles, Shawls, Prints, Towels, Blankets, Quilts, and Flouncings, will be sold on the first two days at BUYERS' OWN PRICES.

'There,' said he, as he closed down his ink-bottle at three o'clock in the morning, 'that, I suppose, is my last day's work in the house of Brown, Jones and Robinson. I have worked, not for myself, but others, and I have worked honestly.' Then he went home, and slept as though he had no trouble on his mind.

On the following morning he again was there, and Messrs Giles, Burrows, and Sloman attended with him. Mr Brown, also, and Mr Jones were present. On this occasion the meeting was held in Brown's sitting-room, and they were all assembled in order that Robinson might read over the sale list as he had prepared it. Poor Mr Brown sat in a corner of his old sofa, very silent. Now and again, as some long number or specially magniloquent phrase would strike his ear, he expressed his surprise by a sort of gasp; but throughout the whole morning he did not speak a word as to the business on hand. Jones for the first few minutes attempted to criticize; but the authority of Mr Sloman and the burly aspect of Mr Giles the paper-dealer, were soon too much for his courage, and he also collapsed into silence. But the three gentlemen who were most concerned did not show all that silent acquiescence which George Robinson's painful exertions on their behalf so richly deserved.

'Impetuous!' said Mr Sloman. 'What does "impetuous" mean? I never heard tell before of an impetuous sacrifice. Tremendous is the proper word, Mr Robinson.'

'Tremendous is not my word,' answered Robinson; 'and as to the meaning of impetuous —'

'It sounds well, I think,' said Mr Burrows; and then they went on.

'Broadcast — broadcast!' said Mr Giles. That means sowing, don't it?'

'Exactly,' said Robinson. 'Have not I sown, and are not you to reap? If you will allow me I will go on.' He did go on, and by degrees got through the whole heading; but there was hardly a word which was not contested. It is all very well for a man to write, when he himself is the sole judge of what shall be written; but it is a terrible thing to have to draw up any document for the approval of others. One's choicest words are torn away, one's figures of speech are maltreated, one's stops are misunderstood, and one's very syntax is put to confusion; and then, at last, whole paragraphs are cashiered as unnecessary. First comes the torture and then the execution. 'Come, Wilkins, you have the pen of a ready writer; prepare for us this document.' In such words is the victim addressed by his colleagues. Unhappy Wilkins! he little dreams of the misery before him, as he proudly applies himself to his work.

But it is beautiful to hear and see, when two scribes have been appointed, how at first they praise each other's words, as did Trissotin and Vadius; how gradually each objects to this comma or to that epithet; how from moment to moment their courage will arise, — till at last every word that the other has written is foul nonsense and flat blasphemy; — till Vadius at last will defy his friend in prose and verse, in Greek and Latin.

Robinson on this occasion had no rival, but not the less were his torments very great. 'Argentine brightness!' said Mr Giles. 'What's "argentine?" I don't like "argentine." You'd better put that out, Mr Robinson.'

'It's the most effective word in the whole notice,' said Robinson, and then he passed on.

'Tons weight of towelling!' said Mr Sloman. That's coming it a little too strong, Mr Robinson.'

This was the end of the catalogue. 'Gentlemen,' said Robinson, rising from his chair, 'what little I have been able to do for you in this matter I have done willingly. There is the notice of your sale, drawn out in such language as seems suitable to me. If it answers your purpose, I pray that you will use it. If you can frame one that will do so better, I beg that no regard for my feelings may stand in your way. My only request to you is this, — that if my words be used, they may not be changed or garbled.' Then, bowing to them all, he left the room.

They knew the genius of the man, and the notice afterwards appeared exactly in the form in which Robinson had framed it.

CHAPTER XXIII

FAREWELL

For the four appointed days the sale was continued, and it was wondrous to see with what animation the things went off. It seemed as though ladies were desirous of having a souvenir from Magenta House, and that goods could be sold at a higher price under the name of a sacrifice than they would fetch in the ordinary way of trade. 'If only we could have done as well,' Robinson said to his partner Jones, wishing that, if possible, there might be good humour between them in these last days.

'We did do quite as well, and better,' said Jones, 'only the money was thrown away in them horrid advertisements.' After that, George Robinson made no further effort to maintain friendly relations with Mr Jones.

'George,' said Mr Brown, 'I hope they'll allow me something. They ought; oughtn't they? There wouldn't have been nothing, only for my four thousand pounds.' Robinson did not take the trouble to explain to him that had he kept his four thousand pounds out of the way, the creditors would not now have any lost money to lament. Robinson was careful to raise no hopes by his answer; but, nevertheless, he resolved that when the sale was over, he would do his best.

On the fifth day, when the shop had been well nigh cleared of all the goods, the premises themselves were sold. Brown, Jones and Robinson had taken them on a term of years, and the lease with all the improvements was put up to auction. When we say that the price which the property fetched exceeded the whole sum spent for external and internal decorations, including the Magenta paint and the plate-glass, we feel that the highest possible testimony is given to the taste and talent displayed by the firm.

It was immediately after this that application was made to the creditors on behalf of Mr Brown.

'He brought four thousand pounds into the business,' said Robinson, 'and now he hasn't a penny of his own.'

'And we have none of us got a penny,' whined out Mr Jones, who was standing by.

'Mr Jones and I are young, and can earn our bread,' said Robinson; 'but that old man must go into the workhouse, if you do not feel it possible to do something for him.'

'And so must my poor babbies,' said Jones. 'As to work, I ain't fit for it.'

But he was soon interrupted, and made to understand that he might think himself lucky if he were not made to disgorge that which he already possessed. As to Mr Brown, the creditors with much generosity agreed that an annuity of 20s. a week should be purchased for him out of the proceeds of the sale. 'I ain't long for this world, George,' he said, when he was told; 'and they ought to get it cheap. Put 'em up to that, George; do now.' Twenty shillings a week was not much for all his wants; but, nevertheless, he might be more comfortable with that than he had been for many a year, if only his daughter would be kind to him. Alas, alas! was it within the nature of things that his daughters should be kind?

It was on this occasion, when the charitable intention of the creditors was communicated to Mr Brown by Robinson, that that conversation took place to which allusion has been made in the opening chapter of these memoirs. Of course, it was necessary that each member of the firm should provide in some way for his future necessities. Mr Jones had signified his intention of opening a small hairdresser's shop in Gray's Inn Lane. 'I was brought up to it once,' he said, 'and it don't require much ready money. Both Mr Brown and Robinson knew that he was in possession of money, but it was not now worth their while to say more about this. The fox had made good his prey, and who could say where it was hidden?

'And what will you do, George?' asked Mr Brown.

Then it was that Robinson communicated to

them the fact that application had been made to him by the Editor of a first class Magazine for a written account of the doings of the firm. 'I think it may be of advantage to commerce in general,' the Editor had said with his customary dignity of expression and propriety of demeanour. 'I quite agree with you,' Robinson had replied, 'if only the commercial world of Great Britain can be induced to read the lesson.' The Editor seemed to think that the commercial world of Great Britain did read the CORNHILL MAGAZINE, and an arrangement was quickly made between them. Those who have perused the chapter in question will remember how Robinson yielded when the senior partner pleaded that as they had been partners so long, they should still be partners to the end; and how he had yielded again when it was suggested to him that he should receive some assistance in the literary portion of the work. That assistance has been given, and George Robinson hopes that it may have been of advantage.

'I suppose we shall see each other sometimes, George,' Maryanne said to him, when she came down to his little room to bid him farewell.

'I hope we shall, Maryanne.'

'I don't suppose we shall ever dance together again at the Hall of Harmony.'

'No, Maryanne, never. That phase of life is for me over. Neither with you nor with any other fair girl shall I again wanton away the flying hours. Life is too precious for that; and the work which falls upon a man's shoulders is too exacting. The Hall of Harmony is for children, Maryanne; — for grown children, perhaps, but still for children.'

'You used to like it, George.'

'I did; and could again. So could I again stop with longing mouth at the window of that pastrycook, whose tarts in early life attracted all my desires. I could again be a boy in everything, did I not recognize the stern necessity which calls me to be a man. I could dance with you still, whirling swiftly round the room to the sweet sound of the music, stretching the hours of delight out to the very dawn, were it not for Adam's doom. In the sweat of my brow I must eat my bread. There is a time for all things, Maryanne; but with me the time for such pastimes as those is gone.'

'You'll keep company with some other young woman before long, George, and then you'll be less gloomy.'

'Never! That phase of life is also over. Why should I? To what purpose?'

'To be married, of course.'

'Yes; and become a woman's slave, like poor Poppins; or else have my heart torn again with racking jealousy, as it was with you. No, Maryanne! Let those plodding creatures link themselves with women whose bodies require comforting but whose minds never soar. The world must be populated, and therefore let the Briskets marry.'

'I suppose you've heard of him, George?'

'Not a word.'

'La, now! I declare you've no curiosity to inquire about any one. If I was dead and buried tomorrow, I believe you'd never ask a word about me.'

'I would go to your grave, Maryanne, and sit there in silence.'

'Would you, now? I hope you won't, all the same. But about Brisket. You remember when that row was, and you were so nigh choking him?'

'Do I remember? Ay, Maryanne; when shall I forget it? It was the last hour of my madness.'

'I never admired you so much as I did then, George. But never mind. That's all done and over now; — isn't it?'

'All done and over,' said Robinson, mournfully repeating her words.

'Of course it is. But about Brisket. Immediately after that, the very next day, he went out to Gogham, — where he was always going, you know, with that cart of his, to buy sheep. Sheep, indeed!'

'And wasn't it for sheep?'

'No, George. Brisket was the sheep, and there was there a little she-wolf that has got him at last into her claws. Brisket is married, George.'

'What! another Poppins! Ha! ha! ha! We shall not want for children.'

'He has seen his way at last. She was a drover's daughter; and now he's married her and brought her home.'

'A drover's daughter?'

'Well, he says a grazier's; but it's all the same. He never would have done for me, George; never. And I'll tell you more; I don't think I ever saw the man as would. I should have taken either of you, — I was so knocked about among 'em. But I should have made you miserable, whichever it was. It's a consolation to me when I think of that.'

And it was a consolation also to him. He had loved her, — had loved her very dearly. He had been almost mad for love of her. But yet he had always known, that had he won her she would have made him miserable. There was consolation in that when he thought of his loss. Then, at last, he wished her good-by. 'And now farewell, Maryanne. Be gentle with that old man.'

'George,' she said, 'as long as he wants me, I'll stick to him. He's never been a good father to me; but if he wants me, I'll stick to him. As to being gentle, it's not in me. I wasn't brought up gentle, and you can't teach an old dog new tricks.' Those were the last words she spoke to him, and they had, at any rate, the merit of truth.

And then, before he walked out for the last time from the portals of Magenta House, he bade adieu to his old partner Mr Brown. 'God bless you, George!' said the old man; 'God bless you!'

'Mr Brown,' said he, 'I cannot part from you without acknowledging that the loss of all your money sits very heavy on my heart.'

'Never think of it, George.'

'But I shall think of it. You were an old man, Mr Brown, and the money was enough for you; or, if you did go into trade again, the old way would have suited you best.'

'Well, George, now you mention it, I think it would.'

'It was the same mistake, Mr Brown, that we have so often heard of, — putting old wine into a new bottle. The bottle is broken and the wine is spilt. For myself, I've learned a lesson, and I am a wiser man; but I'm sorry for you, Mr Brown.'

'I shall never say a word to blame you, George.'

'As to my principles, — that system of commerce which I have advocated, — as to that, I am still without a doubt. I am certain of the correctness of my views. Look at Barlywig and his colossal fortune, and 40,000*l*. a year spent in advertising.'

'But then you should have your 40,000*l*. a year.'

'By no means! But the subject is a long one, Mr Brown, and cannot now be discussed with advantage. This, however, I do feel, — that I should not have embarked your little all in such an enterprise. It was enough for you; but to me, with my views, it was nothing, — less than nothing. I will begin again with unimpeded wings, and you shall hear of my success. But for your sake, Mr Brown, I regret what is past.' Then he pressed the old man's hand and went forth from Magenta House. From that day to this present one he has never again entered the door.

'And so Brisket is married. Brisket is right. Brisket is a happy man,' he said to himself, as he walked slowly down the passage by St Botolph's Church. 'Brisket is certainly right; I will go and see Brisket.' So he did; and continuing his way along the back of the Bank and the narrow street which used to be called Lad Lane, — I wish they would not alter the names of the streets; was it not enough that the 'Swan with Two Necks' should be pulled down, foreshadowing, perhaps, in its ruin the fate of another bird with two necks, from which this one took its emblematic character? — and so making his way out into Aldersgate Street. He had never before visited the Lares of Brisket, for Brisket had been his enemy. But Brisket was his enemy no longer, and he walked into the shop with a light foot and a pleasant smile. There, standing at some little distance behind the block, looking with large, wondering eyes at the carcases of the sheep which hung around her, stood a wee little woman, very pretty, with red cheeks, and red lips, and short, thick, clustering curls. This was the daughter of the grazier from Gogham. 'The shopman will be back in a minute,' said she. 'I ought to be able to do it myself, but I'm rather astray about the things yet awhile.' Then George Robinson told her who he was.

She knew his name well, and gave him her little plump hand in token of greeting. 'Laws a mercy! are you George Robinson? I've heard such a deal about you. He's inside, just tidying hisself a bit for dinner. Who do you think there is here, Bill?' and she opened the door leading to the back premises. 'Here's George Robinson, that you're always so full of.' Then he followed her out into a little yard, where he found Brisket in the neighbourhood of a pump, smelling strongly of yellow soap, with his sleeves tucked up, and hard at work with a rough towel.

'Robinson, my boy,' cried he, 'I'm glad to see you; and so is Mrs B. Ain't you Em'ly?' Whereupon Em'ly said that she was delighted to see Mr Robinson. 'And you're just in time for as tidy a bit of roast veal as you won't see again in a hurry, — fed down at Gogham by Em'ly's mother. I killed it myself, with my own hands. Didn't I, Em'ly?'

Robinson stopped and partook of the viands which were so strongly recommended to him; and then, after dinner, he and Brisket and the bride became very intimate and confidential over a glass of hot brandy-and-water.

'I don't do this kind of thing, only when I've got a friend,' said Brisket, tapping the tumbler with his spoon. 'But I really am glad to see you. I've took a fancy to you now, ever since you went so nigh throttling me. By Jove! though, I began to think it was all up with me, — only for Sarah Jane.'

'But he didn't!' said Emily, looking first at her great husband and then at Robinson's slender proportions.

'Didn't he though? But he just did. And what

do you think, Em'ly? He wanted me once to sit with him on a barrel of gunpowder.'

'A barrel gunpowder!'

'And smoke our pipes there, — quite comfortable. And then he wanted me to go and fling ourselves into the river. That was uncommon civil, wasn't it? And then he well nigh choked me.'

'It was all about that young woman,' said Emily, with a toss of her head. 'And from all I can hear tell, she wasn't worth fighting for. As for you, Bill, I wonder at you; so I do.'

'I thought I saw my way,' said Brisket.

'It's well for you that you've got somebody near you that will see better now. And as for you, Mr Robinson; I hope you won't be long in the dumps, neither.' Whereupon he explained to her that he was by no means in the dumps. He had failed in trade, no doubt, but he was now engaged upon a literary work, as to which considerable expectation had been raised, and he fully hoped to provide for his humble wants in this way till he should be able to settle himself again to some new commercial enterprise.

'It isn't that as she means,' said Brisket. 'She means about taking a wife. That's all the women ever thinks of.'

'What I was saying is, that as you and Bill were both after her, and as you are both broke with her, and seeing that Bill's provided himself like —'

'And a charming provision he has made,' said Robinson.

'I did see my way,' said Brisket, with much self-content.

'So you ought to look elsewhere as well as he,' continued Emily. 'According to all accounts, you've neither of you lost so very much in not getting Maryanne Brown.'

'Maryanne Brown is a handsome young woman,' said Robinson.

'Why, she's as red as red,' said Mrs Brisket; 'quite carroty, they tell me. And as for handsome, Mr Robinson; — handsome is as handsome does; that's what I say. If I had two sweethearts going about talking of gunpowder, and throwing themselves into rivers along of me, I'd — I'd — I'd never forgive myself. So, Mr Robinson, I hope you'll suit yourself soon. Bill, don't you take any more of that brandy. Don't now, when I tell you not.'

Then Robinson rose and took his leave, promising to make future visits to Aldersgate Street. And as Brisket squeezed his hand at parting, all the circumstances of that marriage were explained in a very few words. 'She had three hundred, down, you know; — really down. So I said done and done, when I found the money wasn't there with Maryanne. And I think that I've seen my way.'

Robinson congratulated him, and assured him that he thought he had seen it very clearly.

CHAPTER XXIV

GEORGE ROBINSON'S DREAM

George Robinson, though his present wants were provided for by his pen, was by no means disposed to sink into a literary hack. It was by commerce that he desired to shine. It was to trade, — trade, in the highest sense of the word, — that his ambition led him. Down at the Crystal Palace he had stood by the hour together before the statue of the great Cheetham, ominous name! — of him who three centuries ago had made money by dealing in Manchester goods. Why should not he also have his statue? But then how was he to begin? He had begun, and failed. With hopeful words he had declared to Mr Brown that not on that account was he daunted; but still there was before him the burden of another commencement. Many of us know what it is to have high hopes, and yet to feel from time to time a terrible despondency when the labours come by which those hopes should be realized. Robinson had complained that he was impeded in his flight by Brown and

291

Jones. Those impediments had dropped from him now; and yet he knew not how to proceed upon his course.

He walked forth one evening, after his daily task, pondering these things as he went. He made his solitary way along the Kingsland Road, through Tottenham, and on to Edmonton, thinking deeply of his future career. What had John Gilpin done that had made him a citizen of renown? Had he advertised? Or had he contented himself simply with standing behind his counter till customers should come to him? In John Gilpin's time the science of advertisement was not born; — or, if born, was in its earliest infancy. And yet he had achieved renown. And Cheetham; — but probably Cheetham had commenced with a capital.

Thus he walked on till he found himself among the fields, — those first fields which greet the eyes of a Londoner, in which wheat is not grown, but cabbages and carrots for the London market; and here seating himself upon a gate, he gave his mind up to a close study of the subject. First he took from his pocket a short list which he always carried, and once more read over the names and figures which it bore.

Barlywig, £40,000 per annum.

How did Barlywig begin such an outlay as that? He knew that Barlywig had, as a boy, walked up to town with twopence in his pocket, and in his early days, had swept out the shop of a shoe-maker. The giants of trade all have done that. Then he went on with the list: —

```
Holloway. . . . . . . . £30,000 per annum
Moses . . . . . . . . . . £10,000 per annum
Macassar Oil . . . . . £10,000 per annum
Dr De Jongh . . . . . £10,000 per annum
```

What a glorious fraternity! There were many others that followed with figures almost equally stupendous. Revalenta Arabica! Bedsteads! Paletots! Food for Cattle! But then how did these great men begin? He himself had begun with some money in his hand, and had failed. As to them, he believed that they had all begun with twopence. As for genius and special talent, it was admitted on all sides that he possessed it. Of that he could feel no doubt, as other men were willing to employ him.

'Shall I never enjoy the fruits of my own labour?' said he to himself. 'Must I still be as the bee, whose honey is robbed from him as soon as made?

The lofty rhyme I still must build,
Though other hands shall touch the money.

Will this be my fate for ever? —

The patient oxen till the furrows,
But never eat the generous corn.

Shall the corn itself never be my own?'

And as he sat there the words of Poppins came upon his memory. 'You advertising chaps never do anything. All that printing never makes the world any richer.' At the moment he had laughed down Poppins with absolute scorn; but now, at this solitary moment he began to reflect whether there might be any wisdom in his young friend's words. 'The question has been argued,' he continued in his soliloquy, 'by the greatest philosopher of the age. A man goes into hats, and in order to force a sale, he builds a large cart in the shape of a hat, paints it blue, and has it drawn through the streets. He still finds that his sale is not rapid; and with a view of increasing it, what shall he do? Shall he make his felt hats better, or shall he make his wooden hat bigger? Poppins and the philosopher say that the former plan will make the world the richer, but they do not say that it will sell the greater number of hats. Am I to look after the world? Am I not to look to myself? Is not the world a collection of individuals, all of whom are doing so? Has anything been done for the world by the Quixotic aspirations of general philanthropy, at all equal to that which individual enterprise has achieved? Poppins and the philosopher would spend their energies on a good hat. But why? Not that they love the head that is to wear it. The sale would still be their object. They would sell hats, not that the heads of men may be well covered, but that they themselves might live and become rich. To force a sale must be the first duty of a man in trade, and a man's first duty should be all in all to him.

'If the hats sold from the different marts be not good enough, with whom does the fault rest? Is it not with the customers who purchase them? Am I to protect the man who demands from me a cheap hat? Am I to say, "Sir, here is a cheap hat. It is made of brown paper, and the gum will run from it in the first shower. It will come to pieces when worn and disgrace you among your female acquaintances by becoming dinged and bulged?" Should I do him good? He would buy his cheap hat elsewhere, and tell pleasant stories of the madman he had met. The world of purchasers will have cheap articles, and the world of commerce must supply them. The world of purchasers will have their ears tickled, and the world of commerce must tickle them. Of what use is all this about adulteration? If Mrs Jones will buy her sausages at a lower price per pound than pork fetches in the market, has she a right to complain when some curious doctor makes her understand that her viands have not been supplied exclusively from the pig? She insists on milk at three halfpence a quart but the cow will not produce it. The cow cannot produce it at that price, unless she be aided by the pump; and therefore the pump aids her. If there be dishonesty in this, it is with the purchaser, not with the vendor, — with the public, not with the tradesman.'

But still as he sat upon the gate, thus arguing with himself, a dream came over him, a mist of thought as it were, whispering to him strangely that even yet he might be wrong. He endeavoured to throw it off, shaking himself as it were, and striving to fix his mind firmly upon his old principles. But it was of no avail. He knew he was awake; but yet he dreamed; and his dream was to him as a terrible nightmare.

What if he were wrong! What if those two philosophers had on their side some truth! He would fain be honest if he knew the way. What if those names upon his list were the names of false gods, whose worship would lead him to a hell of swindlers instead of the bright heaven of commercial nobility! 'Barlywig is in Parliament,' he said to himself, over and over again, and loud tones, striving to answer the spirit of his dream. 'In Parliament! He sits upon committees; men jostle to speak to him; and he talks loud among the big ones of the earth. He spends forty thousand a year in his advertisements, and grows incredibly rich by the expenditure. Men and women flock in crowds to his shop. He lives at Albert Gate in a house big enough for a royal duke, and is the lord of ten thousand acres in Yorkshire. Barlywig cannot have been wrong, let that philosopher philosophize as he will!' But still the dream was there, crushing him like a nightmare.

'Why don't you produce something, so as to make the world richer?' Poppins had said. He knew well what Poppins had meant by making the world richer. If a man invent a Katakairion shirt, he does make the world richer; if it be a good one, he makes it much richer. But the man who simply says that he has done so adds nothing to the world's wealth. His answer had been that it was his work to sell the shirts, and that of the purchaser to buy them. Let each look to his own work. If he could be successful in his selling, then he would have a right to be proud of his success. The world would be best served by close attention on the part of each to his own business. Such had been the arguments with which he had silenced his friend and contented himself, while the excitement of the shop in Bishopsgate Street was continued; but now, as he sat there upon the gate, this dream came upon him, and he began to doubt. Could it be that a man had a double duty, each separate from the other; — a duty domestic and private, requiring his devotion and loyalty to his wife, his children, his partners, and himself; and another duty, widely extended in all its bearings and due to the world in which he lived? Could Poppins have seen this, while he was blind? Was a man bound to produce true shirts for the world's benefit even though he should make no money by so doing; — either true shirts or none at all?

The evening light fell upon him as he still sat there on the gate, and he became very melancholy. 'If I have been wrong,' he said to himself, 'I must give up the fight. I cannot begin again now and learn new precepts. After all that I have done with that old man's money, I cannot now own that I have been wrong, and commence again on a theory taught to me by Poppins. If this be so, then farewell to Commerce!' And as he said so, he dropped from his seat, and, leaning over the rail, hid his face within his hands.

As he stood there, suddenly a sound struck his ears, and he knew that the bells of Edmonton were ringing. The church was distant, but nevertheless the tones came sharp upon him with their clear music. They rang on quickly, loudly, and with articulate voice. Surely there were words within those sounds. What was it they were saying to him? He listened for a few seconds, for a minute or two, for five minutes; and then his ear and senses had recognized the language — 'Turn again, Robinson, Member of Parliament.' He heard it so distinctly that his ear would not for a moment abandon the promise. The words could not be mistaken. 'Turn again, Robinson, Member of Parliament.'

Then he did turn, and walked back to London with a trusting heart.

We hope you have enjoyed this Large Print book. Other G.K. Hall & Co. or Chivers Press Large Print books are available at your library or directly from the publishers.

For more information about current and upcoming titles, please call or write, without obligation, to:

G.K. Hall & Co.
P.O. Box 159
Thorndike, Maine 04986 USA
Tel. (800) 223-1244

OR

Chivers Press Limited
Windsor Bridge Road
Bath BA2 3AX
England
Tel. (0225) 335336

All our Large Print titles are designed for easy reading, and all our books are made to last.